PRAISE F(
#1 NEW YORK '
BAH

"In the tradition of LaVyrle Spencer, gifted author Barbara Freethy creates an irresistible tale of family secrets, riveting adventure and heart- touching romance."
*-- NYT Bestselling Author **Susan Wiggs***
on Summer Secrets

"This book has it all: heart, community, and characters who will remain with you long after the book has ended. A wonderful story."
*-- NYT Bestselling Author **Debbie Macomber***
on Suddenly One Summer

"Freethy has a gift for creating complex characters."
*-- **Library Journal***

"Barbara Freethy is a master storyteller with a gift for spinning tales about ordinary people in extraordinary situations and drawing readers into their lives."
*-- **Romance Reviews Today***

"Freethy's skillful plotting and gift for creating sympathetic characters will ensure that few dry eyes will be left at the end of the story."
*-- **Publishers Weekly** on The Way Back Home*

"Freethy skillfully keeps the reader on the hook, and her tantalizing and believable tale has it all– romance, adventure, and mystery."
*-- **Booklist** on Summer Secrets*

"Freethy's story-telling ability is top-notch."
*-- **Romantic Times** on Don't Say A Word*

"Powerful and absorbing...sheer hold-your-breath suspense."
-- *NYT Bestselling Author **Karen Robards***
on Don't Say A Word

"A page-turner that engages your mind while it tugs at your heartstrings...Don't Say A Word has made me a Barbara Freethy fan for life!"
-- *NYT Bestselling Author **Diane Chamberlain***
on Don't Say a Word

"I love *The Callaways*! Heartwarming romance, intriguing suspense and sexy alpha heroes. What more could you want?"
-- *NYT Bestselling Author **Bella Andre***

"Once I start reading a Callaway novel, I can't put it down. Fast-paced action, a poignant love story and a tantalizing mystery in every book!"
-- *USA Today Bestselling Author **Christie Ridgway***

"Barbara manages to weave a perfect romance filled with laughter, love, a lot of heat, and just the right amount of suspense. I highly recommend *SO THIS IS LOVE* to anyone looking for a sexy romance with characters you will love!"
-- ***Harlequin Junkie***

"I adore *The Callaways*, a family we'd all love to have. Each new book is a deft combination of emotion, suspense and family dynamics. A remarkable, compelling series!"
-- *USA Today Bestselling Author **Barbara O'Neal***

"*BETWEEN NOW AND FOREVER* is a beautifully written story. Fans of Barbara's Angel's Bay series will be happy to know the search leads them to Angel's Bay where we get to check in with some old friends."
-- ***The Book Momster Blog***

Also By Barbara Freethy

The Callaway Series
On A Night Like This (#1)
So This Is Love (#2)
Falling For A Stranger (#3)
Between Now and Forever (#4)
Nobody But You (Callaway Wedding Novella)
All A Heart Needs (#5)
That Summer Night (#6)
When Shadows Fall (#7)
Somewhere Only We Know (#8)

The Callaway Cousins
If I Didn't Know Better (#1)
Tender Is The Night (#2)
Take Me Home (A Callaway Novella)
Closer To You (#3)
Once You're Mine (#4)
Can't Let Go (#5)
Secrets We Keep (#6)

Off The Grid: FBI Series
Perilous Trust (#1)
Reckless Whisper (#2), *Coming Soon!*
Desperate Play (#3), *Coming Soon!*

Lightning Strikes Trilogy
Beautiful Storm (#1)
Lightning Lingers (#2)
Summer Rain (#3)

Standalone Novels
Almost Home
All She Ever Wanted
Ask Mariah
Daniel's Gift
Don't Say A Word
Golden Lies
Just The Way You Are
Love Will Find A Way
One True Love
Ryan's Return
Some Kind of Wonderful
Summer Secrets
The Sweetest Thing

The Sanders Brothers Series
Silent Run & Silent Fall

The Deception Series
Taken & Played

SECRETS WE KEEP

The Callaway Cousins #6

BARBARA FREETHY

HYDE
STREET
—PRESS—

HYDE STREET PRESS
Published by Hyde Street Press
1325 Howard Avenue, #321, Burlingame, California 94010

Printed in the United States of America

Cover design by Damonza.com

ISBN: 9781944417444

One

>➤➤❬❬❬

Being back in the firehouse after eight months of travel should have made Hunter Callaway feel good—normal. This was his life, the life he'd led since he'd entered the family firefighting business when he was twenty-three years old. That had been seven years ago. Sometimes, it felt like yesterday. Sometimes, it felt like a lifetime.

But he didn't feel content, not quite sure he was happy to be back, or that he was making the right choice in returning. He still felt restless, a feeling he hadn't been able to shake no matter how many miles he'd put on his motorcycle, no matter how many cities or countries he'd driven through.

Maybe he just didn't want to be a firefighter anymore.

It was a thought that had gone around in his head for months, but he didn't know if it was just the job or if it was more than that. There was something missing inside of himself—a big hole he didn't know how to fill, and it had been there before he'd almost lost his life.

"Well, look who's here—as if we didn't have enough Callaways already," Gary Parker said, slapping him on the back as he gave him a teasing smile. A stocky man with graying black hair and friendly eyes, Gary was a forty-year-old firefighter, who'd mentored more than a few Callaways over the years. "You filling in for MacKinney?"

"Yes, and it's nice to see you, too, Gary," he drawled.

"So, where have you been, Hunter? You come back with a bride, a treasure, a new tattoo?"

"None of the above."

"Well, that's disappointing. Surely, you've got a story or two?"

"A few."

Gary gave him a speculative look. "Dylan said you were looking for something. Did you find it?"

He shrugged. "I had a good time. I needed a break."

"That high-rise fire last year took it out of you, didn't it?"

"It wasn't just that." He knew that most of his fellow firefighters thought that falling three stories down an elevator shaft, breaking his foot, and cracking a few ribs had been the trigger for his sudden hiatus, that he hadn't just needed to heal his wounds but also to get his nerve back.

He didn't think it was about nerve. He wasn't afraid to fight fire; he just wasn't sure he wanted to.

Luckily, he didn't have to comment further as his brother, Dylan, entered the breakroom. Four years older than him, Dylan had dark-brown hair and blue eyes, very much like his own, and most of the Callaway clan, for that matter. As the oldest in the family, Dylan could be a know-it-all but also a protector. Right now, he was in watchful big brother mode.

Out of his five siblings, he and Dylan had always had the most in common, probably because they'd both chosen to become firefighters, following in his father's footsteps as well as his uncle and grandfather and a few cousins.

"How are you doing?" Dylan asked as Gary left them alone to grab breakfast.

"Fine," he said, sensing another interrogation coming his way.

"No first day jitters?"

"I've done this job for seven years. I can barely

remember my first day."

"But this is your first day back in eight months. And you've never worked out of this firehouse."

"And yet it feels like every other shift to me," he retorted, although, that wasn't quite true. He was actually happy to be assigned temporary duty in a new firehouse. He would miss his old crew, but he had his older brother here, and his cousin, Burke, who was the battalion chief at the station. Plus, the temporary gig made him feel like he still had a choice as to whether or not he wanted to go for a more permanent position.

"You talk to Burke yet?" Dylan asked.

"He's tied up in his office. He gave me a wave. I'm sure we'll catch up at some point. How are you doing? How's Tori? The two of you still honeymooning?"

"You know it," Dylan said with a smug smile.

As he could have predicted, his brother was instantly distracted by the thought of his beautiful wife of four months.

"I never really thought I was cut out for marriage," Dylan continued. "But I was wrong. I can't imagine a life that would be better than the one I'm living with Tori."

He saw genuine happiness in his brother's eyes. "I'm glad. Is she still wielding her pen like a sword?" His sister-in-law was a reporter for the *Bay Area Examiner*, determined to do her best to put light into every dark corner.

"Yes. She's rattling some of our city council members with her pieces on the homeless situation. But she doesn't back down from a fight," Dylan said proudly.

"You picked a good one."

"I did, and you deliberately distracted me. We were talking about you."

"You don't have to worry about me. I've got my head together." His words did little to erase the lingering worry in Dylan's eyes. "I can do this job. I wouldn't have come back if I couldn't. I know everyone thinks I lost my nerve, but that was never it."

"I know you can do the job."

"Good. Let's leave it at that. I'm going to get some breakfast and try out the new rookie's cooking skills."

As he moved toward the counter to grab a plate, the alarm went off, followed by the dispatcher's voice, alerting them to a residential structure fire. Breakfast would have to wait.

Within minutes, they were changing into their gear, hopping onto the truck and getting ready to fight whatever fire was ripping apart someone's business, or life, or both.

Despite his earlier words to his brother, he had to admit to a rush of adrenaline and jumpier nerves than he remembered, but this wasn't going to be like the last fire. It was a house, not a high-rise, for one thing.

And he wasn't afraid of fire. He was good at his job. *His restless feelings came from a deeper place, didn't they?*

He was going to find out very soon.

-->>><<<--

As the truck raced through the city streets, Hunter felt his body tighten with every turn. He'd been down these blocks before, which wasn't unusual since he'd grown up in this part of the city. His parents' house was only two miles away, but he hadn't been in this particular Sunset District neighborhood since high school. He'd avoided it for a reason—a very painful reason.

It couldn't be her house. What were the odds?

But he couldn't shake the bad feeling running through him. Nor could he stop the memories flooding his brain. It had been fourteen years since he'd seen her. He'd been sixteen years old and madly in love with the girl with the long, blonde hair, dark-brown, soulful eyes, and soft, full lips that grew pink when he kissed them...

Cassidy Ellison.

He didn't want to remember her, but he'd never really forgotten her.

She'd run out on him the day of the junior prom. She'd

left town with another guy, a boy she'd once vowed was only her friend and nothing more. Obviously, she'd been lying about their relationship—probably about everything. And he shouldn't have spent one second more thinking about her.

But she'd always been in the shadows of his mind. He still had so many unanswered questions. One minute, they'd been crazy about each other, making plans for the summer, dreaming about the future, spending every second they could together. He'd never been able to talk to anyone the way he'd talked to her. They'd been connected in every possible way.

And then she was gone.

At some point, he'd given up on getting answers. He'd moved on. He'd stopped seeing Cassidy's face in every blonde who walked by him. He'd had other women in his life who he cared about. But no one had ever completely replaced her.

A knot grew in his throat, as the truck turned down a street of single-family homes with minimal front yards but some space between buildings, which wasn't always the case in San Francisco. They came to a stop in front of a two-story house with an attached garage that was engulfed in flames, and he was immediately transported into the past.

Cassidy had only let him come in the house once, a quick trip after school when her foster parents had been out, and she'd only done that reluctantly.

But even though he hadn't spent much time inside, he had spent a lot of time kissing her good night on the front porch. His mouth tingled at the memories and as he lifted his gaze to the second-floor window, he could almost see her standing there, waving good-bye to him with a haunted, trapped, worried expression on her face.

He'd thought at the time that her unhappy gaze meant she was missing him already. Yes, he'd definitely had a healthy ego at sixteen. But later he'd come to believe that she'd just wanted to get away from the house, from the family she didn't like, the other kids who felt like strangers and were as unhappy as she was.

He could understand why she wanted to leave the house,

but he'd never understood why she wanted to leave him. The fact that she'd left with Tommy Lucas had twisted the knife in deeper, making what he'd thought they'd been to each other a complete and total farce.

The truck came to a sudden stop, and he yanked his thoughts out of the past. Cassidy hadn't lived here in a very long time. There was no point thinking about her now.

He followed his fellow firefighters out of the truck, falling into the rhythm of the job he'd done all of his life. It was as if the past eight months off had been no longer than a minute.

As they hit the pavement, a woman came running up to them. She was in her mid-thirties, barefoot, wearing jeans and a T-shirt, her hair in a ponytail, a wild look in her eyes.

Dylan intercepted her. "Is this your house?"

"I'm the neighbor from across the street." She waved her hand toward a light-blue, two-story house. "I saw smoke and flames coming out of the windows, so I came over and rang the bell, but no one answered."

"Who lives here?" Dylan asked.

"Geralyn Faulkner. She's an older woman. Sometimes there are kids there, too. I don't know who might be inside," the woman said worriedly.

He stiffened at the mention of Geralyn Faulkner, Cassidy's one-time foster mother. Cassidy had not liked Geralyn at all. He'd seen her around, and she'd always seemed like a nice, motherly woman to him, but he'd never had an extended conversation with her.

Dylan turned to him and Gary, ordering them to check the house while the rest of the squad prepared to attack the fire. He pulled his mask on, then followed Gary into the structure.

The smoke was thick, the heat intense. The fire seemed to be everywhere: clusters of flames eating up curtains and wallpaper, sliding down the stairway in patches, finding more fuel as the sparks landed on the carpet or the wood.

They raced upstairs first, calling out for potential victims, as they cleared the four bedrooms and two bathrooms.

Cassidy had slept in the room at the end of the hall, and while there were still two single beds inside, there was nothing there to remind him of her. In fact, there was little to remind him of anything. The room looked empty, as if no one slept there anymore.

He and Gary moved back downstairs, checking the hall bath, a small den, the kitchen and basement and then tried to head into the attached garage, but the fire was greater here, and they hadn't gotten more than a foot inside the door when an explosion knocked them backward.

He could hear Dylan's voice through the radio, ordering them outside. He struggled back to his feet. He was actually already outside. The explosion had blown them through the door leading out to the side yard.

As he got to his feet, he saw Gary doing the same. He didn't appear to be hurt, giving him a thumbs-up.

He looked back at the garage. The fire was blazing. There was no way they were getting in there.

"Check in, Hunter," Dylan repeated through his headset.

"Gary and I are okay. We're coming through the side yard now. We weren't able to get into the garage."

They made their way out to the front, and then joined the rest of the squad in fighting the fire. Thirty minutes later, the flames were out, but the smoke still hung thick in the air. Half the neighborhood had gathered across the street, watching in worry, hoping that the fire wouldn't spread to one of their homes. Thankfully, they'd been able to contain it to the single structure.

To be certain, they went through the house again, venting walls and ceilings, looking for any lingering trace of fire in the walls. He was the first one to make it into the garage. There wasn't much left inside the smoking room. Whatever had been there had been turned into ashes.

There was a heavy stench of gasoline in the air, which could have been stored in the garage or could have been the accelerant used to start the blaze, which might mean the fire had been deliberately set. Based on his experience, and the way the fire had spread so quickly, he thought it was a good bet.

But who would want to burn down this house?

Cassidy's image came back into his head now that the adrenaline rush had receded. She'd certainly hated living here. Probably the other kids had felt the same way. But she'd lived here years ago. Who knew if the Faulkners even took in foster kids anymore?

According to Dylan, the homeowners had not yet been reached, but the police were looking for them.

As he swung his axe at the wall, it felt good to rip into something, if for no other reason than to chase Cassidy out of his head. He probably went a little further than he needed to and had to jump back when a huge piece of sheetrock came down around him. The wall in front of him fell apart and to his astonishment, something hard and unidentifiable tumbled out from between the wood frames and fell at his feet.

He squatted down to get a better view, his stomach turning over, his heart stopping in shock as he stared in disbelief at what appeared to be human remains: a skull, bones, a rib cage—*What the hell?* He got up, backing away, his breath coming short and fast.

"Hunter?" Dylan strode into the garage. "I've been yelling to you for five minutes. Why haven't you answered? What's wrong?"

He looked at Dylan, then back at what was laying at his feet. "This—this came out of the wall," he said gruffly.

Dylan's gaze narrowed as he came closer. "What is all that?"

He stepped back so Dylan could get a better view.

"Oh, my God," Dylan breathed. "Is that…"

"A skeleton…and it's been here a long time." He had no idea whose bones he'd just found, but his stomach was churning, and fear was rushing through him. Someone had been murdered, their body hidden behind a wall in the garage of the house where Cassidy had once lived. He didn't know how old the skeleton was, but he was guessing it had been there at least a decade.

Cassidy had disappeared fourteen years ago, but these bones didn't belong to her. She'd run away. She'd left this place willingly.

Hadn't she?

He felt sick at the disturbing thought that these remains could be his beautiful Cassidy.

No! There was no way it was her. She couldn't have been killed. She couldn't have been in this house all these years.

He heard Dylan go into the driveway and yell for one of the police officers who'd responded to the fire to come into the garage.

When Dylan returned, he said, "You can go outside, Hunter. I'll take care of this."

"I'm staying."

"Why?"

"Because I have to. I found the body, and..." He couldn't bring himself to say the words aloud.

"And what?" Dylan's gaze narrowed in concern. "What is going on, Hunter?"

"This was her house," he whispered.

"Whose house?"

"Cassidy's."

Dylan's jaw dropped, his gaze widening with shock. "Cassidy?"

"This was her foster home."

"No."

"Yes."

"But she ran away. She told you she was leaving."

"I always thought so."

"It's not her. It can't be her." Dylan's words echoed the refrain going around in Hunter's head.

He was happy to have Dylan's reassurance, but he had a bad feeling in his gut. "What if Cassidy didn't run away with Tommy? What if she never left?"

Two

~~~
→→⫸⫷←←
~~~

Hunter didn't know how he made it through the rest of the day and night. While all he wanted to do was find out who the remains belonged to, he'd had to continue on with his twenty-four-hour shift, leaving the investigation to the police. While the gruesome discovery had spread through the firehouse, he'd asked Dylan not to mention Cassidy, and his brother had agreed, leaving the others to endlessly speculate about how a body had ended up in the walls of that garage.

That question was still rolling around in his head when he finally got off shift early Friday morning. He grabbed his duffel and walked out to the parking lot where his rather dusty but trusty Jeep was parked next to his brother's refurbished Porsche.

Their cars said a lot about their personalities. He liked a rough and rugged, outdoor lifestyle. For him, a car was just a way to get somewhere else. But Dylan had a passion for old classics. He spent hours refurbishing vintage cars that were sleek, sophisticated, and fast. Actually, they both had a liking for speed, but he preferred to drive a car that could also take him off-road. The best adventures always seemed to be off the beaten path.

He threw his duffel bag into the passenger side of his car as Dylan stopped next to him.

"What do you say to some breakfast?" Dylan asked.

"Breakfast would be good, but first I want to go to the police station. I need to know what they've found out about the bones we discovered yesterday."

"I figured you'd say that," Dylan replied with a gleam in his eyes. "And I'm way ahead of you. I called Max a few minutes ago."

"Emma's husband is working this case?"

"Yes. He said to come by, and he'd give us an update on our Jane or John Doe."

"Okay, good. I'm glad Max is on it." His anxiety was still high at the thought that the remains he'd found might belong to Cassidy. No matter how much he had tried to talk himself out of that idea, until he knew for sure, he just couldn't relax. He couldn't stand the thought that those bones could possibly be hers. She was too beautiful, too sweet, too alive—at least she'd always been that way in his head, even after the heartbreaking way things had ended between them.

"I asked Burke to come with us, but he has to go pick out a stove with Maddie," Dylan added.

"That's fine."

"Why don't we take one car? The station is only a few miles from here. I'll drive."

"Of course you will." His oldest brother always liked to drive, to be in charge. Not up to arguing over nothing, he locked his car, then got into Dylan's Porsche.

"I guess your first day back at work didn't go exactly as planned," Dylan said, as he pulled out of the lot.

"No, it did not. I had a bad feeling as soon as we turned down the street, but I never expected to find what I did."

"Cassidy was in foster care when she lived in that house, right?"

"Yes. Her parents died when she was thirteen, and she went into foster care because she didn't have any relatives to take care of her. She was bounced around a few times. She'd been living with the Faulkners for about a month when we met in high school. She was the new kid, and she was super shy and awkward, but God was she pretty. I looked into her big, brown eyes, and I couldn't remember my name." He cleared his throat, seeing the smile on his brother's face. "Anyway, we dated from February to May. And then on the day of the prom, she said she was running away with another kid, and that was that. I never saw her again."

"I remember that part. You got drunk and angry and crazy for a while there. But the sadness in your eyes was what really bothered me, what concerned us all."

"It was a bad time."

"What do you remember about her foster family—the Faulkners?"

"The father was a realtor. The mother was a homemaker. They'd been foster parents for years. I think there were five or six other kids in the house when Cassidy lived there. She didn't say much about the Faulkners, but she did tell me once that she didn't think anyone outside of the house knew who they really were, that they weren't the kind, wonderful people that they pretended to be."

"Did she give specifics?"

"No. She got really unhappy whenever their name came up, so I didn't push. I wish I had now. That skeleton…" He shuddered at the memory. "Who knows what was going on in that house." He took another breath. "It can't be her, Dylan."

"I'm sure it's not."

"Do you think they will be able to identify the body quickly?"

"Max said he was expecting to hear from the medical examiner this morning. Tell me about the kid that Cassidy ran away with."

"He was another foster kid, but he had only been there a couple of weeks. Cassidy said they'd been at another home together, and that's when they'd become friends. She was really happy when he got to the house. She always said they were just friends. And I wanted to believe her. Obviously, that wasn't the case, since she left town with him."

His thoughts drifted back to that horrible day. He'd just picked up her corsage for the prom when he'd gotten her text. He could still remember it word for word: *I'm sorry. I have to leave the city. Tommy needs me, and I need him. I hope you can forgive me one day. Please don't try to find me. Be happy, Hunter.*

He'd called her back. He'd texted her all night long, but she'd never answered, and by the next morning, her phone was dead. He didn't know if she'd gotten a new one or changed her number; he just knew that she was really gone.

He barely remembered the rest of that year. The summer had been hard, too. They'd planned to work at a camp in Yosemite together, but he couldn't make himself go on his own. Senior year had gotten a little easier. He'd dated as many girls as he could, trying to put her out of his head. By college, he'd almost forgotten her smile, her laugh, the taste of her kiss.

But it was coming back now, and he didn't like it. What the hell was wrong with him? It had been fourteen years. He'd had other relationships. Her memory should not be bothering him this much.

"Did you ever try to find her?" Dylan asked. "Stalk her on social media?"

"No. Never. She made her choice. I haven't thought about her in years." He'd deliberately put her out of his head for a very long time, although he had had to struggle a few times on his recent road trip, because they'd spoken so often about seeing the world together. "I'll be fine once I know it's not her. Then it will be a tragic story, but it won't be Cassidy's tragic story."

"True, but I'm not sure you'll be fine. You haven't actually been fine in a while."

He couldn't argue with that, so he let his brother have the last word, happy that they'd arrived at the police station.

They gave their names to the clerk behind the counter

and were told to wait in the small lobby. While Dylan checked out some wanted posters on a nearby bulletin board, he paced around the room, feeling wired and tense, like he'd had too many cups of coffee, but he'd barely had one.

When a nearby door opened, and Max Harrison entered the room, he let out a breath of relief. His cousin Emma's husband wore dark jeans and a button-down shirt, a badge on his waistband. His green eyes were more serious than usual as he shook both their hands, then said, "Why don't we talk inside?" He led them down a hallway and into a small conference room. "This is my partner, Detective Vance Randall—Dylan and Hunter Callaway."

Detective Randall, a fifty-something man with war-weary brown eyes, gave them a nod and motioned them into chairs at the table, an open file in front of him.

"Have you ID'd the body?" Hunter asked as he took a seat across from the detective.

"Yes, we have," the detective replied.

"Well?" he asked impatiently. "Whose bones were in that wall?" His nerves were screaming for the few seconds it took the detective to answer his question.

"They belong to a young male, probably around the age of sixteen or seventeen," Randall returned.

The air went out of him like a popped balloon and it took a second for him to get his breath back.

"I told you it wasn't her," Dylan said, a relieved note in his voice.

"Her?" Max echoed. "Who are you referring to?"

"Cassidy Ellison," he replied. "She was a girl I dated in high school. She lived in the house back then. Do you have a name for the victim?"

The detective glanced at the file in front of him. "Yes. Thomas Mark Lucas."

"No," he breathed. "Not Tommy. Are you sure?"

Detective Randall pulled out a photo and put it on the table in front of them. "We are sure. Did you know this boy?"

He stared at the picture of the rail-thin kid with the dirty-blond hair, and the big, dark, unhappy brown eyes and felt a mix of emotions. He'd hated Tommy for years, because Cassidy had chosen Tommy over him, but seeing his face now reminded him that Tommy had always looked a little broken. It was his vulnerability that had probably made Cassidy want to take care of him, be there for him.

"Yes. I knew him. He was a foster kid living with the Faulkners for a few weeks before he allegedly ran away with my ex-girlfriend. Do you know how long the body was in the house?"

"We're still waiting on forensics for more details, but they estimate the time of death to be approximately fourteen to fifteen years ago," Max replied.

"Which is when I last saw him."

"You said he ran away with your ex-girlfriend?" Max continued.

"It was the day of the junior prom. Cassidy and I were supposed to go together. I got a text saying she was leaving town with Tommy, that he needed her, and she needed him. I called her, texted her; she never answered, and I never heard from either of them again."

"We need to find Cassidy." Max pulled out a pen, grabbing the notepad in front of him. "What can you tell me about her?"

He suddenly didn't want to answer the question. He could see where all this was going. Tommy was dead. He'd been killed and left in the garage of the house. And Cassidy had disappeared at the very same time. The police might think she was responsible for Tommy's death. Or they might think she had been killed, too.

His stomach turned over again. Maybe he shouldn't feel relieved just yet. "What do the Faulkners have to say about all this? Do they have an explanation for how a kid in their care was killed and hidden in a wall in their garage?"

"Donald Faulkner died five months ago," Detective Randall said. "His wife Geralyn was hysterical when she learned of the discovery. She said it wasn't possible, and we had to be wrong. She started screaming and crying and eventually had to be sedated and taken to the hospital."

"Was she living in the house alone now? Is she still taking in kids?" he asked.

"That apparently ended several years ago. Geralyn has been completely on her own in the house since her husband died five months ago, although her sister Monica and twin nieces Dee and Halsey occasionally stay there when they're in the city. She also sees her brother-in-law Evan and nephew Colin. We will be interviewing all of them. We're just at the beginning of this investigation."

"Mrs. Faulkner has to know who did this, or maybe she did it herself. How could a teenage boy have been killed and buried in the walls of the garage without her knowledge?"

"Exactly what we're going to ask her," Max replied. "We obtained a list of the kids who were living with the Faulkners around the time in question. Want to tell me which of these kids you knew?"

Max spread a series of photographs in front of him, and his past came alive in an even more painful and terrifying way, because he hadn't actually looked at her image in fourteen years.

But there she was, with her long, blonde hair, her beautiful features, and her haunted brown eyes. He drew in a heavy, hard breath and then put his finger on her photo. "This is her—Cassidy Ellison."

"And she allegedly ran away with Tommy Lucas?" Max asked.

"I thought so."

"They might have left town together, and Tommy returned at a later date," Dylan interjected.

"That's possible." He didn't know what to think. "Was the house searched for any other bodies?"

"It was," Max said, meeting his gaze. "We had a forensic team go through every inch of the place. We're certain there are no other victims."

"At least, none that were buried there. If the Faulkners

were willing to hide a body in their garage all these years, what else were they willing to do?"

Max tipped his head. "True. Like I said, we're just at the beginning. We'll get all the answers."

"I hope so."

"Even if that makes your ex-girlfriend a suspect?" Detective Randall asked. "It sounds like she was the last person to see Tommy. And she disappeared at the same time."

"She wasn't the last person to see Tommy; that would be the person who killed him, and she did not do that. She was his friend, and she was a sweet, kind-hearted, shy girl. She didn't have any aggression or violence inside of her. And she and Tommy were very close."

"Do you have any idea where Cassidy is now?" Detective Randall asked.

"I already said I never heard from her again. And it seems to me that the one you need to talk to is Mrs. Faulkner."

"We will do that as soon as the doctor allows us to question her," Max said. "But we are also going to try to locate all the individuals who lived at the house during the time period in question. That will include Cassidy."

"I understand. I can't help you. I don't know where she is, and I didn't know any of the other kids." He pushed back his chair and stood up. "Thanks for the update, Max."

He didn't really care what the others thought as he left the room and then the station, not stopping until he got to the parking lot. He paced by the Porsche, taking deep breaths that did little to calm his racing pulse.

It wasn't air he needed; it was answers, and those answers were probably going to have to come from Cassidy...

But how could he see her again?

On the other hand, how could he not?

Three

Cassidy got up from her desk to close the window as a gust of wind blew the landscape blueprints she'd been reviewing all over the floor. Her office, in the back of the Wild Garden Nursery, overlooked the Pacific Coast Highway and the Pacific Ocean. As she looked through the panes of glass, she could see storm clouds on the horizon, whipping the waves into a turbulent frenzy.

It was early June—but it didn't feel like it. The weather had dropped ten degrees from the day before and the high today would be barely sixty degrees. She really hoped the rain would be light and quick. She had a lot of planting to do over the weekend at the Holman Estate in San Francisco, the biggest job of her career as a landscape designer, and she was eager to get started.

Designing and planting gardens had been her dream since she was a little girl, since she'd pulled weeds at her mother's side, and pressed tiny seeds into moist, dark earth and woken up every morning, impatient to see them sprout.

She smiled to herself at the happy memory. She could still see her mom in her head: the big sunhat covering her light-blonde hair and very fair complexion; her laughing brown eyes; her smile that had been as bright as the sun that beat down on them; her voice as soft as the whisper of breeze that lifted her hair off the back of her neck.

Pressing her fingers against the window, she wished she could hear her mother's voice one more time, that she could tell her all that had happened since her death, that her mom could see how she'd pulled herself out of the darkness and actually built a life that was pretty good now.

The Wild Garden Nursery had become the place of her rebirth, so to speak, and located on a hill in Half Moon Bay, a coastal town just south of San Francisco, she'd finally found a safe place to call home.

But it wasn't just home. It was also her place of business, and right now she had work to do.

Returning to her desk, she picked up the blueprints and spread them out in front of her as her office door opened.

"There's a storm brewing," George Mitchell said as he ambled into the room with a slight limp in his gait. At sixty-nine years old, George might have lost a bit of mobility, but his wise hazel-colored gaze was as sharp and as penetrating as it had ever been. "My knees have been swollen since I woke up this morning. You know what that means?"

She bit back a smile, knowing that George wouldn't appreciate her commenting on the fact that he needed to stop spending hours moving plants and planting trees behind the nursery and start delegating his work to the younger employees. "I do know what that means," she said instead. "Rain is coming."

"It's coming, and not just a drizzle. I can feel it in my bones."

An odd shiver ran down her spine at his words. She'd actually been feeling a little uneasy, too, and she didn't know why. Because unlike George, she really couldn't predict the rain. In fact, the clouds usually opened up on her when she least expected it.

"You might want to put off your planting tomorrow at the Holman estate," George added. "I know you're eager to get started, but best not to do that in the rain."

"I'll see how it goes. The Holmans want everything finished by the Fourth of July, which is only five weeks away, so I need to get cracking as soon as possible. There is a lot to do."

"And you're more than up for it." Approval showed in his gaze. "You hooked a big fish, Cassidy."

"Now, I have to deliver."

"You'll deliver. You're an artist when it comes to gardens."

"I've never done anything this complex for anyone with as much money or power or reputation as the Holmans. They'll be hosting parties in that garden. Think of the referrals we could get if I do a good job."

"And that's what you'll do. You're not getting nervous, are you? Because you shouldn't waste a second feeling like you can't do this. The way you mix plants and trees with water features, iron, glass, and rocks—it's like you're a magician. You put things together that shouldn't work and yet they do."

She flushed at his compliment. "I learned from the best."

"I know you're talking about Mary, not me." George perched on the chair in front of her desk. "You look good sitting there."

"It still doesn't quite feel right." Her gaze moved to the photograph of the white-haired woman with the sparkling blue eyes who'd sat at this desk for over thirty years—George's wife and soulmate, Mary.

"When you came on board, Mary knew she'd found the perfect person to take over the business. You were the daughter she never had."

"And she was truly a second mother." She felt a wave of pain—not just for the loss of Mary, who had passed away eight months earlier, but also for the loss of her real mother,

Carolyn, who had died when she was thirteen.

The years in between her mom's death and meeting Mary had truly been the most harrowing, frightening, horrible years of her life. Mary and George had saved her, and she was going to do everything she could to maintain and grow the business they had created so many years earlier. "I want to make both of you proud. You took a chance on me, and I appreciate that so much."

"You've already made me proud. But you have to pace yourself."

"I love my work."

"You should love other things, too. Maybe even find yourself a man."

She smiled at that comment. "You're not going to give me dating advice, are you?"

"Lordy, no." He got up quickly, an uncomfortable expression on his face. "That's the last thing I'd ever do. I just don't want you to work too hard. Did you even have lunch today?"

"I'll get to that; it's only noon."

"Cassidy?"

She looked past George to see Felicia Michaels standing in the doorway. A twenty-year-old college student, Felicia worked part-time at the nursery, answering calls and waiting on customers.

"What's up?" she asked.

"I just got a weird call from a Detective Max Harrison at the San Francisco Police Department."

Her stomach took a sudden nosedive, as she instinctively jumped to her feet. "What do you mean?" She tried to keep the panic out of her voice, but judging by the narrowing of George's gaze, she wasn't quite succeeding.

"He asked for Cassidy Ellison. I said there was a Cassidy Morgan here, but not a Cassidy Ellison."

Her heart turned over. Of course, Felicia would have said that. "Did he say what he wanted?"

"He wanted to speak to you. I got a weird feeling, so I

said you were out. I don't really know why. But he left his number."

Felicia walked forward and handed her a piece of note paper with the name and number scrawled across it.

She drew in a long breath, her pulse racing. *Why on earth would the police be looking for Cassidy Ellison now?*

"Did I do the right thing?" Felicia asked.

"Yes, it's fine. I'll take care of it." She didn't think she'd ever met a Detective Harrison before, but the fact that he was looking for Cassidy Ellison did not bode well for her. She probably should have changed her first name, but it had been the one link to her parents that she hadn't wanted to lose. "How's everything going in the store? Is it busy? Do you need help?"

"It's fine. Jodi and I have things under control," Felicia said, referring to one of their other clerks.

"Good. You can get back to it."

"What's that about?" George asked, as Felicia left the office.

She met his worried gaze. "I don't know."

"Ellison—does that name mean something to you?"

George and Mary had never asked very many questions back when they'd first hired her as a nineteen-year-old in desperate need of a job and a place to stay. They'd gone off a gut instinct that she was a good person who needed help. Not only had they given her a job at the nursery, they'd also let her sleep in the small studio apartment upstairs, where she'd lived for the past eleven years.

She didn't want to lie to George, but she also didn't want to get him involved in her past. "Don't worry about this. I'll take care of it."

"Can't help worrying about you. Wish Mary was here. She'd know what to do."

"I know what to do. It's fine."

"There was trouble in your past. We never wanted to pry, but we could see the shadows in your eyes. We knew you'd been hurt. But you never wanted to talk about it."

"Whatever happened to me was a long, long time ago. I'm sure this is nothing. Anyway, I have to run out for a bit. I have some errands to do."

"Better get those done before the storm comes."

"That's what I was thinking."

She grabbed her navy-blue cardigan sweater off the back of her chair and put it on over her T-shirt and jeans. Then she picked up her car keys and headed out of her office and through the retail shop. Felicia was helping an older woman at the cash register while Freddie, one of their gardeners, was watering plants and rearranging displays. The store and office filled the bottom floor of the two-story building, while her one-bedroom apartment and a storage room occupied the second floor.

Adjacent to the building were two large greenhouses filled with plants and beyond that, fields of flowers and vegetables, which they often sold from a roadside stand along Highway 1, which was at the bottom of the hill, and was the main highway running up and down the coast.

Normally, just walking through the store, inhaling the beautiful scents, feeling the new life all around her made her feel better, but today her mind was not on flowers or plants. It was on the past, and not the happy past that featured her mom. Her memories now were much darker.

As she hit the parking lot, she didn't really know where she was going. She could barely remember what errands she had planned to do today. All she knew was that she felt a desperate need to escape, to get away before the police arrived, although what they could want with her now was unclear. But it had to have something to do with her lost years, the ones she'd locked away in the deepest part of her heart.

She couldn't go back to those years. She'd barely managed to survive the first time.

Not that it had all been bad...

There had been one bright spot, one wonderful person, who'd made her smile and laugh, who'd made her believe for a few minutes that maybe life could be better. But she'd left him; she'd hurt him. It hadn't been fair, but it had been necessary.

As she neared her vehicle, a green van emblazoned with the Wild Garden logo, a car came speeding up the single-lane road, churning up loose dirt and pebbles in its wake.

Thankfully, it wasn't a police car, but a black Jeep Wrangler. Instead of turning into one of the open spots, the Jeep came to a screeching halt in front of her, and a man jumped out.

She was about to tell him he couldn't leave his car there when she saw his face—when she saw his eyes—his stunning blue eyes.

Her heart stopped.

"Cassidy?" he asked in disbelief, as if he couldn't really believe it was her.

She couldn't really believe it was him. "Hunter."

She'd imagined running into him a thousand times. She'd thought about what she would say, what he would say. But now she couldn't get one more word out of her mouth.

All she could do was stare at him with her mind spinning, her palms sweating, her nerves on every last jagged edge.

She'd met Hunter when she was sixteen, when she was desperately lonely, terribly unhappy, but he'd changed all that.

They'd run into each other—literally. Hunter had come around a corner of the school hallway and barreled straight into her. He'd been moving fast—the way he always did—a crowd of boys and girls following behind him, eager to be near one of the most popular boys in the school. Hunter was the star baseball player, the star basketball player. He was funny and handsome and friendly.

When she'd stumbled and dropped her books, Hunter had held out his hand, and she'd stared at it in bemusement, feeling like a complete idiot. She'd been at the high school for a month and until that moment, she'd made a habit of staying in the shadows, spectating, not participating, trying not to be the new kid, who often became the target of bullies and mean girls.

But at that moment, Hunter had put her into the spotlight. And when she'd slid her hand into his, she'd felt a shocking and unexpected heat.

He'd helped her to her feet and when he'd looked into her eyes and given her that lazy, crooked smile that drove all the girls crazy, she'd known her life was never going to be the same.

But she still hadn't expected that Hunter would actually seek her out again, that he would ask her to hang out, that she would become one of those girls by his side. Her classmates hadn't liked that she was by his side, but Hunter hadn't seemed to care that she wasn't part of the popular crowd. And she'd been surprised at how easy he was to talk to, how generous he was, how he opened up her very closed world.

And then there had been the mad attraction between them.

Every time their eyes met, tingles had run down her spine. Hunter's thick, wavy, always mussed brown hair, had made her want to run her fingers through it. His reckless, daring eyes, and his sexy mouth had turned kissing into an out-of-this-world experience. Oh, the things he'd made her want to do, and the things they'd done. When she was with him, she'd been able to be someone else. He'd brought the fun back into her life, made her smile, teased out a laugh even when she'd promised herself she wouldn't get caught up in whatever crazy idea he'd come up with.

And then it had all ended. Her problems at home caught up with the magical relationship she had with Hunter.

She'd had to run. She'd had to hurt him.

He probably didn't think she'd hurt herself at the same time, but she had.

"Hunter," she said again, feeling as if all the thick, protective layers she'd covered herself in were falling apart. He'd grown up since she'd known him. He had a scruffy beard now. His shoulders were broader. His frame was stockier. He was a man, not a boy—an impatient, angry man, who clearly had a problem with her. "What are you doing here?" She had the terrible feeling that the phone call from the police and Hunter's sudden appearance were tied together.

"Looking for you," he bit out.

"Why?"

"You don't know? The police didn't call you?"

"I haven't spoken to the police." A gust of wind lifted her blonde hair and blew it across her face, sending another chill through her. "Why would they want to talk to me? And why are you here?"

"I'm a firefighter."

"Okay." She wasn't sure why that was relevant. "I figured you would probably follow in your dad's footsteps. But what does that have to do—"

"There was a fire yesterday—at the Faulkners' house."

His words drove the breath from her chest.

"I was inside your old home," he continued. "I was in your bedroom."

"I don't want to hear this." She was quite certain whatever was coming next was going to be bad.

As she turned away, he grabbed her arm. "You don't have a choice." His fingers tightened in a hard, punishing grip.

"Let go of me, Hunter."

He ignored her demand, his gaze demanding she look at him. "You have to listen. When I was in the garage, venting the walls, looking for fire, I found a body hidden behind the sheetrock."

Another wave of shock ran through her. "What—what are you talking about?"

"I'm talking about a skeleton. It had been there a long time—probably fourteen years," he said, a hard note in his voice.

She couldn't breathe. She couldn't swallow. And if he hadn't been holding onto her, she thought she might have passed out.

"Don't you want to know who it was?" He gave her a little shake. "Because for twenty-four long hours, I thought it might be you."

"Me?" She barely managed to get the word out between her tight, tense lips. "Why did you think it might be me?"

"Because of the way you left. It was unexpected. It didn't make sense. You never answered your phone when I tried to call you back."

"You tried to call me?"

"Of course I did. What the hell did you think I was going to do when I got your text three hours before I was supposed to pick you up for the prom?"

"I don't know..." Her voice trailed away as she tried to keep up with everything he was saying. *There had been a fire. He'd found human remains in the garage, hidden in the walls. How was that possible?* "Who—who was found in the garage?" she asked, certain she really didn't want to know, but the truth was coming whether she was ready for it or not.

"You know, don't you?"

She wanted to shake her head, but a terrible truth was rocketing through her, the answer to a question she had had for a very long time.

"It was Tommy Lucas," Hunter continued. "The guy you allegedly ran away with. The one you chose over me. The one who needed you more than I did."

Tommy! "No. That's not possible. Tommy isn't dead."

"Unfortunately, he is dead."

Thinking about her friend, her heart broke for his lost soul, his lost life. "Oh, God!"

"That's all you have to say?"

He'd never been so rough with her, so bullying, but she could see the pain in his eyes, and she knew he was as caught up in the past as she was.

"Are you sure it was Tommy?"

"The police identified the body this morning."

"I can't believe it."

"You didn't run away with him, did you?"

"No. He was supposed to meet me at the bus station, but he didn't come. I got a text saying it would be better if we split up. We'd be less easy to find. He told me to go without him, to be safe, and not to look back. I wasn't sure what to do, but I had the ticket in my hand." She could still remember that terrible moment of indecision. *Did she go back to the Faulkners, or did she go forward and save herself?*

"So, you left anyway."

"I had to. I believed what he'd said, that it would be less easy to find us if we weren't together." A horrific thought ran through her head. "They killed him, didn't they?"

"Who?"

She stared into his eyes. "The Faulkners."

Four

⸺➤➤◄◄⸺

"**Y**ou're accusing your foster parents of murder?" Hunter asked.

"Yes, and you're hurting me, Hunter."

He abruptly let go of her arm, and guilt flashed through his eyes. "Sorry. I didn't mean to hurt you."

She rubbed her arm, her mind still spinning.

Tommy hadn't abandoned her. He'd been killed.

And she knew who had murdered him—those horrible people who'd fooled everyone but her and Tommy.

Tommy! Her already bruised and battered heart took another hard hit. *Poor Tommy. He'd barely had a life. He'd deserved so much more.*

She put a hand to her mouth as a wave of nausea ran through her. "I think I'm going to be sick."

"Maybe you should sit down."

It was a good idea. Her legs felt weak. Her world was tilting. Fortunately, there was a bench across the parking lot with a view of the ocean, and she managed to stumble her way over there, not wanting to have this conversation anywhere inside the building. George and her coworkers would have too many questions. None of them knew about her past, and she preferred to keep it that way. Trusting in anyone had never been good for her.

It felt good to have something solid beneath her, but the view, which normally calmed and inspired her, couldn't begin to cut through the turmoil swirling around inside of her. She didn't know what she'd expected when she'd first heard that the police were looking for her, but it certainly had not been this.

Hunter took a seat next to her, his gaze on her and not the ocean.

She turned her head to look at him, seeing a lot of different emotions moving through his eyes as well. "You said that you found the body? That's surreal."

"That's one word for it," he said shortly.

"When did this happen?"

"Yesterday morning. It took them a day to ID the remains."

"I still can't believe it. There's no doubt?"

"It didn't sound like it to me, but you can ask the cops when you talk to them."

The last thing she wanted to do was speak to the police. Their questions were going to rip open all the old scars. "How did you find me?"

"My cousin Emma's husband, Max Harrison, is a homicide detective with the SFPD. He's working the case. I told him about you and Tommy, what little I knew about your living situation back then. He wants to talk to everyone who was living in the house at the time when the murder might have occurred. I told him I didn't know where you were, but he called me a half hour ago and said they found a Cassidy Morgan in Pacifica at a landscape nursery, and I knew instantly it was you, even if you had changed your last name. You were obsessed with flowers and gardens. It was all you talked about, all you ever wanted to do. I jumped in my Jeep and came down here. I'm sure the police will soon be here as well."

"They just called. They were looking for Cassidy Ellison, but—"

"But you know that they'll quickly figure out that Cassidy Morgan and Cassidy Ellison are the same person." His gaze narrowed suspiciously. "Is that why you were in the parking lot? Were you running away again?"

"I don't honestly know where I was going, but I did feel the need to escape. Everything has been going so well. I should have known it couldn't last."

"Are you married, Cassidy?"

"No. I changed my name when I was eighteen. I wanted to put some distance between myself and the past. Start over, be someone else."

"You should have changed your first name, too."

"That would have been smart, but I couldn't. My mom named me Cassidy, because it was her mother's maiden name, the single mom who had raised her, the only grandmother I ever knew. I couldn't break the tie. I never thought anyone would come looking for me after I aged out of the system."

Silence fell between them for a long minute. There were so many unspoken words between them. They were dancing around the heartbreak, the personal anger, but she could see the simmering feelings in Hunter's eyes. He'd never been one to hold back when he had something to say. She supposed she should have appreciated his restraint so far. But that was coming to an end.

"Why, Cassidy?"

It was a simple question, but the answer was oh, so complicated. She looked away from his piercing blue-eyed gaze that had always made her worry that he would see more than she wanted him to see.

"Cassidy. Look at me."

She reluctantly turned back to him.

"Don't you think I deserve an answer?" he asked. "Why did you leave me?"

"I told you in the text. Tommy and I needed to get away from the Faulkners. We couldn't stay in San Francisco."

"But he changed his mind. Why didn't you change yours?"

"I couldn't. It was easier to leave."

"Easier?" Anger sharpened his tone. "You dumped me on the night of the prom. You let me think you and Tommy were together. Do you have any idea what that did to me?"

The glittering pain in his eyes made her realize that while she might have thought he'd long forgotten that day, he hadn't. That surprised her a little.

"You owe me an explanation," he continued.

"An explanation or an apology?"

"Maybe both."

"I am sorry. I would have much rather gone to the prom than gotten on that dirty bus by myself. But I had made my choice, and there was no turning back. When I said it was easier to go, I wasn't talking about you. That part was always hard. I was referring to my situation with the Faulkners. There was a lot you didn't know."

"Like what?"

"I don't want to do this," she said with a sigh. "It's too much to get into now."

"Well, I didn't want to find Tommy's bones in that wall, but it happened, and here we are. This is just the beginning, Cassidy. The police are going to come with even more questions. They're going to ask you about the last time you saw Tommy, why you ran away, why you didn't return to the house when Tommy didn't show up at the bus station. They're going to question if any of your story is true. They'll wonder if you were involved in whatever happened to Tommy and that's why you ran away. They might even think you killed him."

"That's ridiculous."

"I already heard some of their questions. Believe me, it's not ridiculous."

He was right. She was going to end up in the middle of this, especially if the Faulkners started talking and decided she would make a good scapegoat. "Have the Faulkners been arrested?"

"Mr. Faulkner died several months ago. Apparently, his wife got hysterical when she heard about the body and had to be hospitalized. The police haven't been able to question her yet."

"He's dead? Donald is dead?" She felt an immeasurable relief at the idea that Donald was deceased, that he wasn't going to show up next, that she wouldn't have to talk to him ever again.

"Yes, he's dead."

She drew in a breath and let it out. "Well, good."

"Good? What did the Faulkners do to you, Cassidy? Did they abuse you? Hurt you? Is that why you ran away? Is that what you didn't tell me?"

"It doesn't matter anymore."

"It might not have mattered before yesterday, but it does now. Someone killed Tommy, and you're going to be at the top of the list of suspects, along with every kid who lived in that house."

"You think a kid living in their house could have buried a body in the wall of the garage without the Faulkners knowing about it?" she asked in amazement. "That garage was Donald's private place, his workshop, where no one was allowed to go. It was off-limits. If there was a body in there, trust me, Donald knew about it."

"Maybe Geralyn didn't."

"They were a team. She knew whatever he knew." She twisted her fingers together, feeling sad and angry, guilty and confused. If she'd gone back to the house, if she'd tried to find Tommy, maybe he'd still be alive.

"What was happening in that house, Cassidy?"

Hunter's questions were relentless. "I really don't want to talk about it."

"You have to."

"It hurts. Deep in my heart." She looked into his eyes, putting a hand against her chest. "The pain," she whispered. "It's so awful. It rips me apart. I know you didn't like Tommy, but he was a sixteen-year-old boy who hadn't been loved by anyone in a very long time, who had been through hell. To know that his life ended in that house, before he had a chance to ever have a life…it's almost unbearable."

His gaze softened with compassion. "I'm sorry. You're right. Tommy didn't deserve to die, to end up where he did." A pause followed his words. "But you can do more than just feel bad; you can help the police find out what happened to him. If you don't want to tell me, fine. But you need to tell someone."

"I ran away because I was afraid I wouldn't survive living in that house. I know I didn't tell you anything, that you couldn't possibly understand what I was going through. How could you? I kept that part of my life away from you. But knowing now where Tommy ended up, can you understand that the situation was much more complicated than you knew?"

"I'm beginning to realize that," he admitted. "But you should have trusted me, Cassidy. We were close. I thought we were telling each other everything, or, at least, I was telling you everything."

"You wouldn't have liked me if you'd known everything," she said softly, giving him a helpless shrug.

"Well, we'll never know, will we? You didn't give me a chance to help you. You should have. We could have spoken to my parents, to the police. We could have shut down the Faulkners, stopped them from doing whatever they were doing."

"That wouldn't have happened."

"You don't know."

"I do know. I tried, Hunter. I tried to tell the truth, to speak to someone in power. It didn't work. The Faulkners made it look like I was crazy."

"What are you talking about?"

"I'm talking about Molly."

"Molly?" he asked in confusion. "Who the hell is Molly?"

"She was a girl I shared a room with at the Faulkners'. She was fourteen years old. She had black hair, dark-brown eyes, the kindest smile, and for three weeks, she was my friend. But two nights in a row, I woke up and noticed her gone. The third night, she never came back. I asked Geralyn where Molly was, and she told me that Molly had been transferred to a new home, but she wouldn't say why. They cleaned Molly's things out of the room while I was at school the next day. I had a really bad feeling about it, so I went to the social worker who'd placed me at the Faulkners, and I told her what happened. She said she would check into it. I trusted her to do that."

"What did she find?"

"Nothing. She called me in to her office the next day. She told me that there had never been a girl named Molly living at the house, and that the Faulkners had explained that I was having emotional problems and that I had an imaginary friend named Molly." Fury ran through her at that memory. "The social worker made it clear to me that she believed them. She said she'd interviewed several other children at the house, who had no knowledge of anyone named Molly."

"Why would they lie?"

"Because they were scared of the Faulkners. The only one who wouldn't have lied was Tommy, but she didn't talk to him. With everyone against me—even the other kids in the house—I felt very alone. I almost started to believe that maybe I had made Molly up. But Tommy kept me sane. He knew that Molly had been there, and he thought that something terrible had happened to her."

"And all this was going on while we were dating, while we were going to parties and making out and walking on the beach? You never thought to share any of it with me?"

"It wasn't going on the whole time. Molly disappeared two weeks before the prom. I actually asked you if you remembered seeing her when I'd taken you into the house."

"I don't remember that."

"Well, you also didn't remember her."

"I was there once, and, frankly, I was probably more interested in making out with you than looking at who else was around."

She flushed at that memory. She and Hunter had been all over each other back then.

"Anyway." She cleared her throat. "After my discussion with the social worker, Mrs. Faulkner told me that the family doctor was going to prescribe some sedatives for me so that I could calm down. That terrified me. They were going to drug me."

"They couldn't have forced that on you."

"Who was going to stop them? The social worker who thought I was crazy? Then things got worse. Donald Faulkner asked me to go to lunch with him on Saturday, the day of the prom. He said he wanted me to feel more comfortable living in the house and that we should have a private conversation. I freaked out. I was convinced that Mr. Faulkner had done something to Molly. I told Tommy, and he said we needed to run. We couldn't wait. We had to go immediately."

She drew in a hard breath and let it out, then continued. "When Tommy didn't show up, I almost went back to the house, but he'd told me to keep going, to be safe, and the bus was right there. It was either get on it or lose my chance to get away, so I got on board. I figured one day Tommy and I would catch up with each other. Now, I know why that didn't happen. They must have killed him before he could leave the house. He probably suspected he wasn't going to get away and that's why he told me to go without him." She put a hand to her mouth, feeling a rush of nausea. "If I had gone back, maybe I could have stopped that from happening."

"Or you could have died, too. You should have told me what was happening, Cassidy. You didn't even have to tell me the whole story. You could have just said you were in trouble. You were scared. I would have helped you. My parents would have helped you."

There was nothing but sincerity in his eyes. He honestly believed that's what would have happened, but she wasn't so sure.

"I know you would have tried. But the social worker and the Faulkners—they would have convinced your parents that I was making it all up. The Faulkners were well respected in the city. Geralyn volunteered at the high school. Donald was on the city council, remember? It would have been my word against theirs. And I'd already tried to get help."

He frowned. "I would have believed you. If you'd asked me to hide you away, I would have done that. If you'd asked me not to tell my parents, I would have gone along. I was crazy about you, Cassidy. You knew that. We were connected."

The pain in his eyes, in his voice, touched her soul, broke another piece of her heart. In the intervening years, she'd told herself that Hunter probably hadn't missed her all that much, that he'd gone on to other girls, that he'd probably forgotten about her in a minute, but she could see that wasn't true. "I'm really sorry, Hunter. I wanted to tell you. But I was scared. I wasn't thinking straight. Things were happening fast."

"You trusted Tommy over me. You told him everything."

"I didn't have to tell him. He was living my life with me. And when I was with you, I didn't want to talk about the bad stuff. You were my escape. When we were together, I felt almost normal. I thought I could make it a few more years until I could be free of foster care. But after Molly disappeared, the problems with the social worker, the threat of medication, Mr. Faulkner...I panicked. Now I realize that my actions probably got Tommy killed." The horror of his death hit her again. "They made him pay for my leaving. This is my fault."

"It's not your fault. It's theirs—the Faulkners'. And you don't know how or why Tommy was killed. You don't even know if it happened right after you left. Unless you heard from Tommy later?"

"No. I never heard from him again, but I also threw my phone away at the bus station. I didn't want to risk anyone tracking me."

"Where did you go?"

"Santa Cruz. I had enough money for three nights in a cheap motel. It was the kind of place where they don't ask any questions. Luckily, I didn't stay there long. I got a job at the amusement park and eventually found a couple of girls who let me sleep on their couch."

"And you never thought about getting back in touch with me or with Tommy?"

"I didn't know where Tommy was, and I was afraid any contact with you would take me back into the Faulkners' world. I was also busy just trying to survive and stay away from the authorities. When I turned eighteen, it had been over a year and a half since I'd seen you or Tommy. I didn't think anyone would care to hear from me again. So that's it. Now you know."

"I doubt I know all of it, but it's a start. You have to tell the police, Cassidy."

"I'm not sure they'll believe me. Geralyn will tell them a different story. She'll make them think I'm a liar, just like she did before. In fact, she'll probably tell them I was mentally disturbed. She'll say that I killed Tommy and ran away. Oh, God!" She jumped to her feet as the possibilities raced through her head. "I can't do this. I can't see her. I can't hear her lie about me again." She felt an overwhelming urge to run.

"You can face her," Hunter said forcibly, as he got to his feet. "You're an adult now. She can't hurt you anymore. And you have to do this—not just for yourself—for Tommy."

His words were logical, reasonable, but they barely made a dent in the fear running through her. Unfortunately, she didn't think disappearing would be as easy this time around, not if the police were looking for her, too.

"I'll help you," he added.

"Why would you? You hate me."

"I did hate you after you ditched me. But that was a long time ago. And I didn't know this side of the story. I'm also a part of this—not just because we were together back then, but because I found Tommy's bones."

"It's so strange that it was you. What are the odds of that?"

"A million to one? I have no idea. But I'm in this. We need to find out what happened to Tommy—"

"And make them pay," she whispered.

"And make them pay," he agreed.

She wondered if that could really happen. She'd long ago given up on the idea of karma, of people paying for their bad deeds. But Hunter was making her believe there could be justice for Tommy and punishment for the Faulkners. "This is what you did before," she murmured.

"What?"

"You made me think the impossible could happen, that I could have the fairy tale."

"Maybe you could have—if you hadn't run away," he said pointedly.

As Hunter finished speaking, she saw George walking purposefully in their direction. He obviously didn't like the look of their conversation, and since it was on the heels of a call from the police, she couldn't blame him.

"Don't say anything to my boss," she said quickly. "I don't want anyone here to know about this."

Hunter didn't have time to answer before George reached them.

"Everything all right out here, Cassidy?" he asked, his sharp gaze running across Hunter's face, before he turned to her. "You look upset."

"I—I'm fine." She stumbled over the words in a way that would definitely not make her answer believable, but she was still having trouble pulling herself together.

"You don't sound fine." He crossed his arms in front of his chest as he looked back at Hunter. "Who are you?"

"Hunter Callaway." Hunter extended his hand. "An old friend of Cassidy's."

"Friend, huh?" George muttered, not bothering to shake Hunter's hand. "Is he telling the truth, Cassidy?"

"We knew each other in high school," she said, as Hunter dropped his hand and shoved it into his pocket. "Everything is okay. I have to run up to the city for a few hours, though."

"Does this have something to do with that call you just missed?"

"It does. I'll explain when I get back."

"You want me to go with you?"

"No, I need you to run things here. I can do this on my own."

"All right then, but I've got your name," George said, waving a finger at Hunter. "Don't forget that." Then he ambled back the way he'd come.

"You have a protector," Hunter said.

"Yes. George has been like a father to me. He's a good man. He and his wife, Mary, pretty much saved my life."

Hunter gave her a speculative look. "I'd like to hear more of that story."

"One story at a time. I need to talk to the police, and I'd rather not have them come here."

"So, you'll go there. I'll take you."

"I'll drive myself." She needed the time to get her head together. "What's the address?"

He gave her the station address and then said, "I'll follow you."

She didn't bother telling him he didn't need to go at all. That would be a waste of her breath. Clearly, Hunter was going to make sure she spoke to the cops. "All right then. Let's get this over with."

As they walked across the lot, she had one more question to ask. "Has the rest of the house been searched—all the walls?"

His jaw hardened, as his gaze met hers. "Yes. They didn't find any more bodies."

"Thank God," she breathed. But that still made her wonder what had happened to Molly.

Five

Hunter stayed close to the back of Cassidy's silver Prius as she drove into San Francisco, feeling a mix of emotions that ranged from anger to sadness to complete and utter confusion. He had no idea what to make of her story—a disappearing girl, who apparently didn't exist in the foster system, potentially crazy foster parents, the teenaged boy who'd never made it out of that house alive. It sounded like a horror movie. While it made sense on some level, he couldn't imagine a social worker telling Cassidy she was crazy and that she'd made up an imaginary friend.

On the other hand, Tommy Lucas had been killed years ago, and his body hidden away in the wall of the Faulkners' garage, making it impossible to deny that something horrific had happened in that house.

He wondered how they'd gotten away with it. Wouldn't the smell of a decomposing body have triggered anyone to report anything? But Cassidy had said that the garage was off-limits, and if the kids in the house were too terrified to even admit one of the kids there had gone missing, would they have reported a smell coming from the garage? Probably not.

And what about the other missing girl? Was Cassidy right—that the Faulkners had hurt other children?

Or was any of this real? Was Cassidy telling him the truth? Was she a trusted narrator of the story?

She'd already admitted that her social worker thought she was crazy, that her foster mother said she made up people in her head.

Maybe there was something wrong with her.

But every instinct he had rebelled against that thought.

Was that because he really believed in Cassidy, in the girl he thought he knew, or because he just didn't want to have been wrong about her?

No. He wasn't wrong about her. She wasn't crazy or a killer. She was...

He wasn't sure exactly who she was, but he did know that she'd grown up to be a beautiful woman. She wasn't as thin as she'd been in high school. Her jeans and T-shirt had clung to some very nice curves. Her blonde hair was longer and lighter now, but she had the same full, pink lips, he'd spent hours kissing, the same dark-brown eyes that had always held shadows even when he'd sometimes teased a laugh out of her. That laugh had never quite erased the haunted look in her eyes. He'd always wanted to protect her, to take care of her, to wrap her in his arms and hug her until she lost the chill, let down her guard, trusted him completely.

Now, he realized why they'd never gotten to that point. She'd never trusted him—not even a little bit. He wanted to blame her for that. He wanted to still feel the anger that had come with every single thought of her since that day she'd left, but he had more information now, and he was also an adult. He had the perspective of a thirty-year-old man and not a sixteen-year-old kid. He was still pissed off that she hadn't chosen to confide in him, but he could see the extenuating circumstances and the fear that came into her eyes even now when she spoke about the Faulkners.

As they stopped at a light, he saw her gaze move to the

rearview mirror.

Was she thinking of ditching him?

He really hoped not. She couldn't run away from this, and it wouldn't look good if she tried. There was no way she had anything to do with Tommy's death, but the police might have different ideas, especially if Mrs. Faulkner threw the blame on to Cassidy. But Cassidy had been Tommy's friend, and he might be called on to attest to that.

Thinking about Tommy tightened his jaw. He had hated that kid since the day he met him, jealous of his relationship with Cassidy. But now he felt an intense wave of anger and a determined need to help the police find Tommy's killer and get him justice.

When the light changed, Cassidy moved through the intersection at a normal speed, and his tension eased. She wasn't going to run—*at least, not yet.*

His phone buzzed, and he punched the button on his steering wheel to answer the call. His cousin Emma's voice came over the speaker.

"Hi, Hunter. I just got back from the house on Coleman Avenue."

His gut tightened. Emma was a fire investigator, and since her husband was now involved in the homicide case, obviously, she was getting into the arson investigation. "Did you learn anything new?"

"The fire was deliberately set. There were two ignition points—one in the garage, one on the first floor. The materials used were rudimentary—rags and gasoline. He or she didn't leave any clues behind, which is not unusual. As you know, arson cases are very difficult to solve because the evidence goes up in smoke, but in light of your terrible discovery in the garage, my guess is that this was personal in some way."

"Someone wanted those bones to be found."

"Or they just wanted that house to burn to the ground. Max said they have a long list of people to interview because of the large number of foster kids who lived there over the past two decades. Hopefully, one of them will provide a lead."

"Hopefully."

"Did you find your old girlfriend?"

"Yes. Max pointed me in the right direction. I'm actually following her to the police station right now."

"I remember the two of you together. Her name was Cassidy, right? She was a pretty, thin blonde. Although, to be honest, you had a lot of pretty blondes hanging around in high school," Emma said with a teasing note in her voice.

"Cassidy was...different."

"Because she left you?"

"Even before that. She was...I don't know, I can't even describe it. Maybe it was all an illusion."

"I'm sure it wasn't. Are you okay, Hunter?"

"I don't know. I didn't sleep at all last night and today has been chaotic."

"What did Cassidy have to say when you told her about the kid you found?"

"She was horrified. Tommy had told her to leave without him, and she feels guilty that she did that."

"Did you believe her reaction?"

"I did. She's pretty sure her foster parents were involved. She hasn't told me a lot, but from what she has said, that home is beginning to sound like a house of horrors. I hope the police can get something out of Mrs. Faulkner, but I have a feeling she's going to hide in hysteria as long as she can."

"She'll talk. Max is very good at his job."

"I know that. I'm glad he's on the case."

"Be careful, Hunter."

"I'm not worried about some evil foster mother, who must be in her sixties or seventies by now."

"I wasn't talking about Mrs. Faulkner; I was talking about Cassidy. She hurt you once, probably more than anyone in the family realizes."

"Yes, but I didn't know the whole story then."

"Are you sure you know it now?"

"No, but I'm going to find out everything." He cleared his throat. "And I'm not looking to get involved with her again. I just want to know the truth of what happened, and so does Cassidy. That's it."

"Oh, Hunter, when it comes to a first love, the truth is never all there is."

Emma was probably right, but he didn't want to admit it. "I'm almost at the station now. We'll talk later."

"Definitely."

As he turned in to the parking lot, he thought about Emma's words. Cassidy was his first love, but he wasn't sure he'd ever been hers. She'd said he'd been her escape. Maybe that's all he'd been.

Cassidy parked on the lowest level of an underground parking lot adjacent to the station and took some calming breaths before getting out of her car and joining Hunter by the elevator. They didn't talk on their way up to the lobby level, or as they made their way into the station and waited for the clerk to let the detectives know they were there.

Despite the lack of communication between them, she was acutely aware of his presence. He'd told her he was a firefighter now, and she wasn't surprised by that, considering half his family was in the firefighting business, but she wondered what else he did, if he was involved with anyone. Her gaze moved toward his hand. He didn't wear a ring, but that might not mean anything. He could be engaged. He could be living with someone.

She could be, too, as far as he knew. But she wasn't.

While she had let other men into her life, she'd never found anyone she could trust completely, no one with whom she'd been willing to lay herself bare, so no relationship had gone on long. There had always been a wall that she couldn't let anyone over, and she didn't see that changing soon.

On the other hand, she hadn't gotten up this morning,

expecting Hunter to show up at the nursery. And she'd certainly never imagined the shocking and horrific news that he had delivered. Her heart hurt for Tommy, for the loss of his young life, for the lack of justice in his murder. And that ache was followed by guilt. Unfortunately, she knew better than anyone that changing the past wasn't possible. She'd chosen to save herself that day she'd gotten on the bus; now she would choose to get justice for Tommy, even if it meant putting herself in the hot seat.

The door opened, and a man came into the room. He had brown hair and green eyes and wore black slacks and a dark-gray shirt. He gave Hunter a friendly smile and a quick handshake before turning to her. "Ms. Morgan? I'm Max Harrison."

"My cousin Emma's husband," Hunter put in.

"Okay," she said, feeling like it was wrong to say *nice to meet you* in these circumstances.

"Thanks for coming in. Detective Randall is waiting for us in the conference room. We're working the case together, and we have some questions for you."

Her gut clenched at the thought of all those questions. "I don't know anything about what happened to Tommy. When I left the Faulkners' house, Tommy was alive."

"We're still very interested to hear your story. Come with me."

Following him out of the lobby and down the hall to an interrogation room reminded her of being young, homeless, parentless, terrified... And it took every bit of courage she had not to bolt. Not that she could have run with Hunter's solid body right behind her.

Max opened a door and waved her into a small room with a table and three empty chairs. An older man sat at the table, a couple of file folders in front of him as well as a yellow pad, upon which he was scribbling some notes.

He set down his pen and got to his feet as she entered the room.

"Ms. Morgan," he said. "Appreciate you coming in. Mr.

Callaway, will you be accompanying all of our witnesses?"

"Only this one," Hunter replied.

She and Hunter took seats across from Detective Randall while Max sat next to the other detective. "Can I ask where Mrs. Faulkner is?" she inquired.

"She's in the hospital," Max replied.

"Has she said anything about the murder?"

"Not yet. She's sedated."

"That's convenient."

Detective Randall gave her a sharp look. "You don't like her?"

"No, I don't."

"You ran away from her home when you were sixteen, is that correct?" he continued.

"I did."

"Why?"

"Because another girl had disappeared from the house, and I got a bad feeling from Mr. Faulkner. I thought I might be next, so I left."

"Did anyone physically abuse you while you were in the Faulkners' care?"

"No." As she answered his question, she felt like she was talking to the social worker again, trying to explain that there was something wrong in that house, even though she couldn't quite put her finger on exactly what it was. "Look, it doesn't matter what happened to me. Tommy's death is what is important."

"Hunter said that you and Tommy were supposed to have run away together," Max put in.

"Yes. But Tommy didn't show up, so I went without him. I didn't have any contact with him or with anyone from that life after I left."

"Who would have wanted Tommy dead?" Max questioned. "Do you have a theory?"

"Yes. I think it was one of the Faulkners or both of them."

"Not another kid?" Detective Randall asked.

She shook her head. "If another kid had killed Tommy, the Faulkners would have called the police, not hidden the body in the walls of the garage. And no one went into that garage. It was Mr. Faulkner's private space. He made it clear it was off-limits."

"It had to be the foster parents," Hunter agreed. "Cassidy is right. No one else could have hidden the body in the garage without their knowledge."

"You said a girl disappeared while you were living there. Who was that?" Max asked.

"Her name was Molly Bennett. But when I reported her missing to my social worker, she said they didn't have a record of anyone by that name being in the house. But she was there. I roomed with her for three weeks."

"And she just vanished?" Detective Randall asked, clear skepticism in his gaze.

"Yes. And the Faulkners got rid of her stuff the next day. They told the social worker that I had made her up, that she was my imaginary friend. That wasn't true, but their word was valued more highly than mine."

Max and the other detective exchanged a quick look.

"I don't care if you believe me," she added. "But if you want to find Tommy's killer, you might need to find out what happened to Molly, too."

"We'll take all the information you can give us," Max assured her. "Let's start with who else lived in the house with you."

"Besides Molly, there were five other kids in the home while I was there. Jada Washington was a ten-year-old African American girl who was partially deaf. Quan Tran was a fourteen-year-old Vietnamese kid, who had been given up by his adoptive parents, because they thought he had behavioral issues. David Bellerman was a year older than me, and Jeremiah Hunt was a year younger. Rhea Paris was eight or nine. She and Jada shared a room. The four boys were in bunk beds in one bedroom, and for a while it was me and Molly in the other room. The Faulkners had the fourth bedroom upstairs."

"Who else was around the house?" Max inquired. "Were there other family members who came by? Were there house cleaners, gardeners, who were at the house?"

"All of the above. Donald's younger brother, Evan, would come by with his son, Colin. Evan was divorced. I don't know where his wife was, but he seemed to have custody of Colin. I remember Colin as a sullen teenager about three years younger than me, who was obsessed with video games. When he was in the house, he was on the computer in the family room. He'd play games until he had to leave."

Max jotted down notes as she spoke.

"Did they live nearby?" he asked.

"No. They lived in San Jose. Evan ran a bar called Harley's. He always smelled like beer. I didn't talk to him much."

"What about Mrs. Faulkner's sister?" Detective Randall asked. "We've heard she also spent time at the house."

"Monica would bring her twin girls, Dee and Halsey, over. They were about ten, I think. Monica was friendly enough. She lived in Sacramento, so I only saw her once or twice while I was living there."

"What about the neighbors?"

"The Faulkners would sometimes have drinks or a meal with the Graysons, who lived next door, but they always went over there. They never entertained at our house."

"All right. Tell us more about this Molly," Detective Randall said.

"She came in early April, and she was gone by the end of the month. She had black hair and dark eyes; she was part Native American. She didn't know who her dad was. She said her mother was an addict, and every time she went into rehab, Molly would stay with her grandmother, but her grandma had gotten sick, so she was with us. She was two years younger than me. She was very sweet."

"And you don't believe she ran away?" Max asked.

"No, I think the Faulkners did something to her." She

paused. "Hunter told me you didn't find any other bodies."

"No, we didn't."

"But that doesn't mean they didn't hurt her. Why cover up her very existence for a runaway or a kid who was transferred to another home? It never made sense to me," she said.

"We need to look into that," Max said.

"Why didn't the other kids back up your story?" Detective Randall asked.

"That's another mystery to me. I can only assume that they were threatened by the Faulkners, and that's why they kept silent."

"That includes your friend, Tommy?" Max asked.

"He told the Faulkners that he'd seen Molly with his own eyes, but they just laughed at him. He wanted to talk to the social worker, but we were afraid they would split us up if we continued to make trouble. Tommy had been a foster kid his whole life. He knew the drill—even better than I did." She took a breath. "I have to believe that Tommy must have found out something about Molly or threatened the Faulkners in some way."

"What happened the day you left?" Max asked.

"I left the house around ten in the morning. Tommy wasn't there. He'd gone to play basketball with some kids at the park, like he did every Saturday, so it wouldn't look like we were leaving together. Our plan was to meet up at noon. I told Mrs. Faulkner a friend was going to do my hair for the prom, and I'd be back in time to go to lunch with Mr. Faulkner at one."

"Lunch?" Max interrupted. "You were going to lunch with Mr. Faulkner?"

She nodded. "Yes. It was that very odd invitation that made me realize I had to leave. The Faulkners were angry with me for stirring up questions about Molly and suddenly Mr. Faulkner wanted to take me out of the house alone. That had never happened before. I was terrified. Anyway, I went to Golden Gate Park until it was time to meet Tommy. I was at the bus station when I got a text from Tommy that he wasn't coming, that it would be better for us to leave separately, that we wouldn't be as easy to track down. When the bus came, I got on it alone, and that's it. That's all I know. Can we stop now?" She was feeling sick to her stomach, just thinking about what had happened to Tommy after he'd sent her that text.

Max and the detective exchanged another look and then Max said, "That should be enough for now, but we might have more questions as we move forward."

"I'm happy to tell you what I know; I just don't know much. Geralyn is probably the one who has all the answers, but I don't think she'll tell you the truth. She'll lie or plead ignorance or try to blame it on someone else. But she has to know. The body was found in her house. How could she not know?"

"We will talk to Mrs. Faulkner," Max promised. "We'll also talk to the other kids, the relatives and the neighbors."

"I want justice for Tommy."

"So do we. I'll walk you out."

Max escorted them through the lobby, pausing by the front door. "Thanks for coming in."

"I hope I helped," she said.

"What about the fire?" Hunter asked. "I talked to Emma. She said it was arson."

"Emma is working the arson; I'm working the homicide. We have one current case and one very cold case."

"Do you think the two are connected?" she asked.

"It seems likely, but I don't know yet."

As they stepped outside, she shivered, realizing the clouds had gotten darker, and the wind had picked up. The storm was getting closer. She glanced at Hunter as they walked toward the parking garage. He'd been silent during the interview, and while she'd appreciated not having to deal with his anger in front of the detectives, she was curious about what he was thinking.

"Well?" she asked, as they got into the elevator. "Do you think what I said was helpful?"

"I hope so."

"I don't know if anything I told them will matter. I believe Mrs. Faulkner and/or Donald killed Tommy and that's who they need to focus on, not any of the kids or neighbors or relatives. It's so obvious."

"They're covering all the bases."

"I guess." She stepped off the elevator, walking down the ramp toward her car.

"I can't believe that I didn't realize how unhappy you were in that house," Hunter said. "I should have known something was up. You said Molly disappeared two weeks before you left town, and that's when you were talking to the social worker and fighting with the Faulkners, and I was completely oblivious. Was I that selfish? That self-absorbed?"

As she paused by her car, she saw the self-condemnation in his eyes. Hunter had always had high expectations of himself. It was the Callaway way, and while it would have been easier to let him take the blame, she couldn't do that. "I didn't want you to know anything. When I was with you, I just wanted to be with you and forget the rest."

"I really thought we were happy. That's why it was so shocking when you left. It wasn't like we'd been fighting. We'd had a few words about Tommy coming between us, but it wasn't that big of a deal. But then you were gone, and the kid you said was only a friend was the one you wanted to be with. You deliberately let me think there was more between you. Did you want there to be more?"

"No, never. Tommy and I were lost souls. We weren't romantic. I let you think we were, because I figured you'd get mad, and that anger would stop you from trying to find me."

"It worked. I was angry. And I did not want to see you again."

"So, you didn't look for me at all?"

He shrugged. "Where was I supposed to look? I had no idea where you were. And if you ran away from your home, then I doubted you'd told the Faulkners where you were going. I did talk to Lindsay Grayson to see what she knew."

Lindsay had lived next door to the Faulkners and had been her one and only girlfriend, but she hadn't confided in Lindsay, either. They'd just walked to school together and talked about boys.

"Lindsay was as shocked as I was that you left. She thought you were in love with me."

"I didn't tell her anything, either."

He shook his head in bewilderment. "I still don't understand why you didn't say anything to me, Cassidy. You were my girlfriend."

"We were sixteen years old, Hunter. We knew each other for four months. Were we in love or lust—who knows? You were driven by hormones. I was desperate for someone to care about me. It wouldn't have lasted, even if I hadn't left. We were kids."

A dark shadow passed through his eyes. "Is that what you really think or just what you told yourself, so it wouldn't hurt so much?"

"Maybe a little of both," she admitted. "But our past doesn't matter anymore. I can't change what I did, no matter how much I might want to. I'm sorry. But it's done."

"You're right. The past is done, but we can still figure out what happened to Tommy and maybe to that girl who disappeared."

She was surprised by his words. "You believe me about Molly? Because I didn't think either of those detectives believed me."

"Well, I do. I don't think you made her up."

She felt enormously relieved. "Thank you."

"You don't have to thank me, but you do have to start being honest. No more secrets. We need to work together on this, and don't tell me it's not my problem."

"It isn't your problem," she couldn't help saying.

"I found Tommy's bones, and I'm going to help find his killer." Determination darkened his gaze. "That's what's going to happen. I'd like your cooperation. So, what do you say—

can we be partners on this?"

Work with Hunter? Spend more time with him? Be partners with a man she'd once been madly in love with?

Those all seemed like really bad ideas. "I don't know."

"What are you worried about? That I'll fall in love with you again?" he challenged. "Trust me, that's not going to happen."

The biting tone in his voice made it clear he wasn't at risk of falling for her again, but she couldn't say the same for herself. Hunter had gotten under her skin a very long time ago and walking away from him had taken a lot out of her. Getting to know him again was risky. However, with Hunter's connection to Detective Harrison, he was more likely to get information than she was, and she did want justice for Tommy and for Molly.

"All right. I guess we could work together. Although, I feel like this is up to the police to solve. I don't know what we can do on our own."

"We might be able to get people to talk to us that they can't. The other kids might be more willing to reveal things to you than to the cops."

"That's doubtful. Most of them didn't like me much, especially after I got everyone stirred up about Molly. And I don't know where they are now."

"Max will find them. Once he's had his chance to interview them, we might be able to get in the door. And as far as Molly goes, I'm thinking my sister Kate might be able to help. She's an FBI agent and her husband is a former agent turned private investigator."

"That's a good idea." She felt a twinge of hope at his words. She really would like to know what had happened to Molly, although there was the very real possibility that Molly had come to the same sad end as Tommy.

"I'll call Kate later. Are you going home now?"

"I should. But..."

He met her gaze. "Don't do it, Cassidy."

"I don't want to, but I feel like I have to. I need to see the house."

"Are you sure you're up for it? "If you are, I'll take you."

His question hung in the air for a long moment. *Was* she up for it?

Six

"This is a bad idea," Cassidy muttered. If she'd been in her own car, as she'd wanted to be, she would have turned around and left the city as fast as she could, but once she'd said she wanted to go to the house, Hunter had insisted upon driving her there.

Hunter glanced over at her. "You want to abort? Run for the hills?"

There was an edge behind his words, a reminder that she was a runner. When things got tough, she left. He wasn't completely wrong.

But if she'd learned anything from the day so far, it was that she couldn't keep running away, because it was pointless. Eventually the past would catch up.

"Cassidy?" Hunter stopped at a light and gave her a pointed, questioning look. "If you want to go back, just say so."

"No. Keep going."

As he drove through the intersection, she saw Herbert Hoover High School, the place where she and Hunter had first met. The two-story building had gotten a new paint job sometime in the past fourteen years, but the lunch tables in the front courtyard were the same. The parking lot was empty despite the fact that it was only half past two. School must be already out for summer. Instead of daydreaming in class, the kids were off having adventures, seeing their friends, loafing by a pool or a lake.

More memories washed over her. Hunter had found a camp in Yosemite where they could both be counselors. They were going to go to the national park the summer between their junior and senior year. When they weren't working, they'd go hiking, rock climbing, and swimming. They'd be away from family, from the Faulkners, but most importantly, they'd be together. Hunter would bring his camera. He loved taking photos, and she would study the trees, the plants, the flowers, learning all she could about one of the most special places on Earth.

It had all been a beautiful dream, a summer to remember...

She wondered if Hunter had gone without her.

"What are you thinking about?" Hunter's voice cut into her reverie.

She shifted in her seat, glancing over at him. "High school, summer vacation, all our crazy plans."

"They didn't seem crazy at the time."

"Did you go to Yosemite that summer?"

"No. I worked in construction for my uncle."

Which had been the last thing he wanted to do. She wondered if he blamed her for that missed opportunity in Yosemite. Probably.

But those summer plans faded from her mind as Hunter turned right at the next corner. Every muscle in her body tightened, her nerves screaming out warnings to leave now, before it was too late.

Too late for what? Tommy was dead. And the house was...

She sucked in a breath as she saw the blackened structure. The windows in the front were shattered. Some of the walls were gone or there were large gaping holes that anyone could walk through. The fire had been completely destructive, worse than she'd realized.

Hunter stopped the Jeep, and she got out of the vehicle and stood on the sidewalk. Despite the devastation in front of her, she could see the old house as it had once been. She could picture the uncomfortable antique couches in the living room where no one had ever sat. She could smell the tomato sauce that Mrs. Faulkner made at least four times a week, believing the best way to spend her food budget was on some sort of noodle covered in canned tomato sauce. She could hear the heavy footsteps of Mr. Faulkner every night when he came up the stairs, sometimes pausing just outside her door.

She hadn't been abused and probably no one else could understand the fear that those footsteps had brought, but her memories were so vivid, she jumped when Hunter put his hand on her arm.

For a split second, she thought it was Mr. Faulkner who had come back from the dead to put his hands on her.

"Easy," Hunter said quietly. "You don't have to go inside. Everything was destroyed by the fire, the water, or the smoke. There's nothing left."

"What about the garage?"

He shook his head. "You don't want to go in there, Cassidy."

"I don't want to, but I feel like I should."

"It's still a crime scene." Hunter waved his hand toward the police tape that ran around the perimeter of the yard, but there was no one around, no one investigating, and from what she'd heard at the station, everything that could be found had already been found.

"You're not the type to let a little tape keep you out," she murmured.

His lips tightened. "No. It's not the tape. It's what I know you'll see, and you won't be able to un-see it. You can trust me on that. The body might not be there anymore, but the wall where it was hidden is still there, and it will rip your heart out."

"What was in the garage besides..."

"Nothing that I could recognize. Everything was turned to ash. One of the ignition points of the fire was in the garage. There were several explosions—probably the gasoline coming in contact with other accelerants like paint, the kinds of things you'd keep in a garage."

"It's weird because Tommy once said that a few matches, some gasoline, and we could burn the house down and be free. Only problem was, we'd just get sent somewhere else, and who knew where that would be? Of course, it was just talk anyway. We never really considered it."

"Well, someone else had the same idea. Someone who hated the Faulkners as much as you and Tommy did."

"But they waited a long time to do it."

"Or not. Who's to say that one of the kids who lived here more recently didn't do this?"

"That's true. I keep thinking the two events are connected, but maybe they're not. I wonder when the Faulkners stopped taking in kids. Maybe my list won't be of any help to the police. The arsonist could be someone I never met."

"That's possible, but Tommy's murder took place in your time. We have two crimes."

A movement next door drew her eye. A woman came out of the house. She was in her fifties, wearing yoga pants and a fleece jacket. She started for her car in the driveway, but then stopped when she saw them, her expression slowly changing as recognition flashed across her face.

"Cassidy?" The woman took a few steps in their direction. "Is that you?"

"Mrs. Grayson," she said, feeling a rush of warmth. Lindsay's mother, Valerie, had always been very nice to her.

"I can't believe it's you." Surprise moved through Valerie's eyes as she came over to join them. "I always wondered what happened to you, Cassidy. Mrs. Faulkner first told us that you were transferred to another home, but then

Lindsay found out you ran away with one of the other kids. What happened to make you want to run away?"

"It doesn't matter now."

"Are you sure?" Valerie's gaze moved to the burned-out structure and then returned to her. "I was at work yesterday when the fire started. I couldn't believe what I saw when I got home. The police were here last night for a long time, and there was a van from the coroner's office as well. I've been trying to find out what happened, but no one will tell me anything. The neighbor said that Geralyn wasn't home, so I don't understand why the coroner was here. Do you know?"

Cassidy debated telling Valerie the truth. In the end, she decided that the Faulkners had already been allowed to hide too many secrets over the years. "They found human remains in the garage."

Valerie gasped, putting a hand to her chest. "Oh, my God. Who? How?"

"I don't know." She didn't want to mention Tommy. "But the police are looking into it. Geralyn has a lot to explain."

"Geralyn couldn't have known."

"How could she not have known? She lived here for twenty-five years. The body was hidden in the walls of the garage during that time period."

"But she's so nice. And Donald was a good man."

"I don't think you knew the Faulkners as well as you thought you did."

Valerie's gaze sharpened. "Why are you here, Cassidy? Because of this? Because of the body?"

"Yes. I just found out a few hours ago and after speaking to the police, I had to come by and see for myself."

"Where is Geralyn now?"

"She's in the hospital. She's apparently very upset."

"Well, of course, she would be. I'll have to go see her. Or maybe I shouldn't." Suddenly, Valerie was indecisive. "I guess I'll talk to Jim about it," she added, referring to her husband. Valerie's gaze moved to Hunter. "You look familiar. Wait a second. I know you, too. You're Hunter Callaway."

"Yes," he said with a nod.

"You took Lindsay to your senior prom. Your mom had a party beforehand. We came over for the pictures."

"That's right," he muttered.

"You took Lindsay to the senior prom?" Cassidy asked, unable to stop the shock running through her voice.

Hunter looked a bit uncomfortable. "Yes. I told you that Lindsay and I became friends after you left."

"She was quite sad that things didn't work out between you." Valerie gave Hunter a thoughtful look. "You should call her, unless you and Cassidy are together?"

"We're not together," she said quickly. "Hunter is a firefighter. He was here yesterday when the body was discovered."

"I actually discovered the body," Hunter said. "And I really hope you'll talk to the police, Mrs. Grayson. I'm sure they'll want to know everything you know about the Faulkners."

"I don't know that much. We exchanged brief conversations on our way in and out of the house. Occasionally, we had them over for dinner, but our conversations were never that personal. This is just terrible, so awful. I don't know what to think." She paused. "But I'm glad you're well, Cassidy. I'll tell Lindsay. She'll be happy to know that. You know, she lives here in the city. She works at an art gallery. What do you do now, Cassidy?"

"I'm a landscaper. I work at a nursery in Half Moon Bay."

Valerie smiled. "That suits you. I remember when you planted flowers by our back fence. You were so happy digging in the dirt."

She remembered that, too. She'd put the flowers on Valerie's side of the fence, so she wouldn't get in trouble. She'd been able to see them from her upstairs window, and they'd reminded her of the life she'd lived before her parents had died.

"I should go. I have to get my hair cut." Valerie paused.

"The body—it didn't belong to a child, did it?"

"It was a teenager," she answered, again not really wanting to say Tommy's name.

"Oh, no. Not one of the kids. I don't understand how this could happen. I thought I was living next door to good people. I guess you really don't know what goes on behind closed doors. Take care—both of you."

"I wonder if she knows more than she's saying," Hunter muttered, as Valerie pulled out of the driveway.

"I have no idea."

"You were never tempted to confide in Lindsay or her mother?"

"No. I was afraid that Valerie would say something to Geralyn or Donald." She drew in a breath. "So, you and Lindsay dated? I thought you just had a few conversations."

An uneasy gleam ran through his eyes. "That's the way it started."

She wondered why his words brought a stabbing pain of jealousy. Hunter had no doubt dated and loved a lot of women since their brief relationship. But Lindsay had been her friend, and it seemed weird to imagine the two of them together. It felt disloyal. But who was she to judge them? She was the one who'd left.

"Do you have a problem with that?" Hunter challenged, as silence lengthened between them. "What did you think was going to happen when you ran out on me? Did you believe I would spend the rest of my life waiting for you to come back?"

"Of course not. I was just surprised that you would have been with Lindsay. She knew how much I liked you. She was probably the only person who knew that."

He shrugged. "She was a little pissed off that you hadn't told her you were leaving. Maybe that's when her loyalty ended. And we both thought you were with Tommy." He paused. "Why didn't you tell Valerie the body was Tommy's?"

"I don't know. I just didn't want to say his name."

"So it wouldn't be real?"

"I know it's real," she said with a heavy heart. "I just felt like I should protect his privacy. It's silly. His name will be on the news soon. I can't stop that from happening."

"Why would you want to? Isn't it time Tommy's death came to light? That light is the only way Tommy gets justice."

"I really hope that happens."

A drop of rain hit her face, followed by another.

They dashed to the car as the skies that had been threatening all day finally opened up.

She'd been longing for the rain, but once inside the car with Hunter, with the rain pounding on the windshield, she felt very aware of how close they were to each other, how far away the rest of the world seemed to be.

Hunter didn't start the engine and with the rain streaming down the windows, all she could see was him, his ruggedly attractive face, his beautiful blue eyes, his full mouth. Her heart started to beat a little faster, as a long-ago memory tugged at her brain.

They'd been caught in the rain before. Hunter had driven her home after school in his brother Dylan's Mustang. With hail coming down like rocks, Hunter had pulled over by the park and suggested they wait out the storm. But they hadn't just sat in the car and talked; they'd flung themselves into each other's arms.

They'd kissed with the passion and wonder of their sixteen years, completely caught up in every touch, every taste, every whispered word between them. The rest of the world had completely disappeared.

"You remember," he said, a husky note in his voice as he met her gaze. "That day in the rain."

"It was a lifetime ago."

"It was amazing. We kissed for hours."

"It felt like minutes."

Silence followed her words, and then Hunter said, with a reckless glitter in his blue eyes, "Do you think it would be the same now?"

His tantalizing question hung in the air. "It would be different." She felt a little desperate to believe that. "We can't go back. Everyone knows that. It would never be the same."

"Only one way to find out." He reached across the console, his hand slipping around the back of her neck.

"Hunter," she breathed. "This is a terrible idea."

"That doesn't sound like a no." He moved closer.

She should say no. She should push him away, but when he lowered his head oh, so slowly, all she wanted to do was feel his mouth on hers. *Just one more time*, she told herself.

One more kiss...

Seven

---※≫≪≪≪---

She tasted exactly the way he remembered, like sweet cherries, her favorite flavor of lip gloss. Apparently, some things didn't change.

Cassidy's lips parted under his with a sigh, as if she'd been waiting a long time…as long as he had.

He sank into the kiss, savoring the softness of her mouth, the scent of flowers in the strands of her hair that brushed against his cheek. And while he'd meant to stop after one kiss or two, he kept going back for more—just as he had all those years ago. He threaded his fingers through her hair, so she couldn't pull away, not that she seemed to have any interest in doing that. She was matching him kiss for kiss, touch for touch, her hands reaching around his back, pulling him closer.

And he was happy to get as close as he possibly could. He let go of her hair, so he could run his hands up under her shirt, needing to feel the heat of her skin.

She murmured something against his mouth as he explored the curve of her back.

It sounded like encouragement, but who could say for sure?

His blood was roaring through his ears, matching the thundering beat of his heart against his chest. He felt sixteen again—anxious, eager, impatient, filled with desire for the girl in his arms.

The years in between faded away. All he could think about was her. All he wanted was her. Nothing else mattered.

Last time, they'd climbed into the back seat and made love. It was the one and only time they'd been together, but he could still remember it as if it had been yesterday.

He could make it so much better for her now.

But Cassidy was breaking the kiss, pushing him away…

He stared at her in confusion caught between the past and the present.

"We have to stop," she said, a panicked note in her voice.

"Why?"

"Because…I don't want this."

Her brown eyes were shimmering with a desire that belied her words. She might not want to want him again, but she did. "Yes, you do. Isn't it past time for some honesty?"

She straightened. "I'm being honest. This isn't going anywhere—definitely not to the back seat."

"You remember what came next the last time we kissed in a car in the rain."

"How could I forget? But we're not those people anymore."

"You felt remarkably familiar." He paused as she ran her fingers through the hair he'd recently tousled. "It would be a lot better now, Cassidy."

"It was pretty good back then."

She surprised him with the admission. "It was," he agreed. "I'm glad you can be honest about that."

"Clearly there's still some chemistry between us."

"Enough to blow up the lab," he said dryly.

"But we're older, wiser…right?"

"I don't know. At the moment, I'm feeling closer to sixteen again."

"Well, we're not sixteen. And I don't think either of us

needs to complicate our lives any further. We both need to get a grip, pull it together."

"I'm not so sure this kind of complication would be that bad."

He was even less sure when she ran her tongue over her lips, the way she so often did when she was nervous. He'd been able to kiss the nerves away when they were in high school, but now... She was right. He needed to get a grip and pull it together.

"Did you ever tell Dylan what we did in his precious car?" she asked.

He smiled at her question. "God, no. He would have killed me. It was bad enough I took the Mustang without asking him. I had to pay that debt off for a long time, but it was totally worth it. Giving you a ride home on that rainy night was the best idea I'd ever had."

"You must have regretted it when I left two weeks later."

"I was angry, but I never regretted that night. It's still one of the best memories of my life. What about you?"

She hesitated. "Let's just say I haven't forgotten." She shifted in her seat, putting a few more inches of space between them. "How is Dylan? Is he also a firefighter?"

"He is. He's also in love. So is my brother Ian. They had a double wedding in February."

"Really?" Her brows shot up in surprise. "They both beat you to the altar?"

"Yes, and I'm fine with it. I've never been in a rush to get married. Anyway, I work with Dylan now. We're also at the same firehouse as my cousin Burke. Ian is a scientist. I have no idea what he does, but he's changing the world in some way."

"What are their wives like?"

"Dylan married Tori Hayden. I don't know if you remember her. She was in high school with us. Her older brother Scott was one of Dylan's good friends. They reconnected last year and have been inseparable ever since."

"Her name is familiar, but I don't know that I ever talked

to her."

"She's a reporter now, very determined, ambitious, intense, and a great match for Dylan. She has no problem calling him out when he does something stupid. Ian's wife Grace is an elementary school teacher. She's friendly, funny, down-to-earth, which is good for Ian, who tends to walk around with his head in the clouds, his brain on another level."

"What about your sisters? Annie was such a good artist. I remember her sketches were all over your house."

"She's still drawing. She does animations for superhero movies now. She's getting married a week from tomorrow to Griffin Hale. They live down south in San Clemente, but she's having the wedding up here, so all the Callaways can come. Mia lives in Angel's Bay. She's a curator at the local museum there, and she married an ex-soldier, who is now a cop. She has a stepdaughter, and she's also pregnant. She's due in about a month."

"And Kate is the FBI agent."

"Yes. She married Devin a few weeks ago without any family or fanfare. My mother is still pissed off about it, but that's Kate. She dances to her own tune, and she and Devin have been together for a while."

"Your parents are well?"

"They're incredibly healthy, thank God. My dad is retired from the fire department, but he works for my Uncle Kevin doing construction on a part-time basis. Mom is still a nurse, and I don't think she'll be quitting any time soon. The extended family is all around: Uncle Jack, Aunt Lynda, all the kids and their spouses and their kids. It's a big group."

"What about your grandmother? I always liked her. She had the brightest and friendliest blue eyes. She just sparkled."

He felt a twist of pain at the reminder of how his grandmother used to be. "She's not doing so well anymore. She has Alzheimer's. She's been on some medication, a drug trial, that has kept some of the worst at bay, but she's slowly fading. She's one of the reasons I came back."

"What do you mean—you came back? Where were you?"

"I took some time off from firefighting, and I've been traveling the last eight months. I went all through South America and Mexico on my motorcycle."

"Taking pictures?" she asked, a light in her eyes.

He shrugged. "Not really. I took a few on my phone."

"How could you not have taken a camera? It was your dream to photograph the world."

"That was a long time ago. I don't even think about that anymore."

Actually, her words made him question why he hadn't taken a camera. There had definitely been places—moments—on his trip that he could have captured in a better way. But the dream of being a photographer and traveling the world shooting photos had pretty much ended when Cassidy had left. He didn't know why. He could have done it if he'd wanted to. But so much of that plan had been tied up in traveling the world with her, and every time he'd picked up the camera after she left, it had made him think about her, and he'd quickly set it back down.

"I guess dreams change," she said.

"They do," he agreed, eager to get off that topic.

"I'm glad your family is well. I loved going to your house. It was so warm and inviting. There were always kids around, always something cooking on the stove that smelled delicious. Your mom made the best cookies, too. Even though she worked, she made a home for all of you."

"I should have been more appreciative of all she did."

"She must have hated me when I left."

He couldn't deny that his family had been very angry with the way Cassidy had treated him. "They were sorry things didn't work out," he said, not sure why he was protecting Cassidy's feelings, but it felt right.

"They were more than sorry," she said dryly.

"They got over it. So did I. Life goes on."

"Life does go on," she murmured. "I was actually

thinking of my mom earlier today, how she was the one who taught me to garden, who introduced me to the world of flowers. I still miss her."

"I'm sure you do. Did your dad like to garden, too?"

"No, not at all," she said with a sad little laugh. "He liked numbers, data, equations. And as a high school math teacher, I'm pretty sure he would have been disappointed in the grades I got in those classes. I did not inherit his analytical brain." She blinked some moisture out of her eyes. "I wish you could have met them. When we were dating, I used to imagine what it would have been like if I could have brought you home to a happy house, to parents who cared about me."

"I would have liked to have met them."

"But if they hadn't died in a car crash, I probably would have never met you. I would have been living on the other side of the city. Our paths might never have crossed. Maybe that would have been better." She let out a breath. "The rain is letting up. You should take me back to my car."

It was the last thing he wanted to do. He wanted to know more about her life, what had happened after she'd left, how she'd lived, who else she'd loved.

His pulse leapt at that thought, but he couldn't be naïve enough to think there had been no one else for her. She was a beautiful woman.

"Hunter?" she questioned. "You need to start the car."

"I will take you back. I just want you to tell me…"

"What? Tell you what?"

He looked into her big brown eyes. "That you won't run again. That you won't just vanish from my life without a word."

She didn't answer immediately, her gaze growing troubled. "I don't know if I can make that promise. To be honest, I want to run away right now. I don't know where this will all end, but I don't think it's going to a good place. I can't become Mrs. Faulkner's fall girl. I won't take the blame for what they did to Tommy."

"She can't pin this on you, Cassidy."

"She's going to try. As soon as she knows the police have found me, spoken to me, she'll see me as her way out. She'll paint me as the troubled, crazy girl, who made up lies."

"You're an adult now. You can fight her. And you can win."

She smiled. "You always gave great pep talks."

"I know you've had a rough life, Cassidy, obviously much rougher than I ever knew. But you have people in your life now who care about you, don't you?"

"A few, but no one knows about my past. I wanted to keep it away from my life. That was a foolish thought." She let out a breath. "I do need to talk to George, especially if any of this is going to become a problem for the business."

"Why would it?"

"I don't know, but I can't let the Faulkners take anything else from me."

"Then don't let them. Stay and fight. I'll help you."

"I really don't understand why you would want to."

"Because I never had the chance before. You took that away from me, because you didn't trust me."

"I don't know if it was about trust."

"It was all about trust. So, can you trust me to help you and can I trust you not to run?"

She met his gaze. "I guess we'll find out."

"I guess we will." He started the engine and drove down the street.

The rain had eased off to a drizzle now, but the skies were still thick with dark clouds. The storm had subsided, but it definitely wasn't over, and he wasn't really thinking about the weather.

Later that evening, Cassidy stood by the kitchen window in her small apartment, watching as the rain returned with a vengeance, streaming down the windows, pressing pink roses and purple lavender against the panes, providing a kaleidoscope of shimmering color. In that kaleidoscope, she could see her memories spinning around—the good ones and the bad ones.

Her life had always been a series of peaks and valleys, incredible highs followed by horrible lows. But when she'd gotten to the Wild Garden Nursery, she'd found a plateau, a place of stability, evenness. Some might call it boring, but she just felt relief knowing that each day would resemble the one before. Sure, there might be petty problems, but nothing that would bring her anger, grief, or pain—maybe nothing that would bring her incredible joy, either. But she'd always been willing to take that trade-off.

Until now...

Seeing Hunter again...

The terrible news about Tommy...

She was right back where she'd once been, and she felt incredibly fragile, which was not how she liked to feel.

The earth was shifting beneath her feet. Everything she'd put behind her was back in front of her. She wanted to run. She wanted to disappear into the dark night. But she couldn't do that. She couldn't bail on George or the business, and she wanted to show Hunter that she could stay and fight, no matter how difficult it got.

As the kettle began to scream, she moved away from the window and turned off the burner. She poured hot water over her tea bag, inhaling the scents of jasmine and chamomile.

Flowers had always been her haven, her happy place, even when they'd been ground up into an herbal tea.

As she waited for the liquid to cool, a sharp series of knocks came at her door. She jumped at the sound, thinking for a split second that Hunter had come to see her again, but it was George's voice that rang through the air.

She rushed across the room and opened the door for him. As he came inside, water dripped off his jacket. "You're soaked. What are you doing here?"

"I've been worried about you all day. When I saw your light on, I thought I'd come over."

"You should have called. I know you only live at the other end of the property, but it's storming."

"A little rain never hurt anyone. And you know I love storms. Water makes the plants grow."

She smiled at the words he'd said so many times to her, words that he'd once uttered to remind a terrified nineteen-year-old girl that while the storms would come, the sun always followed.

Unfortunately, the sun didn't always shine again for everyone.

"Can I get you some tea?" she asked. "The water is hot."

"Wouldn't mind a cup." He took off his coat and hung it on a hook by the door, then followed her into the kitchen.

As she poured his tea, he settled into a stool at the island. "You want to tell me what's going on, Cassidy?"

She set the mug in front of him. "Not really. But I'm guessing you're going to insist."

"I am going to insist. If you have a problem that has the police involved, I have a right to hear about it."

"You do."

"Are you in trouble?"

"I don't think so, but things have a way of going differently than I expect."

"What has happened?"

"I told you that I was in foster care for several years after my parents died. Well, what I didn't tell you is that I ran away from the last house when I was sixteen. I was terrified of the couple who ran the home, and I managed to stay hidden until I was eighteen."

"Go on."

"I was supposed to run away with a friend of mine—a boy by the name of Tommy Lucas. But he didn't show up at the bus station, and he sent me a message telling me to go without him. I was torn, but I was too terrified to go back to the house, so I got on the bus. I never heard from him again. But yesterday there was a fire at the house where I lived, and the firefighters found a skeleton in the walls—it was Tommy, the boy I was supposed to run away with." She blew out a breath as she finished, the reality of Tommy's death still hitting her hard every time she thought about it.

George's eyes darkened with concern. "And that's why the police were looking for you."

"Yes. I went to see them this afternoon. They asked me what I knew about Tommy, who else lived in the house, who might have had a motive to kill him. I believe it was the Faulkners, my foster parents. Unfortunately, Mr. Faulkner died a few months ago, and Mrs. Faulkner is claiming some sort of mental breakdown. I know they did it, but I'm worried that she'll try to pin it on someone else."

"Someone like you?"

"She might suggest I killed Tommy and ran away."

"And left his body in their house? And they didn't call the police but buried the body in the walls? That's ridiculous."

"She'll find a way to twist the story. She's very good at getting everyone to believe she is who she says she is."

"We need to get you a lawyer."

"That's not my concern right now. I want to get justice for Tommy."

"You still have to protect yourself. What about the man you were with earlier today? You were having a heated conversation. What's his role in all of this?"

"He's the firefighter who found the remains."

"Your conversation looked more personal than that."

George was sharp. "It was personal. Hunter was my high school boyfriend. I ditched him on the day of the prom."

"And he's still angry about it. I saw him grab your arm earlier. Maybe you should stay away from him."

"He's not a danger to me. Hunter is a really good person." Emotion choked her throat. "He has a right to be angry. Anyway, that's what is happening."

"Well, I'm here if you need anything."

"You always have been. You and Mary saved my life."

"You saved ours. You filled a hole that we'd had for a long time. We'd always wanted a daughter, but we were never able to have a child. And what you've done with the business is mind-boggling. I probably would have had to sell out when Mary got sick, if you hadn't taken over."

"I was happy to do it. I love the business. You know that."

"I know you've buried yourself in it. Sometimes, I wonder if it hasn't become a bit of a hideout for you."

"I'm not hiding. I'm working. I'm living my life. Or at least I was..."

"Now you're being dragged back to a dark time."

"Yes, and I don't want to go, but I also don't want to let Mrs. Faulkner get away with killing Tommy. I have to help the police in any way that I can. I just hope I'm strong enough to face her. She's a monster, in my mind."

"The best way to get rid of monsters is to face them. They usually shrink in the light."

"Maybe the imaginary ones. Unfortunately, the Faulkners were very real people."

"What about the firefighter? What are you going to do about him?"

"Nothing."

A disbelieving gleam entered George's eyes. "Seems like the two of you have some unfinished business."

"We were together for about four months when we were sixteen. It was not that big of a deal. We didn't even know what love was."

George gave her a knowing smile. "Is that what you told him or what you told yourself?"

"Both." She sighed. "I thought it was over between us a long time ago."

"But now?"

"I'm not sure." She couldn't help thinking about the amazingly hot kisses they'd shared in the car. "But it should be over."

"Why?"

"Because if it's not, I think there's a good chance we're going to hurt each other again."

Eight

—➤➤◄◄◄—

Hunter woke up Saturday morning to the persistent buzzing of his cell phone on the nightstand. He groaned as he realized it was almost nine. He was usually up at seven, getting in a run or a bike ride on his days off, but he'd spent most of the night tossing and turning, thinking about Cassidy, about kissing her in the car. It had been both a brilliant and a very bad decision.

Grabbing his phone, he saw his mother's number, and sat up in bed. "Hello, Mom?"

"Good morning," Sharon Callaway said with a bright, energized note in her voice. "You weren't sleeping, were you?"

"I was getting up," he lied.

"That's excellent news. Because we're having an impromptu brunch today. Annie, Kate and Mia are here, and I want to get everyone together before they head off for their bachelorette weekend in Napa."

"Mia is going to a bachelorette weekend? Isn't she about to pop?"

"Not for four more weeks. And she'll be with her sisters

if that little baby decides to come early. Jeremy and Ashlyn are here, too. They're going to do some sightseeing in the city, maybe drive down to Santa Cruz and ride the roller coaster. Anyway, brunch is in an hour. I want you to come. I haven't had all six of my kids in the house in I can't remember when, so you need to be there."

"I assume that means Dylan and Ian are coming, too."

"And Grace and Tori. It's going to be fun. I'm going to see if any of your cousins can come as well. Can you make it?"

"Sure, I'll stop by."

"Good. I want us to find a few minutes to talk. Dylan told me what you found in that house the other day."

He sighed. "Dylan has a big mouth."

"He said you were shaken up."

"It's not every day I uncover the remains of someone I once knew."

"Well, I thank God it wasn't Cassidy."

"I see Dylan filled you in on everything."

"I'm your mother. You should have filled me in. I liked Cassidy. I thought she was a sweet girl until she broke your heart. Now, I worry about her coming back into your life."

"You don't have to worry about anything—I'm fine."

"You always say that, Hunter, but my mother's intuition tells me you haven't really been fine in a long time. You've been restless, searching for something."

Her intuition was damn good. "I'll figure it out. And if I'm coming to brunch, I better take a shower."

"I'll see you soon."

He set the phone down on the table, stretched his arms over his head and let out a groan that was filled with some of that restlessness his mom had referred to. She wasn't wrong. He had been in a funk the past year. That feeling of numbness had evaporated with the reappearance of Cassidy, but he didn't know if that was a good thing.

Cassidy had made it clear yesterday that she'd put their teenage relationship behind her. At least, that's what she'd said. Her kiss had told a different story. He didn't know what they were to each other now or what they would be in the future, but he did know they weren't done yet.

--➤➤◄◄--

His parents lived in a two-story home across from the Great Highway and San Francisco's Ocean Beach. He'd grown up in the house, sharing a room with both his brothers for most of his childhood, until his father had cleaned out the attic and made an extra bedroom that Ian had claimed, because he needed quiet in which to study and exercise his ridiculously big brain.

He'd actually been okay with living with Dylan instead of Ian, since his second oldest brother was kind of a neat freak and Dylan was much more chill. Despite the four-year age difference between them, he and Dylan had gotten close during those years, and Dylan had always looked out for him. He wasn't really surprised Dylan had already talked to his mother about Cassidy; he just wasn't looking forward to the interrogation he knew would be coming from the rest of his family.

As he pulled up in front of the house, he parked behind a van of teenage surfers who were unabashedly changing out of their wet suits into jeans and shorts. Smiling to himself, he could picture himself and Dylan hitting the waves on Saturday and Sunday mornings. Occasionally, Kate would tag along, or one or more of their cousins would join in. While his mom and dad didn't surf, they'd often brought the dogs over to the beach for a morning run or packed up sandwiches for an impromptu picnic.

He really had had an idyllic childhood. He'd fought with his siblings, sometimes had petty arguments with his parents, but he'd never been afraid. He'd never been scared to close his eyes, to go to sleep, the way Cassidy had been.

Maybe she'd been right in thinking he never would have understood her situation. He had far more awareness now than he had had as a teenager, and he still didn't completely understand why she hadn't been able to get help from the social worker, why no one had called out the Faulkners on a missing girl, why Cassidy had had to run for her life, and why no one had noticed that both Cassidy and Tommy were gone.

Had the department overseeing their care ever looked for them? Or had they just been two lost kids in an overcrowded system?

He wanted to find out. He wanted someone to be punished for everything that had happened. He didn't just want it for Tommy; he wanted it for Cassidy, too. And maybe he wanted it a little for himself. Because if the Faulkners hadn't been monsters, Cassidy never would have left town. They would have had a real chance to see if what they had would have lasted.

A door slammed behind him, and he turned around to see Dylan and Tori get out of their car. He forced a smile onto his face, knowing that Dylan was already more than a little concerned about him, and he didn't need to give him any more ammunition to play overprotective big brother.

Tori gave him a hug. A pretty, dark-haired woman with deep blue eyes, Tori was not only attractive but very smart, and her sharp eyes didn't miss much. As a reporter, she was always looking for a story, and he really didn't want to give her one, but he suspected Dylan had already done that.

"How are you holding up?" she asked. "Dylan told me everything. I can't imagine how you must have felt opening up that wall…"

"I'm fine. I'm over the shock."

"Of seeing the skeleton or seeing Cassidy?" his brother put in. "I called Max last night, and he said you and Cassidy were at the station together yesterday afternoon."

"Max tracked her down; I brought her in."

"And?" Dylan prodded. "I texted you a half-dozen times last night. Why didn't you answer?"

"Because I was busy." *Busy thinking about Cassidy!* But he wasn't going to tell his brother that.

"I remember Cassidy," Tori interjected. "All the girls were jealous when she snagged you as her boyfriend. She was an outsider, and I think she got some crap about it. Girls can be mean."

His gaze narrowed at that suggestion. "Really? She never said anything."

Tori shrugged. "Maybe it didn't bother her."

He doubted that. But why should he be surprised that she'd kept that from him, when she'd clearly kept a lot of things away from him?

"Are you going inside?" Tori asked.

"In a minute. Go on without me."

"Okay. I hope I didn't upset you."

"You didn't."

"I'll be right there," Dylan told Tori.

When his wife headed toward the house, Dylan gave him a sharp look. "How are you really feeling?"

"I'm fine. I'm just not in the mood for everyone in the family to grill me."

"I only told Tori."

"And Mom."

"That's true."

"So, basically everyone in the family knows?"

"Probably." Dylan gave him an unrepentant smile. "You know how the family works. Get over it."

"Easy for you to say."

"Does this mood of yours have to do with Cassidy? How was it seeing her again?"

He shrugged. "It was…a lot of things. I realize now there was more behind her decision to leave than just another guy she liked better. The Faulkners were not good people. Something bad was happening in that house."

Dylan's smile faded. "Has Max talked to Mrs. Faulkner yet?"

"I don't know. I texted him before I came over, but he didn't get back to me. I was thinking he might be here this morning. Mom said she was asking everyone over. I have a feeling it's going to be a long week of pre-wedding celebration."

"Let's go inside and find out." As they walked toward the house, Dylan added, "Did Cassidy look better than you remember or worse?"

"Way better," he said with a sigh. "I always thought she was beautiful, but now she's really come into her own."

"What does she do?"

"She designs landscapes, gardens. She works at a nursery in Half Moon Bay. She's been there since she was nineteen."

"She's never been that far away."

"No, not far at all."

———⟶≫≪⟵———

As two of her coworkers, Freddie and Dana, finished unloading potted plants and trees onto the deck of the Holman estate, Cassidy took her hands out of the rich, dark soil and stood up, wiping her sweaty brow with a nearby towel. She'd been working on one section of the garden since eight a.m. and it was almost eleven now; she was ready for a break.

"One more pallet of plants," Dana said, walking over to her, as Freddie headed back to the truck. "Then we're done for now. Well, you're not done, but I am."

She smiled back at Dana, a thirty-six-year-old mother of two who worked part-time at the nursery. "I appreciate your help. I know it's hard to leave the kids on the weekend."

"They're with their dad, having some quality time. And I was dying to see this house. It's amazing." Dana waved her hand in the air, motioning toward the four-story Victorian mansion and then to the magnificent views of the Golden Gate Bridge, Alcatraz, Sausalito, and Angel Island.

"It will be more amazing when I get it all done." Right now, she'd only planted one small oval area by the deck. The rest of the yard would have water features, a fire pit, barbecue area, a gazebo, and, of course, plenty of trees and flowers.

"I can't wait to see it, but I hope you don't have to work

the entire weekend."

"I don't mind." She actually liked having something to occupy her mind.

"Is everything okay? Felicia told me the police called yesterday and then you had some intense conversation with a very good-looking man, after which you disappeared for hours."

"Felicia should be minding the store and not my business."

"That's not an answer."

"I have some personal stuff to deal with, but it will all work out."

"Personal stuff? I didn't know you had a personal life, Cassidy. It's been all work and no play as long as I've known you."

"This relationship goes back a long time."

"Which brings us to the attractive man…"

"He's a guy I went out with in high school."

"What happened? Did you dump him, or did he dump you?"

"I broke it off."

"Interesting. And now he's back."

"Not because he's interested in me. Look, I really don't want to get into it."

"All right. I'll shut up. I just want you to be happy."

"I am happy. Look around. This is right where I want to be."

"In someone else's backyard?" Dana asked dryly.

"Not just any backyard. There's a good chance the Holmans' house and gardens will be photographed and publicized. This could be a huge break for the nursery."

"I know, but life isn't just about business. You should have some fun, too."

"This is my fun. Now, go."

As Dana left with Freddie, Cassidy grabbed her thermos of ice water and took a swig, surprised at how hot she was. After yesterday's storms, she'd thought summer was still a long way off, but the temperature was seventy-five, and there wasn't a cloud in the sky. She wanted to take that as a good omen, but she couldn't quite get there. She had a feeling there was another shoe that was going to drop.

Setting down her thermos, she picked up her phone. She had several missed calls from Hunter, and one from George.

She'd call George first. She wasn't quite ready to deal with Hunter again.

"Hi, it's me," she said when he answered. "Just saw you called. Everything okay?"

"It's all good here, but there's a man trying to reach you, and he sounded very distraught. I didn't want to just give out your number, so I got his. He said he knew you when he was a kid, and it was a matter of life and death."

Her heart twisted at that dramatic proclamation. For a split second, she had the ridiculously hopeful thought that it was Tommy, that the police were wrong, that it wasn't his body that they'd found in the garage. "What was his name?"

"David Bellerman. That ring a bell?"

"Yes. He was in foster care with me." He'd also been on the list she'd given to the police. "What else did he say?"

"Just that it was really important that he speak to you. I figured this was about your foster family. What do you want to do?"

"Can you text me his number?"

"Sure. How's it going at the Holmans?"

"Great. Freddie and Dana just left. I have a lot to do, but I'm happy for the good weather and the moist soil."

"What more could you want?" he teased.

"Nothing."

"Don't work too hard."

"I'll see you later." As the text from George came in, she thought about David. He'd been a year older than her and Tommy, but out of all the kids at the house, David had probably known Tommy the best. They'd spent hours shooting baskets in the driveway after dinner.

She had never really trusted David, because he'd always

felt a little like Geralyn's spy. David had been adopted by the Faulkners when he was seven, and he had been treated like the Faulkners' own child, and not like one of those they were getting money from the state to house and feed. She didn't know why they felt differently about David, but obviously they'd had a fondness for him that hadn't extended to the other kids.

If anyone had a different perspective on the Faulkners, it was probably David. It might be worth hearing what he had to say.

Sitting down at the patio table, she punched in his number, her nerves tightening as she waited for him to answer.

"Bellerman," he said crisply.

"It's Cassidy." Just acknowledging it was her felt like she'd taken a step in possibly the wrong direction, but it was too late to backtrack now.

"Well, you actually called me back. I almost can't believe it."

"I assume you're calling about Tommy."

"Yes. I spoke to the police earlier. I could not believe what they told me. I thought you and Tommy ran away together. What do you know?"

"Not much." Her hand tightened around the phone. "We were going to run away together, but Tommy didn't show up. What happened after I left?"

"Mom and Dad went looking for you and Tommy. They were sure you were together."

It was weird to hear David call Geralyn and Donald Mom and Dad. The other kids had always called them by their first names. "Did they contact the police? My social worker?"

"I'm sure they did. But I wasn't involved in that."

"If they went looking for me, it was so they could shut me up—the way they did Tommy. You know they killed Tommy, right?"

"Don't be ridiculous. They might not have been the best

parents, but they weren't killers."

"Then how do you explain Tommy's body ending up in the wall of the garage?"

"I don't know. Maybe one of the other kids did it, or Dad's brother, Evan. He was hanging around that spring. I never liked him, and I don't think he liked Tommy, either."

"None of the kids could have done it. For one thing, they couldn't have gotten into the garage without Donald knowing, and planting a dead body there—no way. Donald had to have known."

"Maybe he was protecting his brother. But I am sure that Geralyn didn't know anything about it. She's a kind, gentle person."

"Oh, come on, David. She might have been that way to you, but she certainly wasn't that way to me or to the others."

"I know she was nicer to me than to you, but I was there the longest. It made sense."

"Have you seen Geralyn?"

"I tried. The doctor wouldn't let me in. He said the only people getting in would be the police, when she was ready, but I could see her through the glass in the door, and she was just staring into space, like she wasn't even there. Her skin was white. It felt like she was a ghost."

"She's faking it, David. She doesn't want to talk to the cops."

"There's no way she's faking it. You didn't see her. I think she had a breakdown when they told her about Tommy."

"Because she knows someone in her family, if not her, killed Tommy."

"I really don't want to believe it was Donald."

"He's the most likely suspect. And it's not like he didn't make other kids disappear."

David cleared his throat. "We don't need to talk about that again, do we?"

"We both know you lied about Molly."

"No one else but you and Tommy said you saw her

there."

"You saw her, too. And if you're going to stick to that old story, then we don't have anything to talk about. I don't even know why you called me."

"Hang on. I don't agree with your feelings about Geralyn, but I think we both cared about Tommy. He was my friend, too. And he didn't deserve what happened to him."

"Fine, you feel bad. What do you want from me?"

"Maybe a little understanding. I'm worried. It feels like someone is out for revenge. The police said the fire was arson."

"I can believe that any number of people would have wanted to burn that house down, but I don't get why you're worried." There was something in his words she didn't understand.

"Five months ago, Dad—Donald, was killed in a car crash. He was driving down the coast highway, and his car just went off the road. It was raining that night, and everyone chalked it up to an accident, but now I'm not so sure."

"Where on the coast did this happen?" she asked, her gut clenching at the thought of Donald having been so close to her home.

"Just south of Pacifica."

Pacifica was north of Half Moon Bay, but it still made her feel odd to know that Donald had been driving down the same highway she'd traveled a thousand times in the last ten years.

"I'm concerned that the car accident and the fire are connected, that someone is out to hurt the Faulkners, and that I might be a target, too, because they adopted me."

She was starting to see where he was coming from. "Now, I understand. How long did you live with the Faulkners after I left?"

"I was there off and on through college. I got my own place after I graduated, when I was in my early twenties."

"But you've kept in touch with them?"

"They were the only family I had after my mom died; of

course, I kept in touch."

"When did you last see Geralyn?"

"Three weeks ago. I've been out of town on business. Before that, I was seeing her fairly often. She's been devastated since Dad died. Her sister came to stay with her for a while. Evan has been around, too. We've all been worried about her very deep depression. We thought she might be suicidal, which is why I can totally believe that she had a nervous breakdown when the fire destroyed her house and the police told her about Tommy. She was already fragile."

"Fragile?" That word didn't describe the woman she remembered at all. "Geralyn has never been a victim, David. Don't try to turn her into one."

"You don't know the woman she is now."

"Well, I knew the woman she used to be, and she was not warm and loving. She was cold and distant. She and Donald took in kids for cash. They didn't care about us."

"That's not true."

"Well, maybe they cared about you, but they certainly didn't care about me. Geralyn lied about Molly's disappearance. She made the social worker think I was crazy. And God knows what Donald was doing out in that garage— what he—or they did to Molly."

"I don't want to talk about her."

"So, now you acknowledge that she existed?"

"I want to concentrate on what's happening now. We need to figure out who set the fire, who might have killed Donald if it wasn't an accident, and what happened to Tommy."

"But Molly could be part of it." A sudden thought occurred to her. "Maybe she set the fire. Maybe she didn't die. She could have run away. She could have come back and torched the house."

"Or you could have done the same thing. Your hatred for the Faulkners was well-documented, and it's obvious you feel the same way now."

"Is that why you called me—to see if I'd confess?"

"No. I called you because you were Tommy's best friend in the world, and aside from everything else, the kid deserves a memorial service."

She hadn't even thought about that, and another wave of guilt ran through her. "You're right. Tommy does deserve a funeral."

"We should do something."

"I can take care of it."

"You weren't the only one who cared about him, Cassidy."

"If you cared about him, why didn't you try to find him?"

"Because I thought the two of you were together. All this time, I thought you and Tommy were just living your lives. I thought you were both happy. Anyway, we might be on different sides when it comes to Geralyn, but this isn't about her. Can we meet later today?"

"Meet?" she stuttered, surprised by the request. Their conversation hadn't been great so far and he wanted to keep it going? "Why?"

"To make plans. To talk things through. There are not many people in my life I can talk to about any of this, and I'm betting you feel the same. I'll be at Jack's in the Marina at five thirty tonight. Come by. Have a drink."

"Can we talk about Molly?"

"We can talk about whatever you want."

"I'll think about it." She ended the call on that note, feeling even more unsettled by their conversation.

David thought someone was out to get revenge, and if he was right, he might be the next target. But it wasn't up to her to protect him, or even to try to help him get through anything. He had never been that nice to her. They had never been friends. Even now, he couldn't admit that Molly had lived in the house. Despite what he'd just said, she doubted he would talk about Molly if she went to the bar, so why go?

She did want to do something for Tommy, but she didn't need David's help to do that, although it was nice of him to offer. Maybe he wasn't a horrible person. Could she really blame him for being the Faulkners' favorite kid? David probably had the most information about the Faulkners. If they kept talking, he might inadvertently reveal something.

Was it worth the risk?

David might be trying to lure her out of the shadows, so he could pin everything on her.

Tapping her fingers restlessly on the table, she thought about calling Hunter. He wanted to work with her. He wanted to be partners. She'd tentatively said yes the day before, but she'd certainly had second thoughts since then.

Picking up her phone, she opened a text, then hesitated. How many mistakes was she going to make when it came to Hunter?

She'd already hurt him once, entangled him in her problems. Even though he felt a duty to get justice for Tommy, wouldn't it be better for Hunter if he went on with his life and didn't get sucked into the darkness that surrounded the Faulkners and her?

Nine

➤➤◄◄◄─

His parents' house was filled to the rafters with Callaways. It took Hunter almost an hour to make his way through the living room as he stopped to chat with his Uncle Jack and Aunt Lynda, his cousin Nicole and her husband, Ryan, and their two kids Brandon and Amanda. He was happy to get a small smile out of Brandon whose communication skills and behavioral problems had definitely improved since he'd been reunited with his twin brother Kyle.

He also spent a few minutes with Aiden and Sara, marveling at how their two kids were now active toddlers, and how happy the two of them were. Their love story had started when they were kids, growing up next door to each other, although they both said it had been more of a hate story back then and the love had taken a long time to come. They'd had to grow up before they could see what they had.

He wondered if that could possibly be true for him and Cassidy. Although, they had the reverse story: love first—then hate. Not that he really hated her anymore. Truth be told, he didn't know how he felt.

Making his way into the combined family room and

kitchen, he saw his grandmother Eleanor sitting on the couch with his brother Ian and Ian's wife Grace. Eleanor suffered from Alzheimer's but seemed to be alert today as she listened to Grace, although he wondered if she really had any idea who Grace was. There were so many people in the room, his head was spinning.

Squeezing past his cousin Sean and Sean's wife, Jessica, with a friendly nod, he grabbed a beer out of the fridge. When he turned around, the guest of honor, his sister Annie, gave him a smile.

"It's about time you got here, Hunter."

"I've been here for an hour. It took me that long to get through the house." Looking at his sister he saw nothing but pure joy on her face. Annie was glowing with love.

"I know. It's crazy in here." She laughed as she jumped out of the way to avoid being run over by four-year-old Chloe, Aiden's daughter, who was chasing the family dog. "Mom said only family, but surely we must have half the neighborhood in here."

"This is all family, and we're all here for you."

"I told Mom not to make a big deal. We're going to see each other for the rehearsal dinner and the wedding next weekend."

"She takes any opportunity she can get to bring the family together." He pulled off the top of his beer and took a swig. "Where's Griffin?"

"He's coming up on Tuesday. He wanted me to have time on my own with my family and friends. Plus, the bar is super busy these days. Since he reopened the Depot, it has been packed every night."

"I suspect you've had a hand in that, or have you been too busy developing your action movie?"

"I've been busy with it all," she said, delight in her eyes. "So much has changed in the last six months; sometimes I have to pinch myself to believe it's all real."

"It's real. Just look around."

She laughed. "Last year, I was feeling lonely and restless

and not sure what I wanted to do, where I wanted to live, and then I decided to go into the ocean and face an old fear, and I met Griffin. He saved my life, literally and figuratively."

"I still can't believe you got into the water, much less got attacked by a shark. You do attract trouble, Annie."

"I don't always have the best luck, but that shark brought Griffin into my life, so I can't complain. He didn't like me at all at first, but I slowly worked my way into his heart."

"You're a force of nature."

"Just like you. How does it feel to be back fighting fire?"

"My first shift was fairly eventful, so I can't answer that question yet."

"I heard. Do you want to talk about it?"

"I really don't."

"Can we talk about Cassidy then?"

He groaned. "Dylan told you about Cassidy?"

"Well, actually, Mom did. Any lingering sparks from the old days?"

"There's too much going on to think about sparks."

"You don't think about sparks; they're just there. And I remember Cassidy. I saw how looney tunes you were about her. And then after she left, you got crazy and did all kinds of stupid stuff."

He put up a warning hand. "We don't need to rehash any of that."

"Well, just be careful. First loves are hard to shake off."

"Are you two talking about Cassidy?" Emma asked, as she joined them, her blue eyes as inquisitive as ever.

"I'm glad you're here, Emma. Is Max with you?" he asked, avoiding her question.

"No, Max is working the case. He's interviewing kids from the foster home and still hoping to speak with Mrs. Faulkner at some point. By the way, I got an interesting call this morning from someone I have not talked to in a very long time."

"Who's that?"

"Lindsay Grayson. I didn't realize she lived next door to

the Faulkners."

"And she just called you out of the blue?"

"So she could ask me for your number. Apparently, you spoke to her mom yesterday. She wants to catch up with you. I didn't want to just hand out your number, so I got hers." Emma reached into her pocket and pulled out a piece of paper. "It's up to you if you want to call her back. I tried to find out if she knew anything relevant to the fire, but she said she spends little time in that neighborhood and hasn't spoken to anyone at the Faulkner house in years."

Knowing that Lindsay probably had no information to give, he really didn't want to talk to her. They hadn't parted on the best of terms. Lindsay had always wanted more from him than he had to give. Although, she might know something about Tommy's murder that she didn't realize she knew. She had lived next door to the Faulkners until she went to college. She might even remember Molly, which would certainly make Cassidy happy. Not that he needed to be thinking about making her happy.

In fact, he suspected that calling Lindsay would make Cassidy quite unhappy. He smiled to himself, remembering how jealous she'd looked when she'd discovered that he'd gone out with Lindsay. Her reaction had been like a salve to his wounded heart. But it had probably just been a momentary reaction. She couldn't possibly care that much. She'd obviously put him out of her mind all these years.

Although, those kisses they'd shared in the car yesterday had showed the attraction between them was still very strong. But even so, he shouldn't go down that road again.

"Hunter?"

He realized both Emma and Annie were staring at him with speculative expressions. "Thanks for this." He shoved the paper into his pocket. "I'll let you guys talk about your trip." Moving away from Annie and Emma, he spotted Kate coming through the kitchen door and immediately cut her off. "Hey," he said, giving her a hug.

"Hey yourself. How are you?"

"I'm great and not interested in talking about Cassidy," he said preemptively.

Kate laughed. "I swear that was not going to be the first thing I asked—maybe the second."

"Where's your better half?"

"Devin is in DC. He'll fly out on Thursday for all the wedding hoopla."

"Are you sorry you didn't have any of this hoopla?"

"Not even for a second. I just don't go crazy over wedding stuff, but I am thrilled to help Annie do her thing."

"I get it. Listen, I need a favor."

"That sounds intriguing."

He pulled her into the hallway where they could get a little privacy. "I know you've heard about the body I found."

"Yes. I'm really sorry you had to discover that."

"Well, the police are looking into the boy's murder, and Emma's team is working on the arson, but I'm also interested in the disappearance of another girl at that foster home. Cassidy swears a girl named Molly went missing years ago, but everyone claimed that the girl didn't exist, and that Cassidy made her up."

"How does an entire family agree on the non-existence of an individual while your ex-girlfriend does not?" Kate asked suspiciously.

"That's a good question, but what I'd like your help on is tracking down this girl. Her name is Molly Bennett. She has black hair, brown eyes, might be of Native American heritage, and was fourteen years old when she disappeared fourteen years ago. Cassidy said she was at the Faulkners for about three weeks, but social services had no record of her ever being there."

Kate's expression turned serious. "I'm happy to use my resources to look into this, but I might need more to go on, like where she was born, parents' names, and schools she attended."

"I'll talk to Cassidy and see what else I can find out."

"The two of you are friends now?"

"I don't know what we are, but I do want to know what happened to the kid who died and also to this girl."

"Well, we're leaving for Napa in a few hours, but text me whatever you can get from Cassidy, and I will have a friend of mine start working on it while I'm away, and then as soon as I get back, I'll jump on it, too."

"I really appreciate it."

She shrugged. "I'm happy to help. I just hope you know what you're doing, Hunter."

"I know what I'm doing. I've been taking care of myself for a long time. Everyone in this family needs to chill."

"That would be easier if you were a bit more open. You got hurt in that fire and then you went on the road. It just feels like something is off with you. You haven't been yourself for a long time."

"And I'm working some things out, so give me some space. It's not like you tell us everything you do. In fact, you rarely tell us anything."

"Point taken."

"It's up to me to figure out my own life."

"Will that life include Cassidy?"

He didn't answer her question, distracted by the buzzing of his phone. His pulse jumped at the message from Cassidy. *Can we talk today? Call me or come by my job site. Here's the address.*

"Hunter? Earth to Hunter?"

He looked up at Kate. "What?"

"It's her, isn't it? It's Cassidy." She gave him a knowing smile. "You have the same look on your face now you had in high school."

"It is from Cassidy, and I have to go. Have fun on your trip. I'll catch up with you when you're back. And if your friend finds anything out before then—"

"I'll let you know. Be careful."

He gave a careless shrug. "Not really in my nature."

"I know. That's why I said it."

The address Cassidy had sent him took him into Pacific Heights, an upscale San Francisco neighborhood of mansions, many of which were set back behind circular drives or iron gates. At this particular four-story home, the gates were open, and Cassidy's Wild Garden van was in the driveway. Suspecting he'd be most likely to find her in the back, he avoided the front of the house and headed down the drive.

The backyard was a definite work in progress. There was a lot of dirt and building materials off to one side. Stakes had been laid around various parts of the yard. A massive deck off the back of the house boasted potted plants and pallets of small flowers. Bricks were stacked and waiting to be placed somewhere, perhaps around one of the garden areas.

As he moved farther into the yard, he saw Cassidy on her knees working on an oval area by the deck. Her blonde hair was pulled back in a ponytail, and her work jeans and tank top were dusted with dirt and stray twigs. Her face was red from probably both the sun and the exertion, but she looked happy. This was her element. Planting always made her smile.

He remembered one Saturday when his mom had asked for Cassidy's help in the garden. She'd been over the moon with the invitation. He, of course, would have preferred to take her to the beach, rather than help her and his mom plant vegetables. But Cassidy had been so excited, he hadn't been able to say no.

She'd made a point of checking on that garden every time she came over, impatient to see a bloom of some sort. Unfortunately, she'd left before the garden had started to flourish. He could still remember looking at it through his bedroom window and wanting to go rip out every tomato and zucchini he could find just because she wasn't there to see them.

He hadn't really understood Cassidy's love affair with gardening back then, but now he could see that planting something and watching it grow gave her back the control she'd lost over her life. Not only that, it gave her a chance to make something good happen, to put some light into her dark world.

Watching her work, he could see the passion for what she did in every movement, and it made him question where his passion for his job was. Did he love firefighting the way she loved gardening? He certainly loved parts of it, and he was good at his job. It gave him satisfaction to save someone's property, sometimes their life, but sometimes he couldn't save either. Sometimes it was hard to witness so much destruction day after day. Whereas Cassidy was bringing new life to the world in her planting. She was creating something new, and it felt a bit more inspiring.

He took a step forward and a branch crackled under his feet. Cassidy whirled around, jumping to her feet, as if preparing for fight or flight.

"It's just me," he said quickly.

She put a hand to her heart. "I thought you would text me before you came over."

"Sorry."

"It's fine. I didn't hear you come into the yard. How long have you been standing there?"

"Just a minute. You looked busy; I didn't want to interrupt you."

"I can get lost in my work." She picked up a nearby towel and brushed the dirt off her hands.

"I'm glad you contacted me, Cassidy."

"I had a moment of temporary insanity."

He grinned at her dark words. "Or maybe you were actually being smart. Two heads are better than one. But if I hadn't heard from you, I was going to get in touch. I just saw Emma."

She immediately stiffened. "Is there news?"

"Nothing yet. Max is conducting more interviews today. Mrs. Faulkner has not yet been interrogated. But someone unexpected did call Emma."

"Who was that?"

"Lindsay Grayson."

"Lindsay called Emma? Why? I didn't realize they knew each other. Was she looking for me?"

"Actually, she was looking for me. Emma told Lindsay she'd give me her number."

"Did you call her back?"

"Not yet. I was going to, but…"

"But what?" she challenged, a harder light coming into her eyes.

"It felt like a conversation you should be there for."

"She called you, not me."

There was a definite edge to her voice. "She was your friend."

"It seems like maybe the two of you were better friends."

"You sound jealous."

"I'm not. That's ridiculous. You probably dated the entire cheerleading squad after I left."

"Which would be none of your business, since you did leave."

She frowned. "Right. But it feels a little odd. Lindsay was my friend. She knew I liked you. She heard me talk about you. It's just weird that the two of you…" She cleared her throat. "It doesn't matter. It's not my business. I don't care at all. And it was a long time ago anyway. You should call her back on your own. She might want to talk to you in private."

"Are you done? Wow, I used to think you were on the quiet side, but that's changed."

She made a face at him. "I'm a bit unnerved these days."

"I get it, but here's the deal. Lindsay and I became friends after you left, and then senior year we started hanging out more. I wasn't interested in having a girlfriend, but she was easy to have around. It wasn't until I asked her to the senior prom that I realized she was more interested than I was, but I didn't want to hurt her, so I took her to the dance. And after that, I told her I thought we should just be friends. I was graduating. She still had two more years of high school."

"I'm betting she wasn't happy about that."

"She wasn't. She was angry. But that was that. And there's one more thing. I never slept with her."

Cassidy stared back at him. "You could have."

"I know I could have, but I didn't. Are we clear?"

Ten

→➤➤◄◄←

"We're clear." Cassidy felt a stunning sense of relief that Hunter hadn't slept with Lindsay. She didn't know why the idea had bothered her so much, but it had.

"Do you want to call her together?" he asked.

"I guess." As she looked into Hunter's compelling and pointed gaze, she found herself getting distracted by his face, his dark-blue eyes, his full, sexy mouth, the scruff of beard on his jaw, the waves in his brown hair.

She'd spent most of the night and half the day telling herself he hadn't looked that good, but that was certainly a lie. He looked even better than she remembered. While the boy of her dreams had been hot, the man in front of her was even more attractive. His shoulders had broadened, his frame had filled out, his jaw had gotten stronger and more determined. In jeans and a T-shirt, he looked incredibly fit, with powerful, muscular arms and long lean legs. She could only imagine what was going on under those clothes.

Her heart started to race and sweat damped her palms as a wave of desire ran through her.

The worst part was that Hunter knew what she was

feeling. She could see it in his eyes. No matter how much of her life she had been able to hide from him, she'd never been able to hide the fact that she wanted him.

"Cassidy?"

His husky voice almost undid her. She had no idea if he'd said more than her name in the last five minutes, because she'd completely lost track.

She moved toward the patio table, reaching desperately for her water, hoping the long drink would bring some much-needed cooling.

"Are you all right?" he asked.

"I'm just warm. It's amazing how hot it is after the storm yesterday. I've been working since dawn. I guess it just caught up to me."

"I don't think it's the work or the weather that's bothering you."

As she sat down at the table, he took the chair across from her. "You're feeling overwhelmed," he said.

"A bit." She was happy that he'd gone for overwhelmed instead of suggesting she was lusting after his body.

"It's understandable. I feel the same way."

She gave him a doubtful look. "You? Hunter Callaway, overwhelmed? I don't think so. You've always been in control, in charge, confident, the kind of guy who goes after what he wants and gets it. I can't believe that's changed."

"Is that how you think of me?"

"Did I say something that wasn't true?"

"I wanted you, but I didn't get you."

"That wasn't because I didn't want you, too." The admission was probably a bad idea, but it seemed like it was past time to be honest. "But I was living a double life, and I wasn't really the girl you thought I was. I was pretending to be someone I wasn't. I think I always knew deep down that our time together would be short."

"You made it short. You decided when it ended."

"I know. But we can't keep going over old ground. It's pointless."

"That's true."

She took a sip of water. "Sorry I don't have anything to offer you to drink. The Holmans gave me full access to the yard, but not the house."

"I'm fine." He looked around the yard. "This is a magnificent house. The views are spectacular."

"And worth a fortune," she said, happy he'd changed the subject. "The Holmans bought this house last year for twelve million dollars."

"That's a lot of cash."

"I'll say. I can't even imagine how much money they must have to make such an investment."

"And you're doing all the landscaping? That will be profitable."

"It will definitely put the nursery in the black. But more importantly, it will hopefully bring us more high-end customers. We've struggled a bit the last few years. Mary was sick for a while, and after she died, George couldn't keep up with things. He made some bad decisions, but we're getting back on our feet now, and this job will really help."

He gave her a thoughtful look. "I was thinking when I saw you digging in the dirt how happy you looked, just like when you planted that vegetable garden with my mom."

"She was very nice to include me."

"She wasn't being nice. She wanted a helper, and none of her kids liked to garden."

"I thought about that garden after I left. I wondered if all the vegetables came in."

"They did. We were eating salads every night for dinner. Well, the rest of the family was. I couldn't look at a tomato or zucchini without thinking about you."

His words touched her heart. "I thought about you a lot, too. I wondered if you would go into photography or follow in your dad's footsteps. You always seemed a little torn about whether your destiny should be ordained by your family name. It looks like your dad won out."

"I didn't do it for him, but I had to do something, and

firefighting is the family business."

"I suspect you're good at it."

"I was doing better before I fell down an elevator shaft."

"What? When did that happen?"

"Last year. It happened during a high-rise fire. I only fell three stories. It could have been worse."

"How badly were you hurt?"

"Broke my foot and a bunch of ribs. While they were healing, I took time off and did some traveling."

"That's when you went to South America."

"Yes. The day I found Tommy's remains was my first day back on the job, and the fire at the Faulkners was the first call. It felt somewhat fateful."

She shook her head at that bit of irony. "I can't even imagine. You remembered right away that it was my house?"

"I did. The past came rushing back."

"I felt the same way when you drove into the parking lot of the nursery. The fourteen years in between just vanished."

He met her gaze. "It's a hell of a thing. Tommy drove us apart and now he brought us back together. He probably wouldn't like it that I was the one who found his remains."

"Oh, I don't know about that. He didn't dislike you nearly as much as you disliked him."

"I'm not sure I believe that."

"He didn't like me the way you did. He was like a brother. You can believe that or not, but it's the truth."

"Then I'll believe it. If we don't lie to each other from here on out, it will probably make things easier."

She nodded. "I agree. I texted you to come over, because I also got a call from someone in my past—David Bellerman."

"What did he have to say?"

"He expressed shock and horror. He spoke to Max earlier. He doesn't want to believe that his parents had anything to do with Tommy's death. Did I mention that David was officially adopted by the Faulkners?"

"No, you didn't."

"They got him when he was six or seven. They treated him much better than the rest of us."

"Then he has a different perspective."

"He does. He thinks Donald's brother, Evan, or one of the kids might have killed Tommy, but he didn't have anything to back up that theory."

"Has he tried to see Geralyn?"

"Yes, but he couldn't get in, either. He expressed sadness about Tommy's death, which I guess doesn't surprise me that much. They both loved basketball, and they'd shoot baskets every night. The old hoop over the garage got a lot of action. It didn't even have a net, but they didn't care. David said we should have a memorial for Tommy, and I feel guilty that I didn't even think about that."

"Things are happening fast."

"I know, but David thought about it."

"You can still organize something if you want to."

"I do want to. Anyway, David said something else that was disturbing."

Hunter leaned forward in his chair. "What's that?"

"He speculated that Donald's death might not have been an accident. Apparently, Donald's car went off the Pacific Coast Highway and crashed on the rocks. It was raining, so it was considered an accident. But now with the fire being arson, David is wondering if someone is out for revenge, and whether the events are tied together. He's worried that he could be a target, because of his special relationship with the Faulkners."

"That's interesting. I wonder if he told the police that."

"I would think so. He seemed pretty worried about it. He wants me to meet him tonight for a drink. I didn't commit either way. He still refuses to admit that Molly existed, but maybe I should go. He might know something that I don't know. He was there after Tommy and I disappeared. He knows what his parents did, how they acted."

Hunter nodded, a gleam in his eyes. "We should definitely meet with him."

She let out a sigh. "I know you want to go but…"

"There's no but; I am going."

"I'm just afraid we're getting in too deep. Maybe we should back away from this, from each other. You have your life; I have mine. Nothing we do will bring Tommy back."

"It's not about that; it's about justice, and I know you want that. Stop trying to push me away."

"I don't want to hurt you again."

"I told you how not to do that—don't run away without a word. And I don't think you're as interested in protecting me as you are in protecting yourself."

"Maybe that's true," she admitted. "I've been in survival mode a long time."

"Look, I don't know what's going to happen with any of this, but let's take it one step at a time." He pulled out his phone. "We can start by calling Lindsay."

As Hunter punched in Lindsay's number, Cassidy took another sip of water, mentally preparing herself to hear Lindsay's effervescent voice. The girl had always talked fast, with an energy that never seemed to flag. On their walks to school, Lindsay would talk nonstop, only occasionally waiting for her to acknowledge a comment before jumping into whatever else was on her mind.

She'd actually liked that Lindsay talked a lot, because it meant she didn't have to say much. She could just listen, and that was easier for her.

Maybe that's why Hunter had been a good fit, too. In high school, he'd certainly had a lot to say, and he'd always had so many friends around, it had been easy to just be by his side or in his shadow.

Was that why he liked her? Because she'd been comfortable in the background?

She frowned at that thought.

He gave her a questioning look. "What?"

"Nothing," she muttered.

Lindsay's phone rang several times and then went to voicemail. Hunter hung up. "We can try her later."

"That's fine. I don't think Lindsay will know anything anyway."

"She did grow up next door. You and Lindsay used to walk to school together. Didn't Molly go with you?"

"No. She was being home-schooled, I think. Or maybe she was in the middle of transferring between schools." She paused, frowning at her own lack of recollection. "Why don't I remember that?"

He shrugged. "You had other things on your mind. But speaking of details, I asked my sister Kate to see what she can find out about Molly, but she asked for more information. What else do you remember about her? Did she ever say where she came from, what her parents' names were, how they died, anything that would help us trace her?"

She thought for a moment. "She was born in New Mexico, but her mom brought her to San Francisco to live with her grandmother. Her grandmother's name was Lily. She worked in a jewelry store where she also sold the necklaces she made." An old image ran through her mind: Molly sitting in her bed, running the silver and turquoise pendant up and down the silver chain. "Molly had a necklace that her grandmother had designed for her. It had a beautiful turquoise stone. It felt tribal. Molly said it was supposed to protect her from evil. I don't think it worked."

"What else?"

She tried to remember what other things Molly had told her when they'd turned out the lights at night and talked in the dark until one of them fell asleep. "Her mother—I don't remember her name—she was a waitress when she wasn't in rehab."

Hunter stared back at her, a grim expression tightening his lips. "So, Molly's mother was alive when she was at the Faulkners?"

"I think she was. I don't know. There was one other thing. Her grandmother was sick. She was in the hospital. That's why Molly was at the Faulkners'."

"Is it possible that Molly ran away, just like you did, and

the Faulkners didn't want to own up to it? Maybe her grandmother got better, and she ended up back with her."

"I really hope that's the case, but she was only fourteen. It was hard enough to do at sixteen; I'm not sure she could have made it on her own at her age. And I still don't know why everyone pretended she didn't exist."

"We need to find her."

"I would love to find her, but I haven't given you much to go on. Do you think your sister can locate her with what little information we have?"

"I hope so. We do have one other clue—the jewelry store where Molly's grandmother worked. Someone might remember one or both of them."

"I'm sure there are dozens of jewelry stores in San Francisco."

"But maybe not a lot that sell artisan-type jewelry. It sounds like Molly's grandmother used her Native American background in her jewelry making."

His words gave her a glimmer of hope, but she was afraid to latch on to it. "That's true, but it was fourteen years ago. The store could be closed. Or it's possible no one would remember her."

"That's seeing the glass half empty, Cassidy."

His words brought a reluctant smile to her lips. "You said that to me before—when we were kids."

"It doesn't hurt to be optimistic."

"It actually can hurt a lot. You have farther to fall."

"Or you might get a new idea if you're not mired in pessimism. Is there anything else you remember?"

"I don't think so."

"I'll text Kate the information we have so far. It's a start. If we can't find Molly, maybe we can find her mother."

She saw the determination in his eyes and was reminded again that when Hunter went after something, he usually won. "You're all in on this, aren't you?"

"I told you that yesterday."

"I thought you might have changed your mind after

sleeping on it."

"To be honest, I didn't get much sleep. I had a lot to think about. What about you? How was your night?"

"Long," she admitted. "Which is why I'm running out of gas now."

"How much more do you have to do? Can you call it a day?"

She glanced at her watch. It was almost two, and she had been at it since eight. "I think so."

"Good, because if you want, we could check out some jewelry stores until it's time to meet David."

"You want to do that now?" she asked, a little startled by how quickly everything was moving.

"I'll get on the internet while you finish up here and see what stores might be worth visiting. It's a long shot, but we might get lucky. If nothing else, we'll look at some jewelry."

"All right. I need about twenty minutes."

"Take your time. I'm not going anywhere."

His words sent a tingle down her spine. At some point, she was going to have to say goodbye to Hunter. She had a feeling it was going to hurt even more this time around.

Eleven

—➤➤➤«««←—

When she'd finished putting her things away, Cassidy climbed into the back of her van and grabbed a clean shirt with the Wild Garden logo on it and quickly changed. She wished she could do something about her dusty jeans, but she hadn't brought along another pair of pants. She could, however, pull out her ponytail and run a brush through her hair.

Taking a quick glance in the rearview mirror, she wished she looked a little better than she did. Her lip gloss had vanished hours ago, and she hadn't bothered with any eye makeup, thinking the plants she'd be working on all day certainly wouldn't notice. Her cheeks were nicely warmed from the sun, and there was a sparkle in her eyes that had more to do with Hunter than anything else.

Oh, well, it didn't matter. She and Hunter were not going on a date; they were just working together. Although, how that was actually going to work was a mystery to her. It had taken all of her willpower the day before not to jump into the back seat of his Jeep and recreate the best night of her life.

And even with all the mental reminders that that had

been a good decision, a tiny part of her felt like she'd missed out on something amazing.

But maybe she'd also missed out on more heartbreak.

Playing it safe wasn't the worst idea in the world, and it had certainly been her mantra for the last decade. She didn't want to change that now.

With that resolve in mind, she got out of the van and locked the doors behind her. They didn't need to take two cars downtown, and Hunter's Jeep would be easier to park than her van. She'd leave it in front of the Holmans' house and pick it up later.

As she got into Hunter's car, she heard him on the phone.

"Thanks for the update," he said. "I'll let Cassidy know."

"Let me know what?" she asked, as he set the phone down on the console between them. "Who were you talking to?"

"Max. They're expecting to talk to Mrs. Faulkner within the hour."

She was both thrilled and alarmed by that fact. She wanted Geralyn to be caught and punished, but she was afraid of what Geralyn would say as well as what she wouldn't say.

"This is good, Cassidy."

"I hope so. Did he say anything else?"

"He spoke to Quan Tran. Quan teaches martial arts in San Rafael. He said he hasn't been in touch with the Faulkners since he was eighteen. He thought you and Tommy ran away together. But if someone in the house did kill Tommy, he thought it was probably Evan, Donald's brother. He said that Evan had pulled his son Colin and Tommy apart during some fight over a video game."

"I don't remember that, although Colin did play a lot of video games, but Tommy didn't get into fights. He knew better than that. It would mean getting kicked out of the home."

"Maybe he wanted to get kicked out of the home."

"He probably would have wanted that if we hadn't been together. But he wouldn't have wanted to leave me there alone. We made a vow to stick together when Molly went missing." She paused. "David mentioned Evan to me, too, though. Something about him obviously bothered the boys."

"Max said they're trying to track him down, but he and his son are apparently on a fishing trip this weekend. There is one other interesting tidbit—Quan is a volunteer firefighter." A gleam entered his eyes. "Who better to start a fire than someone who knows how to put it out?"

"That's a leap. I don't know if I can see Quan as an arsonist. He was a quiet kid. He didn't speak much at all. He was like a turtle who was trying to hide under his shell. He was always looking down, almost afraid to make eye contact." As she spoke about Quan, she began to wonder if her defense was actually making Hunter's case. Quan had not been happy at the Faulkners'. Maybe he had chosen to retaliate years later. "I guess it is possible, though."

Hunter shrugged. "It was just a thought. I don't know if his job is significant or not. Max also said that Quan was not surprised by the news; he'd already spoken to David before coming to the police station."

"David must be calling all the kids."

"Well, at least Quan. Were they close?"

"I spent as little time as possible with the boys, especially after Molly disappeared, so I can't say. We can ask David tonight. In the meantime, do you know where we're going?"

"Yes." He nodded toward the envelope on the console where he'd jotted down some addresses. "I found five possible jewelry stores. I thought we'd start downtown and then work our way back through North Beach, ending at the Marina where we'll be meeting David."

"That's a good plan, very efficient." Hunter had always been good at making plans, whereas she'd been afraid to think too far into the future.

"Hopefully, we'll find a clue."

"Our chances are slightly worse than finding a needle in a haystack."

"Ooh, now the glass is like a quarter full," he said dryly.

She rolled her eyes. "Just calling it like I see it. Do you ever feel pessimistic, Hunter?"

"I try not to let myself get to that point. If things are going bad, I'd rather try to change them than just be depressed."

"What if you can't change them?"

"Well, then I might take a shot of whiskey or more likely I'd get my bike and go for a really long ride."

"Bicycle or motorcycle?"

He shot her a smile. "Either. I like the bike for exercise, but a motorcycle was my trusted steed on my recent travels."

"Why aren't we on the back of that motorcycle now?"

"I traded it in for this Jeep when I got back."

"Why?" she asked curiously.

"The motorcycle was good for traveling; it's not as practical in real life."

"And you're back to real life."

"Definitely," he said, a bit heavily.

"Was it hard to return to firefighting after your accident?"

"No, it was remarkably easy. It felt like I'd never left." He glanced over at her. "No one seems to accept that answer when I give it, though."

"Like your family?"

"Yes. They keep looking for some hidden problem. I can't totally blame them. While I was rehabbing, I decided to travel, and I didn't include anyone else in my plans. They didn't know I was even going until I texted them a group message to say I'd see them in a few months."

"Seriously? You didn't talk to them before that? You're all so close."

"I knew there would be questions, and I didn't feel like answering them."

She thought about his answer. "Something was going on in your head that you didn't want to share. What was it?"

Hunter didn't answer right away, concentrating for a moment on maneuvering through the crowded downtown streets. Then he said, "I was feeling restless. I needed to expand my world beyond the city, the family. I was on medical leave anyway; it seemed like a good time to go."

"Did you have fun?"

"I enjoyed myself," he said with a nod. "Every day was a new adventure. I saw things I couldn't have even imagined. Being in places where I didn't speak the language should have made me feel isolated, but in some ways, it forced me to get more in touch with myself. I had to be okay in my own company."

"I'm not surprised you had the fearlessness to go on your own, but I'm a little surprised that you didn't take some people along with you. You've always had a lot of friends. You're like the center spoke in a wheel. People revolve around you."

"I wouldn't say that, Cassidy."

"It used to be that way."

"That was high school. I'm not as popular now."

With his charming grin coming at her, she didn't think that was true at all.

"I wasn't lonely," he continued. "I made friends along the way. I had conversations I wouldn't have had if I'd been with friends. I'm very glad I did it. It was good to be on my own for an extended period of time. I realized how I had gone from one thing to the next without ever taking a minute to think about it."

She cocked her head, casting him a thoughtful look as she considered his words. She didn't want to be like his family and go looking for some hidden problem, but maybe his family wasn't wrong, because there was something in his tone... "What conclusions did you come to? Did you decide to make some big changes in your life?"

He gave her a quick, somewhat ironic smile. "No. I'm doing exactly the same thing I was doing before, at least temporarily."

"What does that mean?"

"I don't have a permanent job at the moment. I'm filling

in for another firefighter who is on medical leave. When he comes back in six weeks, I'll have to make another decision as to whether I want to take a permanent job or do something else entirely."

"What would you do?" she asked curiously.

"I have no idea. That's the problem. I'm conflicted. Firefighting is in my blood. But…"

"But," she prodded when he fell silent.

"I don't know if it's in my heart. And I can't believe I just said that out loud. Because I haven't said that to anyone."

She was touched by that admission. "Well, I'm not your family and I don't really care if you're a firefighter or not, so maybe that made it easier to say out loud."

"Maybe. I don't want to say that the last decade of my life has been for nothing. I don't want to feel like I've wasted years being a firefighter. But there's a hole inside of me, and the job isn't filling it. But then I wonder if any job would fill it. Maybe I want too much."

"You always did want a lot." She gave him a small smile. "Your optimism tends to generate a lot of ideas."

He smiled back at her. "That's true. I've had a lot of different dreams—travel photographer, professional cyclist."

"A cyclist?"

"Definitely. I thought I could probably win the Tour de France if I put some effort into it," he joked.

"Well, sure. And you would have looked good in the spandex shorts."

"I would have looked good," he agreed with a cocky grin.

"You could still do photography. What happened to that camera your mom gave you in high school? We used to take it out every weekend and shoot all over the city."

"It's probably in a box in my closet. I haven't used it in a long time, probably not since you left."

She felt a little sad at that thought. "That's too bad. You used to love taking pictures."

"I loved taking pictures of you," he corrected. "Without my favorite subject, it wasn't nearly as much fun."

"So, getting back to your career choices—"

He groaned. "Let's not get back to those. Let's talk about you. How do you like living in Half Moon Bay?"

"I love it. It has a small-town vibe that's charming, and I know a lot of shop owners now, so it feels like I'm seeing family when I go to town. George has a golden retriever named Boomer, who loves to walk on the sand with me. I do that with him a lot."

"Just you and the dog? No men in the picture?"

"Not at the moment." She left it at that, not willing to share that there hadn't been anyone in a very long time. "What about you? Any women in the picture?"

"Not at the moment," he said, echoing her words.

Silence followed. They'd ventured into dangerous territory by acknowledging their single, available status, and she was very glad to see Hunter turn in to the parking lot under Union Square. They'd shared enough personal information for the time being.

As they got out of the car and walked toward the elevator, she said, "I still think this is going to be a wild-goose chase."

"I'd rather be chasing a goose than sitting around waiting for the police to figure things out."

"I suppose it is better than that. I really wonder what Geralyn is going to tell them. I'm pretty sure I'm going to end up under the bus."

"Finding Molly or someone who knows what happened to her would be a good way to get you out from under that bus," he reminded her.

She wanted to prove him wrong and think positively for a change, but it seemed like it would take a miracle to track down Molly now.

—➤➤◄◄—

Two hours into their hunt for a clue to Molly Bennett, Hunter was beginning to feel some of his earlier eagerness fade. They'd visited four jewelry stores in the downtown area. They'd seen a lot of expensive stones and shiny diamonds but very little turquoise. They'd had no better luck at two stores in North Beach and were now walking back to the car before heading to the Marina and the final store on their list.

He knew it had been a long shot, but he'd really wanted to take some kind of positive action, and he'd also wanted to spend time with Cassidy. That part had been fun. She'd been a pretty good sport, even though he knew she was fighting her pessimism just to prove him wrong.

"Wait," she said suddenly, grabbing his arm.

"What?"

She pointed to the hill in front of them, to the steep, winding stairs that went from the bottom to the top. "Those are the steps, aren't they? The ones they call *a thousand steps to heaven*. We could never find them. Remember? We kept getting lost. But here they are." Excitement lit up her brown eyes. "Let's go up."

There was no way he was saying no to that suggestion, especially not when her hand slid down his arm and her fingers wrapped around his.

She was so caught up in the steps, she probably wasn't aware of what she was doing, but he certainly was.

They jogged across the street, pausing at the bottom of the stairway, where a very old engraved sign said the stairs were dedicated to the dreamers, to those who were willing to pursue their goals, no matter how high or how far away they might be.

"This sounds a little too optimistic for you," he teased. "Now, if the stairs were going down into the darkness, the depths of—"

"Stop," she said. "I want to go up. Although, it's a lot of stairs."

"The view will be amazing."

"I hope I'm in shape for this."

"You can do it. I'll be right behind you. If you stumble, I'll catch you. And if you need a push, I'll push you."

She stared back at him, an odd glint in her eyes. "It's not right that you always have to take care of me."

"Are you kidding me? All I ever wanted to do was take care of you, but you wouldn't tell me what your problems were."

She frowned. "Fair point. But while I didn't tell you about problems at home, you still took care of me when we went out. You never left me alone at a party. You helped me get through calculus. You carried me to the car when I cut my foot on glass at the beach."

Her words took him back in time. "That's true."

"See? I did let you help me sometimes. But I don't remember a time when I helped you."

He thought about that. "You listened. You didn't judge. No idea was too crazy. You made me think I could do anything."

"Me—little old pessimistic me?"

He liked that they could laugh together again. Even though Cassidy had been shy around groups of people, she'd been much more outgoing with him, and she'd always had a quick wit. They had laughed as often as they'd kissed—well, maybe not quite that often, but still a lot.

"Why don't we go up together, side-by-side?" he suggested. "The stairs are wide enough."

"I like that."

They headed up the steps. Cassidy started to breathe a little hard about three-quarters of the way up the hill, but she didn't complain; she just put her head down and kept going.

Fitness was part of his job, so he had no trouble with the stairs, but he did have trouble trying not to get caught up in the wonderfulness of the woman by his side. While it was nice to remember their good times, he really shouldn't let himself forget the bad times. *Wasn't that just asking for more problems?*

"Almost there," Cassidy said breathlessly, pushing herself up the last few steps.

The top of the hill offered a bench and an incredible view

of the city—from the ocean at the west to the Golden Gate Bridge, Angel's Island, and Alcatraz, and then off to the east—the Bay Bridge, the Berkeley and Oakland Hills.

"This is amazing," she said. "Totally worth the effort."

"I agree."

Cassidy lifted her gaze to the sun, closing her eyes for just a moment, and he loved the fact that he could stare at her unabashedly for those few seconds. While she was enjoying the moment, he was enjoying her.

She opened her eyes and said, "Don't you wish you had a camera now?"

He pulled out his phone. "I've got one. Stay right there." He snapped a photo of her against the amazing background.

"Are you getting the bridge behind me?"

He muttered, "Yes," but he was really just focusing on her face. He realized now why he had loved taking pictures of her. He'd been trying to freeze her in time, keep her with him always.

Had he sensed even before she left that she might one day disappear?

He was beginning to think he had.

"Let me take one of you," she said, pulling out her own phone.

"Let's make it a selfie." He walked over and put his arm around her shoulders.

They smiled together into the lens. And in that moment in time, it felt like his world shifted. Something clicked back into place.

He was suddenly afraid that what he'd been missing all these years was *her.*

Twelve

⇒⇒⇒⇐⇐⇐

It was almost five when they got to the final jewelry store in the Marina. While it was probably a lost cause at this point, Hunter wanted to check it off the list, and they still had a half hour before they were supposed to meet David.

"One last shot before we call this plan a bust," Cassidy said, as they walked down the street. "It was a good idea, but it was a very long shot."

"I like long odds. When you win, you win big."

"You're used to winning; I am not."

"That might have been true once, but I don't think it's true anymore. You're doing well in your business. You had to have beaten out a lot of other designers to win your current job at that big estate."

"I did have to compete for that one. I came up with three different plans before I found one they loved. And, frankly, they only gave me a shot because the Holmans' housekeeper knew Mary and said they should give me a chance to pitch. They had a lot of other architects and designers who wanted the job, but somehow they picked me."

"Because they recognized your talent. A connection

might have gotten you into the pitch, but you did the rest."

"Well, I'll be proud when it's done, and everyone is happy."

His steps slowed as they neared the front of the jewelry store. "Here we are. This looks interesting." The window display featured silver and turquoise jewelry: several sets of earrings, two necklaces, and a bracelet.

"It does," Cassidy agreed. "That necklace there reminds me of the one that Molly wore."

She was referring to a turquoise pendant with strands of silver woven around the stone as if it were a protective shield.

"Let's check it out." He opened the door and waved her inside.

There was an older woman standing by the cash register, finishing up a transaction with a gray-haired gentleman, who was having something gift wrapped for his wife. While they were waiting for the clerk to be free, they wandered around, perusing not only the jewelry but also hand-designed scarves as well as some beautiful watercolor paintings.

Cassidy took a very long look at one painting in particular. It featured a Native American girl standing by a window, looking out at a mountainous vista. Around the girl's neck was a silver chain. She was in profile, one side of her face in the light, the other in the shadows.

"This kind of looks like Molly, wearing her necklace, looking out the window of our bedroom," Cassidy murmured. "She wanted to escape as much as I did. Sometimes, we'd bump into each other, trying to get to that window."

"I remember you standing by the window every night after I dropped you off. I'd wait until I saw you there, until you waved good-bye."

She turned her head to look at him. "I always felt better when you were there after I went upstairs. I didn't realize you waited, though. I usually raced up the stairs, so no one would try to talk to me."

"I always waited." As her eyes shimmered with moisture, he felt an ache in his heart, followed by an anger at himself for letting her emotions get to him. He wanted to get answers. He wanted to help her. But he couldn't let himself fall for her again. As much as he wanted her to trust him, he wasn't entirely sure he could trust her.

"Can I help you?" the clerk interrupted, as her former customer left the shop. "Are you looking for something in particular? That painting is lovely, isn't it?"

"It's beautiful," Cassidy said. "It reminds me of someone I used to know."

"Art will do that."

"We're actually looking for someone who might have worked here a very long time ago," Cassidy added.

"Well, I've been here twenty years," the woman replied. "My sister owns the store, but I run it for her. My name is Helen Barkley. Who are you talking about?"

"Her first name was Lily and she had a granddaughter named Molly," Cassidy said.

Helen's face paled. "Oh, my goodness. I haven't heard those names in a very long time. Lily died years ago. She got cancer. It was very fast. She was only in her early sixties."

"Do you remember Molly as well?" Cassidy asked, excitement in her voice.

"I don't remember that name, but I do recall Lily's granddaughter. She was a sweet thing. She had long hair down to her waist. Sometimes she'd ask me to help her braid it, but I was never very good at it."

Cassidy shot him an impossibly hopeful look.

He'd wanted her to be optimistic, but now he was worried about the fallout. They might find Molly, but they might also find out she was dead, and that might hurt Cassidy even more. But he'd started them down this path, and there was no turning back.

"Lily's daughter was trouble, though," Helen said. "She even tried to steal something from the store one day. I remember it so vividly. Lily grabbed her daughter by the arm and yanked her purse open and took the necklace right back. I'd never seen her so angry. She told her daughter that she had dishonored her and that she needed to get help. If she didn't do that, she shouldn't come back. I'm not sure she ever did." Helen paused. "Now I know why this picture feels familiar to you. The little girl looks like Lily's granddaughter. How did you know her?"

"I was in a foster home with her—when her grandmother was sick. She wore a beautiful turquoise necklace, similar to the one in your window."

"Those pieces are gorgeous, aren't they? I recently acquired them. They're part of a collection by a designer named Kenna; it's a Native American name for a girl born of the flames."

A chill ran through him at the mention of fire.

Cassidy also appeared a bit rattled by Helen's words. "Have you met the designer?"

"I have not. My daughter does all the ordering now. She found those pieces. I can ask her for more information, or you can probably find it online. I think the designer has a website. You said you were here looking for Lily, but it's the little girl you want to find, isn't it?"

"She wouldn't be a little girl anymore," Cassidy replied. "She'd be close to thirty now. But, yes, we are looking for her. I don't suppose you'd have any idea where she might be? Did Lily have friends or other family who came around?"

"I don't know. I'm sorry. I haven't thought of them in years."

He saw the disappointment run through Cassidy's eyes, but they were as close to Molly's family as they'd ever been, and he wanted to press a bit further. "Do you remember where Lily lived when she worked here?" he asked.

"She lived in an apartment in lower Nob Hill. I dropped her off there a few times."

"Would you remember the address?"

"You're really pushing my memory skills. Let's see. I think it was on California Street. Yes, that's right. It was next door to a church, one of those churches with the really pretty names. I think sky was in the name somewhere. In fact, Lily volunteered at that church. You might find some people there who remember her, or who might still be in contact with her daughter."

"Thank you," he said. "That's a very big help."

"No problem. I'm curious. How did you know to come here?"

"We've actually been to several jewelry stores," he admitted. "We thought we were about out of luck." He turned to Cassidy. "Ready to go?"

"In a second. I'd like to buy a necklace in the window display," she said, leading the clerk to the front to show her which one she wanted.

While Cassidy was making her purchase, he pulled out his phone and looked up churches on California Street and found a Church of the Sky. His heart leapt. That had to be the place. They were closing in on Lily's past. Hopefully, it would get them closer to Molly.

—————

"Molly was real." Cassidy said the words as soon as they walked out of the shop. "Her grandmother was Lily. She used to hang out in this shop. It's all coming together."

"It is."

"Why aren't you more excited?" she asked, her bright eyes dimming.

"I'm excited."

"You're not jumping up and down."

"I just wish we could go to that church right now and ask some questions."

"Why can't we?"

"It's closed. I looked it up while you were buying the necklace. But there is a service tomorrow morning at ten thirty."

"Then it looks like we're going to church. Should we call Max and tell him what we've found?"

"Let's wait until tomorrow. We might have more to

report after we talk to some church members. Or if he calls us before that about Geralyn, I can fill him in."

"It is weird that we haven't heard from him yet. It has been hours."

"Hopefully, that means it's a long, productive interview." He checked his watch. "Looks like it's time to meet David. Should we walk there? It's only about three blocks."

"Yes. Let's not mention Molly to David. He wouldn't acknowledge her existence when we were on the phone earlier, and I don't want him to know anything until we find her."

"That makes sense, but..."

"What?" she asked warily.

"I just want you to prepare yourself for the possibility that Molly might not be alive. This story might not have the happy ending you're looking for."

"Now who's being negative?" she returned. "I'm very aware that she could be dead. But until I know for sure, I'm going to take a page out of your book and think positively."

"Well, I can't argue with my own book," he said with a laugh.

"No, you can't. Right now, I'm just thrilled to have third-party confirmation that Lily and Molly did exist. The story that Molly told me about her grandmother and her mother was true. I didn't make it up."

"I never thought you did, for what that's worth."

"It's worth a lot. Could you hold my bag?"

"Sure." He took her purse while she retrieved the necklace she'd just purchased from the gift bag. "I'm going to wear this to our meeting with David."

He smiled at the mischievous gleam in her eyes. "Good idea."

"I'm pretty sure I'm not the only one who noticed Molly's necklace. She wore it all the time. She wouldn't even take it off when she got in the shower. And this necklace looks remarkably similar. I'm not going to say anything about it. I just want to see if David has a reaction."

"I like the way you think." He handed her back her purse, and they headed to Jack's.

A few minutes later, they walked into the bar. Cassidy suddenly put her hand on his arm. The unexpected touch sent a jolt right through him, but she didn't seem to be aware of their sudden connection; her gaze was on a table by the window.

"It's not just David," she said. "It's Quan and Jeremiah, too. I didn't know they were all going to be here."

There was panic in her voice. Her past was coming to life in those three men, and he could feel her need to flee. "It's going to be all right. You're not alone. I'm here."

She looked at him with a painful struggle in her eyes. "I don't want to do this."

"You don't have to do this, but I know you can do it. No matter what they say about Molly, you know the truth. The truth gives you power."

"You're right. It just feels so weird seeing them again. Like I'm sixteen again, and they're all ganging up on me."

"This isn't about Molly; it's about Tommy. Maybe you're all on the same side."

"I seriously doubt that, but I guess I need to find out." She squared her shoulders, lifted her chin and then headed across the room.

He quickly followed.

Out of the three guys, the only one he recognized was the balding David Bellerman, who'd had a receding hairline even when they'd played on the high school basketball team. He hadn't known David beyond that since David had been a grade ahead of him.

The man next to David was Asian with dark hair and eyes and was quite thin; he assumed that was Quan. The third guy with the dark-blond hair and linebacker build had to be Jeremiah.

David got up when he saw Cassidy. "Cassidy, you came. And you brought someone." His gaze narrowed. "You look familiar."

"Hunter Callaway," he said.

"Right. We played basketball together. It's been a long time."

David extended his hand, so he shook it. He didn't think David had aged all that well. In addition to losing his hair, he'd put on some pounds around the middle and his skin was very pale.

He turned to the other two men. "I don't think we've met."

"Quan Tran," the Asian man said with a nod.

"Nice to meet you."

"Jeremiah Hunt," the third man said shortly. "I thought you were coming alone, Cassidy."

"And I thought David was coming alone," she replied. "Does it matter?"

"This is family business," Jeremiah said.

She uttered a harsh, disbelieving laugh. "What family could you possibly be talking about?"

"The Faulkners," Jeremiah said.

"They weren't my family."

"Why don't we all sit down?" David suggested, grabbing extra chairs from a nearby table.

As they sat down, Jeremiah said, "Look, we get that you didn't like the Faulkners, Cassidy, and that you and Tommy decided to run away, but they took care of us. And while you were only there a few months, we lived in that house a long time."

"I don't know what you want me to say," Cassidy replied. "The Faulkners killed Tommy while you all were living in that house."

"They did not do that," Jeremiah said.

"They didn't," David echoed, both men appearing very certain in their opinions.

Hunter couldn't help noticing that Quan didn't seem as eager to make that statement.

"If they didn't kill Tommy, who did?" he asked. "Got any ideas?"

"Like I said, this is family business," Jeremiah repeated, giving him a pointed look through mean, beady eyes. "Why don't you give us some space?"

"Cassidy and I are a package deal. You want to talk to her, you talk to me."

"Are you her bodyguard?" Jeremiah drawled.

"I'm her friend."

"He was her boyfriend before she dumped him and ran off with Tommy," David put in, obviously eager to get that dig in.

"That's enough." Cassidy put up a hand. "I didn't come here to get into a fight, so Hunter and I can leave."

"No," David said. "Please don't go, Cassidy. We do need to talk."

"Where are the girls?" she asked. "Jada and Rhea? Why aren't they here? It seems like all of you have kept in touch."

"Jada and Rhea moved to Los Angeles several years ago," David said. "I spoke to both of them on the phone. They were horrified, but they barely remembered Tommy. They were young, and he wasn't there very long."

"Just long enough to get killed," Cassidy said, her hand creeping to her necklace.

Hunter didn't think she was making a deliberate point of touching the pendant, but her gesture did bring Quan's attention to the necklace, and he seemed to stiffen.

"Everything okay, Quan?" he asked sharply.

Quan flinched, quickly averting his gaze, as he drank what appeared to be a vodka tonic. "Fine," he muttered.

Cassidy dropped her hand, exchanging a quick look with him before turning her attention back to the guys. "So, what do you want to talk about, David?"

"I was wondering if you'd heard anything else from the police about the case."

"I heard they were going to talk to Geralyn, but I don't know if they did. Do you?"

David shook his head. "I went by there again after I spoke to you this morning. The nurse told me she was still sedated. I didn't run into the police, but they might have shown up later."

"She's not capable of murder," Jeremiah said. "I think we all know that. So how are we going to get her out of this?"

"I don't want to get her out of this," Cassidy said hotly. "Maybe you're all still under her spell, but I'm not. There's no way Tommy got buried in the wall of the garage without Donald or Geralyn or both of them knowing about it."

"We think it was Evan or Colin," David said. "Dad's younger brother was around that day. He was drinking a lot. He got into a fight with his son Colin and then with Dad. I heard them arguing in the garage before I left for baseball practice."

"How does that involve Tommy?" she asked.

David looked over at Quan. "Tell them what you heard."

"I heard Colin and Tommy talking about going in the garage after Evan and Donald left the house. Colin said there was something in the garage that Tommy might want to see."

Cassidy frowned, folding her arms across her chest. He could see she wasn't buying their story, and he was glad, because it sounded to him like they were trying out possible defenses for Geralyn.

Cassidy looked at Jeremiah. "What about you? Were you there that day?"

"How do we know what day it was?" Jeremiah countered.

"We all think it was the day Cassidy left," David put in. "Because we didn't see Tommy after that, remember?"

"Right. I didn't hear any arguments. I didn't see anything, but Geralyn couldn't have killed anyone."

"So, you're discounting Geralyn, but not necessarily Donald?" Cassidy asked.

"I think David is probably right—that it was Evan," Jeremiah said. "Evan had a bad temper, especially when he was drinking, and he was always drinking when he came over."

"That's true," Quan said with a nod.

The men seemed to agree on everything. He was curious what they'd thought when Cassidy had left. "What happened after Cassidy disappeared?" he asked.

The three men looked at him in surprise, as if they'd forgotten he was there.

"I don't remember," Quan muttered.

"My parents went to look for her," David said. "I told Cassidy that earlier."

"What about the police? Did they come to the house?"

"I didn't see any cops. I think they might have gone down to the station to talk to them."

"Did the Faulkners think Tommy and Cassidy were together?" he continued.

"We all did," David said.

"They were tight," Jeremy put in. "They were always sitting off to the side, telling secrets to each other."

"Did the police interview any of you about their disappearance?" he asked. "It seems odd to me that the police wouldn't investigate."

"Foster kids run away all the time," Jeremiah said. "No one cares that much."

"I don't think the Faulkners told the police Tommy and I were gone," Cassidy said. "They probably continued to take money for both of us for years."

"I could see that," Quan said. David shot him a dark look. "I can," Quan reiterated. "I don't think they were murderers, but I think they liked the money they got from the state."

"And they didn't really want Tommy or me to be found," Cassidy said. "Because then I would have brought up Molly."

"Your imaginary friend?" Jeremiah sneered. "Aren't you a little old to still believe in that?"

"She was real. I have proof," Cassidy declared.

"What do you mean you have proof?" Quan asked.

As the three men focused in on Cassidy, Hunter got a bad feeling about her recent revelation. If one of these guys had had something to do with Tommy's death, then she might be putting herself in the line of fire.

"It doesn't matter," she said. "But I know the truth. And, someday, everyone else will, too."

"Let's get back to Tommy," David said. "Regardless of who killed him, we should have a memorial for him. I don't know if he was religious…"

"He wasn't," Cassidy said. "I think he'd like to be cremated. He never wanted to be in the ground." Her voice broke, and she wiped her hand over her eyes. "I'm sure he didn't want to be in a wall, either."

A morbid silence followed her words.

"I'm sorry," she said, taking a sip of her drink. "It's just hard to think about."

"It's awful," Quan said. "I'm sorry, Cassidy. I know we don't agree on who killed him, but I am sorry. He didn't deserve to die."

"Maybe Cassidy killed him," Jeremiah put in. "It makes sense. You could have killed him and run away."

"Oh, sure, and Donald would have been happy to let me hide the body in his garage for fourteen years," Cassidy replied. "Don't be stupid, Jeremiah."

"Don't call me stupid. You were the crazy one, making up shit all the time," Jeremiah snapped back.

"I didn't make anything up, and the fact that none of you can now acknowledge that you lied about Molly makes me realize that you're willing to go to any lengths to cover anything up. I don't trust one word any of you have said here. And we're done. I'm going to take care of Tommy. You can all do whatever you want. But I'd prepare yourselves for the truth, which is that your beloved Geralyn and Donald were murderers."

"Cassidy, wait," David pleaded. "We're all upset, but we need to stick together."

"We were never together. And this is pointless." She shoved back her chair and stood up. "Are you ready, Hunter?"

"Sure," he said, impressed with her confident, assertive speech. Cassidy might have had a moment of weakness when she'd seen all of the men together, but she'd gotten past that.

He followed her out of the bar. She was walking fast, and he had a feeling that energy was fueled by a lot of emotions, so he didn't bother to tell her to slow down. Obviously, she needed to walk some of the adrenaline off. They actually passed the Jeep without her noticing, but he didn't call her back. He just stayed next to her, until she finally came to the light on the corner of Van Ness and gave him a look of confusion.

"We didn't park this far away," she said.

"No. We passed the car about ten blocks ago."

"Why didn't you say something?"

"I had the feeling you needed to walk."

The wind whipped strands of her hair in front of her face, and she brushed them away. "They made me so angry."

"I know, but you handled them well."

"I wasn't going to mention Molly, but I couldn't stop myself."

"I get it."

"They're still unified in their denial of her existence."

"Maybe because they're used to sticking together. It might be interesting to talk to Quan on his own. He seemed to be the most reasonable."

"But he's also the volunteer firefighter, remember?"

"That might not mean anything."

"What did you think, Hunter? What was your impression of them?"

"Jeremiah is a hothead. He doesn't like you at all. He wasn't a fan of Tommy's; he seems to care about the Faulkners, though. David is definitely trying to be your friend as well as Tommy's and still be a loyal son. Quan is in the middle. He seems to blow hot and cold, depending on who's talking. But when you touched your necklace, he had a definite reaction."

"I thought so, too. I don't really know why they wanted to see me. I can't figure it out. I had already told David what I thought about the Faulkners. What was the point of this conversation?"

"I think the point was to find out what you knew, maybe what any of them knew. David is clearly trying to protect Geralyn. He's looking for a way to do that. And I do worry that in bringing up Molly you might have put a target on your back."

"Why? They don't care what I say about Molly."

"They might care more when you say you have proof of her existence. Think about it—if the Faulkners lost a kid in their care…"

"Then they could be guilty of more crimes—like murder," she finished. "I'm an idiot."

"No. You were standing up for yourself. Nothing wrong with that. In fact, I think you needed that moment."

"I did need it. I enjoyed it." She gave him a guilty smile. "But I might have made things worse. We're supposed to be getting justice for Tommy, not for me."

"They might be tied up together. Here's a mundane question. Are you by chance hungry?"

"I'm starving. I haven't eaten since breakfast, which was a really long time ago."

"There's a good pizza place on the way back to the car."

"Pizza sounds perfect, as long as you don't order pineapple and ham."

He laughed at the memory. "You almost stopped dating me when I did that."

"I wouldn't go that far, but it was not good."

"I think you ate it."

"Because I was trying to impress you. But I don't think fruit and pizza go together."

"Well, you can pick whatever you want tonight. You've earned it."

"Thanks for having my back."

"No problem."

He'd almost said, *always*, but he'd stopped himself just in time. While he did want to help her, and they were getting along at the moment, *always* wasn't necessarily in the cards.

Thirteen

—➤➤◄◄◄—

The Italian restaurant with the pizza oven and delicious smells of garlic and oregano was just what she needed. The vibe was warm, friendly, and casual, with plenty of families surrounding them. They managed to nab a table by the wall under a photograph of the original owner of the restaurant: Mateo Rossi, a short, bearded man, with a happy smile.

"I feel like Mateo is watching us," Cassidy said, as she sipped her iced tea.

"Because he wants the customers to feel like family." Hunter tipped his head toward a saying on the wall that read: *When you're at Mateo's, you're home.*

"Have you been here before?" she asked.

"A few times. My apartment actually isn't too far from here."

"Do you live alone?"

"I do. My days of bunking with Dylan are over."

"Because he got married?"

"Actually, we split up about a year before that. We both realized we were over having a roommate."

"But you still work together, so I assume you're close."

"We're in a good place. He likes to stick his nose into my business, tell me what to do, but other than that..."

She could see the affection in his eyes. "You love him."

"I guess."

"You said before that Annie is getting married this coming weekend?"

"Yes. At which time, I will officially be the last single Callaway in the immediate area. There are a few cousins outside San Francisco who haven't found marital bliss yet."

She wondered if his single status bothered him more than he was letting on but getting into Hunter's romantic life was probably a dangerous subject. She needed to leave it alone.

"You look more relaxed now," he commented, running his finger around the top of his beer mug as he gazed back at her.

"I feel better. Still hungry, though. Hoping our deluxe vegetarian pizza comes soon."

He laughed. "I should have known when I gave you free rein on the menu that I'd be eating a lot of vegetables."

"They're good for you. And the restaurant only serves organic from local farms, which is also nice."

"Do you still plant vegetables?"

"We have a garden at the nursery devoted to vegetables and another one to herbs. I've been experimenting with the herbs, thinking about making my own brand of tea or turning them into a lotion. It's just a little hobby. I don't really have time, but it's fun to think of creating something new."

"Did you ever go back to school?"

"I took the GED when I was eighteen and got my high school diploma. Then I went to community college for a while and took a lot of classes in landscape design. I sometimes think about going back and getting a degree in landscape architecture, so I could create the blueprints, not just follow them, but that would take a lot of time. Maybe one day. My plate is really full right now."

"You've made a good life for yourself, Cassidy. And you're different. You're more confident. You've found your voice. You've come into your own."

"I do feel like I'm getting closer to who I want to be when I grow up," she said lightly. "It's taken me a long time, and I still have moments of doubt, like when I first saw the guys at the bar. I panicked a little. I thought about bailing. I guess I do have a tendency to run when things get dicey."

"But you stuck it out and you stood up to them. They didn't know what to make of you. I think you scared them a little."

"They shouldn't be scared unless they had something to do with Tommy's death."

"Maybe they did," he suggested. "They're certainly trying hard to come up with other suspects."

"You don't think that's to protect Geralyn?"

"Could be, or there might be another motive. I feel like we should try to talk to Evan and his son Colin. They seem to be coming up a lot."

"Max told you they're out of town this weekend."

"Which is convenient. Do you think there's any possibility the guys could be right about Evan?"

"I don't know. Evan did have access to the garage. He did have a hot temper. His son Colin and Tommy did fight over video games. I can't say that what the guys just told us was wrong, but I keep coming back to the part where the body was hidden in the garage all those years. And that just seems like it has to tie to Donald at the very least."

"I agree."

She let out a sigh, feeling exhausted by the spinning wheel they were on. "Let's talk about something else for a while."

"That sounds good to me. Read any books lately?"

She laughed. "I have, actually. One was a memoir by a woman who worked on the Gardens of Versailles for twenty-eight years."

"Sounds fascinating. It's all flowers all the time, isn't it?"

"Not all the time. I also read a fiction series with a really sexy vampire as the hero. That was hot."

"You like vampires, huh?"

"I like books that take me into another world. What about you?"

"I've been reading a book about the Wright brothers, how they got their first plane off the ground. It's amazing the challenges they went through, the obstacles they faced."

She pressed her fingers together as she gave him a thoughtful look. "So, you're not just looking for answers on a road trip, you're also looking in books?"

"I like to read about people who accomplish big things. I'm not necessarily looking for an answer."

"Maybe just inspiration. You said before that you don't know if you want to still be a firefighter."

"I shouldn't have said that."

"Well, you can't take it back now. What's really going on with you? Why are you so conflicted? Do you feel like your family pushed you into the job? Are you bored? What's the deal?"

He stared down at his beer for a moment, then lifted his gaze to hers. "I honestly don't know. I don't hate my job. It's important work, and I do it well. The guys in my squad are great. Even the ones who aren't related to me feel like brothers. The firehouse is home."

She considered his words. "Maybe home isn't what you're looking for. You've always had a home: a family, brothers…perhaps you need something else."

"I don't know what that would be. To be honest, I don't even know if it's really the job that's the problem."

"Maybe it's all the weddings."

"I've never been in a hurry to walk down the aisle; it's not that. And thank God our pizza is coming, because I don't think you're qualified to be my shrink."

"That's true. If anyone needs a shrink, it's probably me," she said, as the waiter set down their pizza.

"Have you ever spoken to a professional?" He scooped a large slice of pizza onto his plate. "This looks great, by the way, even if it is covered in zucchini and mushrooms and a bunch of other healthy stuff."

"It's all good for you. And, no, I've never talked to anyone. It was too dangerous when I was young, and by the time I could have taken the risk, I was feeling much better. I had a good life going; I didn't want to look at it too closely." She took a bite of the pizza, delighting in the cheesy flavors. "This hits the spot."

"I hope you can keep up, because I'm pretty hungry."

"I can keep up. When you're in foster care, you learn to eat fast."

"When you have five siblings, you also learn to eat fast."

She grinned, thinking how much she had missed his teasing smile—how much she had missed him. He'd always made her feel happy. He'd always made her feel like anything was possible, and tonight was no exception.

Despite his suggestion she keep up with him if she wanted her fair share of pizza, she didn't want to eat too fast. She didn't want to leave this cozy table. *She didn't want to leave him.*

That was a terrifying thought. They could never go back to who they were. Hunter had just said how much she'd changed. He'd changed, too. Although, maybe not as much as she had. He was still confident, charming in a self-deprecating way, sexy as hell...

She turned her attention to her pizza, knowing she should not let herself get caught up in a fantasy that was not going to come true. She knew better than most that not every story had a happy ending.

As they ate, they talked more about books and movies and some friends from the old days. Hunter said he still biked on the weekends and ran every morning before the sun came up. He'd always been much more athletically inclined than she was, and while she couldn't relate to his desire to work out, she could definitely appreciate the results. She had a feeling he'd look really good without a shirt on, which took her into another unwanted but tantalizing fantasy.

Unfortunately, her fantasy was interrupted by the wail of

a baby at the next table, which set off another child on the other side of them.

"I don't think I've heard so many babies cry at one time since I visited my mother in the infant nursery at the hospital," Hunter said. "We should get our check."

She wiped her mouth with her napkin, having finished up her third slice of pizza, which was two less than Hunter, but she was more than full.

Hunter was right about the screaming kids. While they'd been eating, Mateo's had gotten more crowded, and the wait for pizza was apparently causing some children to have a meltdown. Even though it was loud and chaotic, she liked it. The sound of families out together had always tugged at her heart, reminding her of her early childhood with her parents. They'd been a happy trio before the accident that had taken her parents' lives.

"Cassidy?"

"Sorry, did you say something?"

"What were you thinking about?"

"Happier times with my mom and dad."

"You never talked about them much."

"It hurt too much. And I had so many mixed emotions. I wasn't just sad; I was angry that they'd left me alone. I couldn't put all those feelings into words, so I didn't."

"That makes sense. Tell me one thing about each of them that you remember, and it can't have to do with gardening."

She smiled. "Let's see. My dad loved cookie dough. My mom and I could not make cookies without him stealing half the dough. He never wanted to eat the cookies after they were in the oven."

"A man after my own heart. Love the cookie dough. What about your mom?"

"She liked to sing—in the car, in the shower, while gardening, cooking—you name it, she had a tune going."

"Was she good?"

"She was enthusiastic."

"Did you sing with her?"

"Sometimes when we were in the car. She'd crank up the radio, roll down the windows, and we'd let it fly. It was fun. But while I can carry a tune, I would not call myself a good singer." She rested her arms on the table. "Now it's your turn. I know your parents are very much alive but tell me something about them that I don't know."

"Okay." He thought for a moment. "My mom spent a summer in Paris right after college. She lived with another girl and took cooking classes. She thought she might become a chef, but said she quickly realized she wasn't that talented. So, she came home and became a nurse."

"It sounds like she had a good adventure first. What about your father?" While she'd spent some time with Hunter's mom, Sharon, she'd had only a few words with his dad, who had often been at the firehouse when she was visiting.

"This one will surprise you," he said. "My dad was an actor when he was in college. He even performed in a play in San Francisco when he was in his twenties."

"No way. Your father? He doesn't seem like the acting type, although he did have a loud, deep voice. I bet that was good for the stage. Why did he quit?"

"He got married, had six kids, and worked a demanding job. He put the needs of the family ahead of his own. He was that kind of man."

"Six kids is a lot," she murmured. "I always wanted a sibling, but my mom said she had a terrible pregnancy with me and she just couldn't risk having another baby."

"Do you want to have kids some day?" he asked curiously.

"I would," she admitted, immediately thinking of some little Hunters running around with dark hair and blue eyes. "And you?"

"Sure. If I met the right person."

"Right." She cleared her throat. "We should get our check." She waved to the waiter, who came over with the bill.

"I've got it," Hunter said, pulling out his wallet.

"I can split it with you."

"Have I ever let you pay for anything?" he countered.

"We're not dating, Hunter. You're not...you know...getting anything for this."

"I didn't get that much in high school," he said dryly. "We went out for two months before...you know."

"It was worth the wait, wasn't it?"

"More than worth it," he said, a glint in his eyes. "And, as proven yesterday, there are still a few sparks."

"That we're going to put out every time they appear," she said firmly. "You're a firefighter; you should know how to do that."

"I also know how to stoke a fire. In fact, I'm pretty sure I remember exactly what you—"

"Stop. We're not going to talk about that."

"I wasn't actually thinking about *talking*."

"Or doing." She picked up her iced tea, thinking she definitely needed a drink to cool her down. Before the tea could hit her lips, two kids went running by the table, one smashing into her chair, knocking the glass out of her hand and sending cold liquid all over her T-shirt.

"Oh, my goodness, I'm so sorry," a woman said, grabbing both boys in a tight grip. "Let me pay for your dinner or your shirt or something."

"It's fine." She dabbed at her shirt with her napkin, but it didn't help much. She was completely soaked.

"I feel so bad," the woman said with apology in her eyes.

"It's nothing, really. Don't worry about it."

The waiter came over, offering her a stack of napkins, but what she really needed was a new shirt. "It's all good," she told the waiter and the woman. "I just need to go."

Hunter put cash down for the bill. "I don't need any change. We can leave."

As they exited the restaurant, she paused to wring out her shirt. "I really wish I hadn't gotten that last refill."

"Sorry about that."

"It wasn't your fault. The kids were just playing. It's

going to be a long drive back to Half Moon Bay," she muttered as they walked to his car. "Although, maybe I can change into my sweaty shirt from earlier today."

"I have a better idea. Why don't we stop at my apartment? It's only a mile or so from here. I can give you a T-shirt or sweatshirt to get you home."

Going to Hunter's apartment seemed like both a bad idea and a good one.

"It will take five minutes," Hunter added. "Don't waste time arguing."

She slid into the passenger seat and decided to take his advice. She really wanted to change out of her shirt, and she wouldn't mind getting a peek at Hunter's home. But that's all she was going to do—change clothes and take a look around.

The icy-cold tea shower had doused the sparks between them, and she wasn't about to let them come back to life, no matter how appealing the idea might be. She hadn't just grown in confidence over the past several years; she'd also learned how best to protect what little was left of her battered heart. And if there was one man who could break it, it was Hunter. She couldn't give him that chance.

Within minutes, Hunter pulled into a short driveway, stopping in front of a closed garage door. "We can leave the car here while you change."

So, Hunter wasn't planning on having her stay long, either. She told herself that was a good thing.

As she got out of the car and followed him toward the front of the building, a figure suddenly came out of the shadows.

Startled, she put her hand on Hunter's arm, as he instinctively shielded her from whoever was there.

Then she heard a woman's voice say, "Hunter? It's me. It's Lindsay."

She moved around Hunter to see her old friend, only Lindsay was no longer a fourteen-year-old girl. She was a beautiful brunette wearing a short dress and high heels that showed off her bare legs.

"Lindsay?" she said in surprise.

"Oh, my God, Cassidy. Is that you?" Lindsay squealed.

"What are you doing here, Lindsay?" Hunter asked.

"I saw that you called me earlier. I thought I'd come by. And here you and Cassidy are together. Wow! It feels like old times."

Cassidy nodded, but in her gut, she was thinking it felt nothing like old times.

Fourteen

-–>–>>>–<<<–<––

"Let's go inside," Hunter said, a trace of tension in his voice. He led them up the stairs and into his building, then up another flight of stairs to the second floor.

She'd been curious about where he lived, but now with Lindsay in between them, Cassidy was feeling a lot more curious about the relationship that Lindsay and Hunter had had. Hunter had said that he'd never slept with Lindsay, that he hadn't felt the same way about her as she'd felt about him, but he hadn't given her any other details.

It shouldn't matter to her, but it did. Lindsay was the one girl she'd confided in. She'd told Lindsay after she'd slept with Hunter. She'd told Lindsay that she was in love with Hunter.

But once she was out of the picture, Lindsay had apparently not cared about any of that.

Hunter opened the door and waved them inside.

She glanced around his apartment, noting the comfortably large gray sectional sofa, the oversized TV on the wall, the golf clubs in the corner, and a racing bike hanging off the wall. Through the open bedroom door, she could also see a king-sized bed that hadn't been made.

Hunter's home was very much like him—carefree, casual, sporty, and inviting. Only, it would have felt more inviting if Lindsay hadn't been there. And seeing Lindsay in her pretty dress and heels and beautifully styled hair and makeup, Cassidy felt like a mess, very aware of her still sopping T-shirt and the jeans with the dirt and grass stains.

"I'll get you a shirt," Hunter said, heading into his bedroom.

"Someone dumped iced tea on me," she said, in response to Lindsay's questioning look.

"You were having dinner together?"

"We got some pizza."

"You look different, Cassidy. Your hair is a lot lighter, longer."

"I spend a lot of time in the sun. I'm a landscape designer."

"You and your gardens," Lindsay said with a smile. "That's appropriate. I work in an art gallery."

"That fits you, too. You always liked to draw."

"I don't do much of that anymore. I sell other people's work." Lindsay shifted her weight, crossing her arms in front of her ample breasts. "Did Hunter tell you we went out a few times back in high school?"

"He mentioned it. So did your mom. She said you went to Hunter's senior prom."

"He was heartbroken when you left. So was I. I thought we were best friends. I couldn't believe you wouldn't say good-bye to me. Hunter felt the same way. You abandoned him. And you didn't just leave, you went with Tommy."

She frowned at Lindsay's characterization of her departure, but she couldn't really deny any of it.

"Although, I guess you didn't leave with Tommy. I spoke to the police earlier, along with my parents, and my sister. They told us that Tommy's remains were found in the Faulkners' garage. We were stunned. Do you know what happened? Was he killed before you left? Is that why you ran away?"

"No. I had no idea Tommy had been killed until yesterday."

Hunter returned with a T-shirt. "Will this work?"

"Sure. Thanks. I'll go change." She was actually happy to have a minute to get her head together. Lindsay's attitude was a mix of *happy to see you* and *wish you'd never come back.* She couldn't quite get a read on her.

As she moved into the hall bathroom, she didn't close the door all the way, curious to hear what Lindsay would say now that she was out of the room.

"I missed you, Hunter," Lindsay said. "But you look good, really good."

Cassidy's heart twisted at the sultry note in Lindsay's voice.

"So do you," Hunter replied in a polite tone.

"It's been a long time, and once again it's Cassidy who brings us together. That's ironic."

"What are you doing here, Lindsay?"

"I want to help."

"Do you know something that could help us figure out who killed Tommy?"

"I don't know. But I definitely think we should talk about it."

Cassidy had a feeling Lindsay wanted to do more than talk. Deciding she'd heard enough, she closed the door and stripped off her shirt, replacing it with a navy-blue shirt with an SFFD logo.

Wearing Hunter's shirt made her feel like his arms were around her, which was a silly thought. It was just a shirt, nothing more.

She splashed some water on her face, ran her fingers through her hair, and then gave herself a brief pep talk. She didn't have any reason to be jealous of Lindsay and Hunter. She'd left. She'd made her choice. He could have dated whoever he wanted. And she had no reason to hide out in the bathroom. She hadn't done anything wrong. And she'd been invited into his home. Lindsay was the one who'd shown up unexpectedly.

She might have been a little afraid to come out of the shadows when she was in high school, but as Hunter had pointed out over dinner, she'd changed. She had confidence now, and maybe it was about time she showed Lindsay the new Cassidy, too.

––➤➤◄◄–––

Hunter stared at Lindsay with a frown, not quite sure what to make of her sudden reappearance in his life, the flirty gleam in her eyes, the hint of nervousness in her smile. And the fact that Cassidy was steps away only made the situation more uncomfortable.

"Is this too weird?" Lindsay nervously played with the ring on her right finger.

She'd always loved rings, always fiddled with them when she was tense or on edge, and just as he remembered, she had three on each hand, but the third finger on her left hand was bare.

"It's weird," he agreed. "But it's not your fault."

She seemed relieved by his words. "You're right. It's not my fault." She shot a glance toward the hallway where Cassidy had disappeared. "I feel like Cassidy is angry about the fact that we went out together. What did you tell her?"

"Not much, and I don't think she's angry."

"She is the one who left. I would have never gone out with you if she hadn't. I was her friend."

He would have never asked Lindsay out if Cassidy hadn't left, because he'd barely noticed her until he realized she was the one person who was also missing Cassidy, which had given them an unexpected bond.

"I always thought we could have been something...if Cassidy's shadow hadn't been between us," Lindsay added.

He didn't feel that way at all, but he couldn't see the point in arguing that fact, and he was more interested in talking to Lindsay about her experience with the Faulkners than their past dating situation. "Let's talk about Tommy. Did you ever notice anything unusual going on at the house next door?"

"No. Cassidy never said much, but I knew she wasn't happy there. Donald and Geralyn were friendly enough to me and my parents. They came over a few times for dinner, but they never brought the kids. I only spoke to Tommy a couple of times and that was usually when he was looking for Cassidy or wanted to get Cassidy to go somewhere with him. I can't believe he was killed in that house. I'm kind of glad it burned to the ground. It's really hard on my parents knowing they've been living next door to monsters all these years, and they had no idea."

"Do your parents think the Faulkners killed Tommy?"

"What else can they think?" She dropped her voice down a notch. "Do you think they hurt Cassidy? Is that why she ran?"

"You'll have to ask her that," he said, not wanting to reveal anything Cassidy had said to him.

"Cassidy never said that she was being abused or threatened. I wish she'd been more candid. Maybe I could have helped her. Maybe she wouldn't have had to run away."

"I don't think you could have stopped anything; you were a kid."

"We both were. I hope you're not blaming yourself now."

She took a step forward, getting closer than he wanted.

"I don't blame myself," he said.

"That's good. You suffered so much when she left you. I hope you haven't forgotten what she put you through."

He cleared his throat and moved away as Cassidy came back into the room, wearing his T-shirt.

"Did I miss something?" Cassidy asked.

"Not really," he replied. "We were just talking about Tommy, about the Faulkners being the most likely suspects."

"They were the adults in the house," Lindsay said. "Although, Tommy wasn't that big. One of the other boys could have done something to him. I know Jeremiah didn't like him."

"Why do you say that?" Cassidy asked.

"We hung out a few times after Tommy and you disappeared. Jeremiah said he was glad you were both gone. He said you were trouble, and you were messing things up in the family."

Based on what he'd heard at the bar from Jeremiah himself, Lindsay's words rang true.

"But I can't imagine Jeremiah killing Tommy," Lindsay said. "Or being able to hide him in the garage. You know, there was a time when we thought there was a dead skunk under the house. Now I'm wondering..." Her mouth curved down in distaste as she visibly shuddered. "Anyway, I hate even thinking about it."

"You don't need to think about it," he told her.

"Well, I want to help. Let's keep talking," Lindsay said, giving him another flirty look.

Cassidy frowned, then said, "I need to go home. But you two can stay and chat."

"I need to give you a ride to your van," he reminded her.

"I can call for a car to take me to the Holmans' house."

"No. I'll take you," he said firmly. "Why don't we talk another time, Lindsay? It's been a long day."

"All right," Lindsay replied. "You have my number. I hope you'll call. I mean it when I say I want to help."

"Before we break this up," Hunter cut in, knowing he was probably going to piss Cassidy off with his words, but who knew when they'd have a chance to talk to Lindsay again, and they needed as much information as they could get. "Do you remember a girl named Molly living at the Faulkners' house?"

Cassidy sucked in a quick breath, giving him a worried look before her gaze turned to Lindsay.

"Molly?" Lindsay repeated on a questioning note. "I don't remember the name, but there were a lot of kids who went through the house, and to be honest, my mom didn't really like me playing over there. She thought some of the kids were kind of rough. The only one she really liked was you,

Cassidy. She thought you were a lost soul, and she wanted to mother you. That's why she let us walk to school together and why she let you work in the garden."

"Your mom was very nice to me. Molly lived in the house for only three weeks. She had long, black hair and dark eyes. She was of Native American heritage. She wore a turquoise necklace around her neck."

"Like that one?" Lindsay asked, motioning to the necklace around Cassidy's neck.

"Yes. Just like this one."

"I think I remember seeing a girl with long black hair in one of the upstairs windows. But I don't believe I ever spoke to her. What happened to her?"

"I don't know," Cassidy said. "The Faulkners told me she was moved to another home. When I went looking for her, the story changed, that she had never existed. And all of the kids went along with the Faulkners' lie."

"Why would they do that?"

"I'm pretty sure they didn't want to disappear like she did."

"Is she why you ran away?" Lindsay asked.

"Molly was part of it."

"I wish you'd told me about her. Why didn't you?"

"I don't know. You were part of a different life—a life outside the house, just like Hunter was. And I felt the need to keep the two parts separate. But it's all merging together now."

"Well, I'm glad you're all right, Cassidy. Is there a man in your life?"

"No, but I'm busy with work, so it's all good."

Lindsay smiled at that piece of information. "I'm glad you're happy. I'll let you two go. Promise you'll stay in touch."

"We will," Hunter said, with Cassidy nodding her head in agreement.

The tension seemed to have dissipated in the last few minutes with Cassidy opening up about Molly, and it was a much more comfortable silence that accompanied them down the stairs.

"Did you park far away?" he asked Lindsay. "Do you need a ride?"

"No, I'm just across the street. I'll see you both later."

"Okay." He kept an eye on Lindsay until she got in her car, and then he and Cassidy got in the Jeep and headed toward Pacific Heights.

Cassidy didn't say anything for the first few minutes, but he had a feeling words were coming; he just wasn't quite sure what those words were going to be. Waiting for her to speak started to get on his nerves, so he broke the silence. "Are you okay? Want to talk about anything Lindsay had to say?"

"What she said about Jeremiah rang true. I don't think he and Tommy got along."

"How did Donald and Tommy interact? Were they hostile? Was there a lot of friction?"

"Not until Tommy took my side on the Molly situation."

"I don't think you ever told me Tommy's story. Where did he come from? How did he end up in foster care?"

"He was abandoned, left at a fire station when he was two years old. He wasn't old enough to tell anyone who he was. The firefighter who took him in—his name was Tommy, and that's the name he was given. He was in foster homes his entire life. I think he was born with fetal alcohol syndrome. He had trouble with school work, couldn't always concentrate, was sometimes hyperactive and distractible. So he was never adopted; he just kept getting moved from house to house."

"That's rough."

"I first met Tommy at a group home run by a church. I was moved there after the family I was with decided to stop fostering kids because the mom got pregnant with twins, and she had to go on bedrest. The group home was pretty bad. It was four to a room, in bunk beds. Some of the kids were mean. Tommy watched out for me. I'd only been in foster care since I was thirteen, so I was kind of an innocent. At any rate, that place got too crowded, and I got sent to the Faulkners. I was there four months before Tommy showed up. The rest you know."

He thought about her story, about Tommy's story, and realized again how very privileged he'd been. "I always took my family for granted. I shouldn't have."

"No, you shouldn't have, but everyone does. I did, too, until they were gone. Losing them was the most difficult, painful, horrible thing I've ever had to go through." She paused. "The second hardest thing was leaving you, losing you."

His gut clenched at her words. He wanted to take her in his arms, but he was driving.

"Oh, hell," he said, wrenching the wheel to the right.

"What are you doing?" she asked in alarm.

He pulled over to the side of the road, threw the Jeep into park and then put his arms around her. He drew in a deep breath, inhaling the scent of her hair, the beautiful essence that was all her. "I wish you'd never had to go through so much pain," he murmured, stroking her back.

She'd been stiff in his arms, but at his words, she sank into his embrace, resting her head on his shoulder.

"Don't be so sweet, Hunter. You're going to make me cry. And I've cried too many tears already."

He pulled away, so he could look at her. "I don't want you to cry. I just want you to know you're not alone."

"I do know that. I just don't know why you would want to stick by me after everything that went down between us."

"Because I want to. Don't overanalyze it."

"Okay, I won't overanalyze; I'll just say thanks." She sat back in her seat. "You should take me to my car now."

"All right."

A few minutes later, he pulled into the driveway behind her van. The house was dark, and he kept the lights on, so she could see her way. "Do you want me to pick you up at the nursery tomorrow—before we go to church?"

"The church—I almost forgot about that."

"You still want to go, don't you?"

"I do, but it's silly for you to drive to Half Moon Bay. I can meet you at the church."

"Come to my apartment instead. I'd rather go in one car, in case that's just the first stop, and we have other places to go."

"Do you think we'll get a lead on Molly?"

"I'm hoping."

She gave him a smile. "Me, too. Thanks again, Hunter. For everything. Good night."

"Night." As he watched her get into her van, he realized he didn't really want her thanks; he wanted a lot more. He just didn't know if they could ever get beyond their past.

Fifteen

Cassidy thought about Hunter as she wove her way through the dark city streets, finally making her way to the ocean and the Pacific Coast Highway. The sunny day had given way to a foggy night, and fingers of dark mist clouded her vision as she drove south toward Half Moon Bay.

The weather seemed to be following her mood. One minute, she felt bright and hopeful; the next minute, she was lost in a dark maze. Hunter was the light that kept drawing her out of the shadows.

But was that fair to him? He didn't need to be involved in any of this. He had a good life, an amazing family, lots of friends. And she was just like what she'd been before—a dead-weight anchor, dragging him down.

That's what one of the cheerleaders had told her once, that Hunter would have been prom king if he hadn't been taking her to the dance. Hunter probably hadn't cared about being prom king, but the girl's words had stung, because they'd had truth to them. She had held Hunter back. Her fears, her shyness, his need to protect her...what kind of a relationship was that?

She wished she could say it was different now. She had changed, but a lot of the world around her had not. She was still mired in ugly, dirty business, and she didn't want to bring Hunter down with her.

She blinked as a pair of high beams lit up her car, almost blinding her. She sped up a little, but the car behind her stayed right on her tail.

She wanted to pull off and let them go by, but there was no shoulder, no extra lane along this part of the road that clung to the edge of a high bluff.

She pushed down on the gas again, going far faster than she wanted to go.

The other car did the same. She couldn't see who was driving; she couldn't even tell what kind of car it was, but she was starting to think it wasn't just a tailgater.

David's words from earlier that day rang through her head.

Donald had died when his car went off the road on the coast highway.

Oh, God!

Was that what was happening now? Was someone trying to kill her? Was it going to look like she was upset or drunk or reckless and just missed a turn?

And then no one would ever know what had happened to her.

She'd disappear…*just like Molly…just like Tommy.*

But she couldn't let that happen.

The car behind her tapped her bumper, and she gripped the wheel tighter, as she sped up again. If she could make it a few more miles, she could get past this deserted part of the coast; she could be around other cars, other people.

She grabbed her phone out of her purse and hit Hunter's number.

She'd just told herself to break away from him, but if she lost this battle on the highway, she couldn't stand the thought of no one knowing what had happened to her.

"Hunter," she said.

"What's wrong?"

"Someone is following me down the highway. They're trying to run me off the road. If something happens to me, tell the police, tell them it wasn't an accident."

"Where are you?"

"South of Pacifica." She screamed as the car behind her hit her harder, and the tires squealed as she tried to regain control. Somehow, she managed to stay on the road.

"Cassidy? Cassidy?"

She heard the panic in his voice. "I'm sorry to bring you into this. I didn't know who else to call. George's heart isn't good. I didn't want to tell him. It's not fair."

"I'm on my way. Can you pull off the highway?"

"No. But if I can make it three more miles, he'll run out of cliff. I can't talk. I have to concentrate."

"Keep the phone on. You can do this, Cassidy. Just stay toward the middle of the road as much as you can."

She set the phone on the console, grateful for his positive voice coming across the speaker.

He kept up a nonstop pep talk, encouraging her to move back and forth across the lanes, so she would be more of a moving target. That seemed to be working. Although, even as she thought that, a huge bump from the car behind her bounced her off the low wall, which thankfully stopped her from going over the side.

She swerved back into the middle, her heart beating so fast, she could barely breathe. And then she saw the lights.

"I'm almost there, Hunter."

"You can do it, babe. Just keep driving."

His words gave her more confidence. She sped ahead again, thrilled when she passed the first of several restaurants. And then there were hotels, parking lots, and turnouts. She slowed enough to take a fast turn into one of those lots, coming to a stop under a big shining light. A group of people exiting the restaurant gave her a startled look, but she didn't care. She was too busy looking in the rearview mirror. The car behind her was gone. It had not followed her into the lot.

She was safe. Apparently, they'd decided to let her go.

Hunter's shouting voice finally penetrated her consciousness. She picked up the phone. "I'm okay. I turned in to a restaurant parking lot. They kept going."

"Good job. Did you see the car?"

"I think it was an SUV. It was big and dark. It had its high beams on, so I couldn't see the driver or the license plate." She blew out a breath, the reality of what had just happened sinking in. "Someone just tried to kill me, Hunter."

"But they didn't. You made it."

"This time. Who could it have been?"

"Maybe someone we talked to today."

She thought about the three men from her past, about Lindsay, about the woman who might have known Molly. Her hand went to the necklace that she'd worn boldly as a reminder of a girl no one wanted to remember. "I must have made someone nervous."

"They think you're getting too close to something."

"Donald died when his car went off the road. Maybe David was right, and the same thing happened to Donald that happened to me, only I managed to survive."

"We need to talk about that. I'm probably fifteen minutes away from you."

"You're driving down here?"

"Yes. Do you want to wait for me or go home and I'll meet you there?"

"You can go home. I'm all right now. There's no danger on this section of the road. I can make it home."

"No way. I'll meet you at the nursery. Leave the phone on. We'll keep talking."

"It helped hearing your voice," she told him as she nervously pulled back onto the highway. She was glad she still had the connection with him. "You don't think they're waiting for me at my house, do you?"

"No, I think it's over—for tonight."

She didn't care for his ominous words, but she couldn't deny them. "You know what the scariest part of this is?"

"I can't imagine."

"Whoever just tried to kill me is not Geralyn or Donald. All these years, I thought they were the evil people, but maybe I was wrong."

"They could still have been evil. They just might not have been the only ones."

⟶⟫⟪⟵

Hunter made it to the nursery ten minutes after Cassidy arrived. He'd talked to her the entire time she was parking and walking into her apartment, so he shouldn't still be worried that she was okay, but when she opened the door, he felt a rush of relief that was almost overwhelming.

He pulled her into his arms, needing to feel her body against his, needing to know she was truly all right. The last hour had been a nightmare, not knowing what she was facing, whether she'd be able to get out of it, if she'd survive. He didn't think he'd ever been that scared.

"You're crushing me, Hunter."

He eased his grip on her, but he didn't completely let go. "Sorry. I'm just glad you're all right. I have to say I've faced some dicey situations in my life, but hearing what you were going through and not being able to be there—"

"It was selfish of me to call you. I just didn't want anyone to not know what had happened."

"It wasn't selfish. It was smart. And now I want to call Max."

"There's nothing he can do. I didn't see the car. There are no cameras along that stretch of road."

"There might be by the restaurant you pulled into."

"Possibly, but there were a lot of cars in there, which is why I stopped."

He ran his hands down her arms, his gaze sweeping her face. There wasn't a scratch on her, but her brown eyes were wide and still a little shocked. There was, however, a gleam of pride in her gaze. "You handled yourself really well."

"I should thank you for that. You were my first driving instructor."

"I forgot about that. We used to go to the parking lot by City College, so you could practice."

"And I was terrible. I gave you whiplash on a quick stop."

"But you kissed me and made me feel better." He was happy to see that memory replace the fear in her eyes. "When did you get your license?"

"Not until I was twenty. I didn't want to go near the DMV or any other governmental building until I was officially an adult, and I let it go a few years after that, because I didn't have a car. George and Mary actually got me driving. They wanted a delivery person, and they thought that should be me. It was probably good I was in the big van tonight."

"Was there any damage?"

"I didn't even look. I just came inside. I didn't want to run into George while I was feeling so crazed."

"Does he live in the house on the hill?"

"Yes, just up the road." She let out a breath. "I was going to make some tea. Do you want some?"

"Sure. Can you put a shot of whiskey in it?"

"Sorry, I don't have any alcohol in the house."

He followed her into the kitchen, noting the cozy warmth of her apartment. There were indoor plants everywhere, of course, as well as soft couches and armchairs, colorful hand-knitted blankets on the furniture, and lots of books—some in the bookcase, others strewn across the coffee table.

He slid onto a counter stool. "This place feels like you."

"I've been here a long time. George and Mary lived here when they first opened the nursery. They built the house on the hill shortly after their tenth wedding anniversary and moved over there, turning this into a storage room, until I showed up needing a place to stay."

"You said Mary passed away?"

"Last year. She was sick for a while, so it was probably a

blessing, but George is lost without her. They had a great love story. They met when they were thirteen years old and got married at nineteen and were together for fifty more years before she passed. Thank goodness George has the business to keep him occupied. Otherwise, he'd really be depressed."

"It's good he has you, too. I get the feeling you're like a daughter to him."

"He and Mary never had kids, so they liked being able to teach me the business, especially because I wanted to learn everything I could about it. But you're no stranger to a good love story. Your parents have been married for a long time, too."

"Thirty-six years and still going strong."

"What do you think keeps them going?"

"They both find each other hilarious," he said dryly. "Which is quite a feat, because my dad is not really that funny. My mom is witty, but it's not like she could do standup. But I swear whenever I go over to the house, one or the other is laughing at something."

Cassidy pushed a mug of tea across the counter. "I like that. I forgot how to laugh for a long time. I almost wasn't sure I could do it anymore, and then one day, something really funny happened at work, and it was like whatever rope had been tied around my funny bone was suddenly gone. I just let out this crazy belly laugh that almost turned into a snort, and I shocked myself as much as everyone else."

They'd talked so much about the darkness of her past, he was happy to know it had gotten brighter. "I'm going to have to see if I can hear one of those laugh/snorts."

"That's not going to happen. It's not pretty." She dipped her tea bag in and out of her mug. "I feel better now. It almost feels like I imagined the whole car chase thing."

"But you didn't. And I have to say it scared the crap out of me."

"Me, too. I'm not used to being in danger, although I know you are."

"It's different when it's me, when I have some semblance

of control over what might happen. But knowing you were in terrible danger and there wasn't a damn thing I could do about it—that was the worst. But don't apologize again for calling me. I'm glad you did."

"I'm glad I did, too. You gave me the courage to fight."

"I think you would have fought no matter what."

"I feel bad you drove all the way down here."

"Bad enough to let me sleep on your couch tonight?"

She licked her lips. "Uh, I don't know. That seems a little…"

She didn't have to finish her sentence. He knew what she was going to say. "I promise to stay in the living room. I don't want you to be alone tonight, and we were going to meet up in the morning anyway, so…"

"I guess you could sleep on the couch. It's actually pretty comfortable."

"It looks like it. And I can sleep anywhere." He paused. "I won't bother Max tonight, but we need to talk to him tomorrow. Let him know what's going on."

"All right." She sipped her tea. "I was thinking that I probably annoyed quite a few people today. The guys weren't happy with me. Lindsay wasn't thrilled to see me, either."

"I wouldn't say that."

"Oh, come on, Hunter, she still likes you. I don't know what happened between you, but she was flirting with you when I went into the bathroom."

"Are you sure you're not jealous?"

"It's possible that there's a part of me that doesn't like the fact that you were with her. It feels like a betrayal on her part—not yours, because I left you. But she knew how I felt about you. It's like she was waiting for me to be out of the picture. And now she's jumped on the chance to see you again. I don't think she came by because she wanted to know who killed Tommy; I think it was all about you."

"I can't say I completely disagree with you," he said slowly. "I figured out a little too late in high school that she liked me more than I liked her."

"I think she still has feelings for you."

"I hope not. But we don't need to see her again."

"That might not be our choice. I have a feeling Lindsay is going to stay as close as she can."

"I hope she's grown up enough to realize when someone is not interested in her."

"Some men are hard to let go of." She cleared her throat. "I'm going to get you a pillow and a blanket." She set down her tea and moved around the counter.

He caught her by the arm. "Cassidy."

"What?" she asked, a wary note in her voice.

"Some women are hard to let go of, too."

"You should let go, Hunter. Look at all the trouble I bring you."

"Well, you could try to balance that out." He got to his feet, then moved his hand on her arm to the back of her neck. "I want to kiss you."

"I could hurt you again," she whispered. "I wouldn't want to, but it might happen."

"Or I could hurt you. You might fall in love with me all over again."

"Would you really want that, Hunter?"

He had to admit it was a question he wasn't sure how to answer. This woman had broken his heart once. *Did he really need to give her the chance to do it again?*

But looking into her eyes now, he couldn't remember the pain, only how good it had felt to be with her. And he wanted that feeling again.

"I think it's worth the risk. We don't know what tomorrow will bring. But we have tonight. Want to live in the moment?"

"This moment?" she asked with a helpless smile. "Yes. I'd like to stay in this moment for as long as possible." She framed his face with her hands. "I really missed you, Hunter."

Her words completely undid him. "I missed you, too."

He pressed his mouth against hers. She tasted like tea, like sweet, spicy herbs, and as he slid his tongue between her lips, her heat enveloped him. He couldn't get enough of her. He wanted to taste and touch every inch of her. He wanted to stop thinking, stop worrying, stop pretending like he didn't give a damn about her anymore. Because he did; *God help him, he did.*

Sixteen

An overwhelming rush of desire and need swept over Cassidy as she kissed the man who had stolen her heart at sixteen. She'd thought she was over him. She'd thought she could handle being his ex, his friend, but that had been a foolish thought. Everything that was wrong in her world tilted back to right as his tongue danced with hers, as his hands ran under the T-shirt he'd given her.

He backed her up against the kitchen counter, but not even the cool granite did anything to cool the heat sweeping through her. She'd felt exactly like this that day in the rain fourteen years ago, when being with Hunter was an all-consuming need.

Like then, she'd dismissed all thoughts of logic, common sense, self-protection. All the complications of her life had faded into one simple, driving desire to connect with Hunter in every possible way. The consequences might be brutal, but at this moment, she didn't care.

He broke away from her mouth to pull her shirt over her head, and she was eager to help him, wanting his hands on her breasts, wanting his mouth there, too.

He was happy to oblige, his tanned, rough hands immediately cupping her breasts as his mouth touched her lips and then slid down the side of her neck, sending shivers through every nerve ending.

"Cassidy," he murmured.

The sensual, husky tone of his voice melted her heart. She'd always loved the way he said her name. He'd asked her why she hadn't changed her first name, and she'd told him the story she'd told herself, that it meant something to her family.

But wasn't he the reason? Wasn't it that she heard his voice saying her name in her dreams? That she hadn't wanted to lose that last connection with him?

As his hands moved down her body, his fingers playing with the snap on her jeans, she grabbed the hem of his shirt, and urged him to take it off. As the material came off, she pressed her hands against his chest, loving the feel of his ripped muscles under her fingers. Hunter had definitely developed a more powerful body since they'd last been together, and she wanted to feel all that power around her, inside of her.

She lifted her gaze to his and saw the same need she felt in the fire burning in his blue eyes. She gulped, feeling a little nervous. It had been a long time.

What if it wasn't the same, wasn't as good?

What if it was better?

"Stop," he murmured. "Don't overthink it."

"Are we crazy?"

"Probably. But it feels crazy good."

"It does."

"Let's take this into the bedroom."

At his words, she licked her lips, suddenly realizing that she was woefully unprepared for this. "I—I don't have anything. I'm not on anything."

Awareness dawned in his eyes. "No problem."

"Really?"

He took out his wallet and pulled out several condoms.

She smiled. "Just like the last time, you're much more

prepared than I am."

He grinned back at her. "Whenever you're around, I feel the need." He stole another kiss. "But I don't want to rush you." He kissed her again, not giving her a chance to answer. "It's whatever you want," he said, before covering her mouth again.

She playfully pushed him away. "Good, because I want..." She let that dangle as she leaned in for another kiss. "You." She grabbed his hand and led him into the bedroom.

At the end of the bed, she paused long enough to unhook her bra and pull it off, loving the way Hunter's eyes lit up. Then she shimmied out of her jeans and panties, feeling remarkably confident. She didn't know what would happen tomorrow, but tonight...she had no doubt that tonight would be great.

"Beautiful," he murmured with male appreciation.

"And you're...slow. I can't be the only one who's naked."

"I could spend the next hour just looking at you."

"I doubt that," she said with a little laugh, as she put her hand on the waistband of his jeans. "These might be getting tight."

He laughed back. "You're right. The looking might have to come later."

"Much later," she agreed, as she helped him off with his pants, knowing that she wanted to do some looking of her own, but right now she just wanted to touch and to feel.

Hunter tossed several condoms onto the bed. "For later. I want to warm you up first."

"I'm already burning, Hunter."

"Let's see about that." He pushed her back onto the soft mattress, then covered her body with his. He kissed her mouth, then moved his way down her body until she was grabbing handfuls of the comforter, as she bit back a scream of delight. The man definitely knew how to push her buttons.

Then it was her turn to explore, to touch and taste, to torment with pleasure, and she loved every minute of it.

She did all the things she'd wanted to do with Hunter the

first time they'd made love, but she'd been too shy, too inexperienced, too insecure to risk doing it wrong. Now, there was no holding back. She could love him exactly the way she wanted to, and Hunter urged her on, saying her name again and again as they climaxed together.

Then she had the second crazy thought of the night—she felt like she'd finally come home.

⎯⎯►◄⎯⎯

Hunter watched the early morning sunlight play off the ceiling as he held Cassidy in his arms. Her head was on his shoulder, her silky blonde hair spread across his chest, her arm around his waist. They'd made love twice, and while she'd fallen asleep, he'd been unable to doze off, not wanting to miss a second of their time together. He just wanted to look at her, to hold her, to watch her breathe.

She looked peaceful. Her cheeks were pink, her lips still red from their passion, her long black lashes hiding her beautiful eyes.

He'd remembered her this way before. In those days after she'd left, all he could think about was how they'd been together. But now he had to admit that those memories were a dim comparison to reality.

It hadn't been as good as he remembered; it had been better. It had felt incredibly…right. Like he'd found what he'd been looking for all these years. Wariness followed that thought.

Had missing Cassidy been at the core of his restlessness all these years?

Was that why he hadn't found what he was looking for in South America, in Mexico, anywhere on the roads he traveled?

He didn't want to believe that.

He'd had relationships since high school. He just couldn't remember any of those women now. His heart and his head were filled with Cassidy. She'd once been his girl. Now she was his woman.

But as much as he liked that thought, he knew it wasn't true. She'd never really been his girl. She'd hidden so much of herself from him. And even now, he didn't think he knew all her secrets. She'd been generous with her body, even with her heart. But would she ever really trust him enough to tell him everything, to be completely vulnerable?

Maybe that was asking too much of anyone. How many people would he trust in that way?

Only her name rang through his head.

But did he trust her? Wouldn't he be stupid to go that far? She'd left him before. She could do it again.

Cassidy shifted in his arms, and as she blinked her eyes open and gave him a sleepy smile, he knew that the future didn't matter, not when this moment was so perfect.

"Is it morning?" she asked.

"It is. How did you sleep?"

"Good. What about you?"

"Great," he lied.

"This is the first time we've ever spent the whole night together. I'm glad you had more than one condom."

"Me, too, and there's one left."

"We have things to do this morning."

"Not quite yet," he said, rolling onto his side, so he could face her. "We have time."

"I wish we had nothing but time. I wish reality didn't always have to ruin my dreams."

"Last night wasn't a dream; it was reality."

"I know, but I feel like today isn't going to be quite as dreamy. The past is waiting outside the door."

"Not everything in the past was bad. Maybe the good is waiting there, too."

"Your optimism is irresistible."

"Only my optimism is irresistible?" he teased, cupping her warm curves with his hand. "I must be doing something wrong."

As his fingers strayed, she sucked in a breath of air, and

her eyes glittered. "You have been doing everything right. And, yes, there are other parts of you I find incredibly irresistible."

"Want to show me?"

"I thought you'd never ask," she said, planting her sweet lips on his.

Hunter would have stayed in bed for another hour, if his phone hadn't started ringing quite persistently, and Cassidy hadn't used the opportunity to slip out of bed and grab a shower.

He pulled on his briefs before venturing out of the bedroom to retrieve his phone from the kitchen island. He had three missed calls, all from Max. He'd planned on calling him to report what had happened to Cassidy the night before, but it appeared there might be other news.

Frowning, he called Max back, wondering what could be so pressing on a Sunday morning. Maybe Mrs. Faulkner had finally found her voice.

"Max, what's up?"

"I have some bad news," Max said heavily.

His gut clenched, but he told himself whatever the news was, it couldn't be that bad since Cassidy was safe. "What's happened?"

"Geralyn Faulkner disappeared from the hospital last night."

"What? How did that happen? I thought there was a guard on her room."

"There was. Something was put in his coffee. He became violently ill and rushed to the bathroom. When he got back, Geralyn was gone. We've checked the security cameras, but it appears that the footage was hacked and erased."

"How is that possible?"

"Unfortunately, the system had not been updated in a few years, and there were holes."

"Well, that's just great. What did she say before she escaped? You told me you were going to talk to her yesterday afternoon."

"I tried, but as soon as I started asking questions, she began to cry, became hysterical, and the doctor ended the interview."

"She's just faking it."

"She was definitely medicated after her breakdown with us. I saw the doctor give her an injection. She was taken out of the hospital approximately three hours later, so I suspect she was still in a sedated state."

"But whoever took her doesn't want to hurt her; they did it to help her. I'm guessing it was one of the now adult foster children I met with last night."

"Who did you meet with?"

"David Bellerman, Jeremiah Hunt and Quan Tran. David had reached out to Cassidy. When we got there, the other two were there as well. None of them wanted to believe Geralyn was guilty of Tommy's murder. They seemed rather angry that Cassidy wasn't getting on board with them."

"She should be careful."

"She knows that now. Late last night, on her way back to Half Moon Bay, an SUV tried to run her off the road. It was around ten. It happened just south of Pacifica, no witnesses, no other cars on the road. Fortunately, she managed to hang on until she got back to a more populated location and then they sped off."

"That sounds a lot like Donald Faulkner's tragic accident."

"Cassidy had the same thought. She also said that David told her he believed someone was trying to get revenge on the Faulkners, first with Donald, then with the fire. David thought he might be the next target because he was the only kid adopted by the Faulkners, and they apparently treated him better than the others."

"That would make more sense than the attack on Cassidy. Why go after her?"

"Someone doesn't like the fact that she's hell-bent on proving the Faulkners killed Tommy."

"She needs to back down on that. You both do. Leave the investigation to us."

"We just had a conversation with them. It didn't seem like it would be dangerous."

"Well, I'll talk to David again, see what I can find out."

"If I was going to bet on who sprung Geralyn Faulkner, I'd bet on one of those three guys, with David at the top of the list."

"I'll keep that in mind. But in the meantime, watch your back, Hunter. And maybe think about staying away from Cassidy. From what Emma has told me, it doesn't sound like she was good for you the first time around."

"I appreciate your concern, but I can take care of myself, and the last thing I'm going to do is stay away from Cassidy."

"Who wants you to stay away from me?" Cassidy asked, as he set down the phone.

"I didn't see you standing there. How much did you hear?"

"Only the last part. Who were you talking to?"

"Max."

"Why does he want you to stay away from me?"

"He's just concerned about me. It's a family thing."

"You told him someone tried to kill me last night?"

"I did."

"Well, no wonder he's concerned," she said with a sigh. "I understand that, and he's probably right. I've been worried all along about dragging you into the mud with me, and clearly others share my concern."

"I can take care of myself, and you're not dragging me anywhere I don't want to go." He paused. "But there is something else to worry about."

Concern filled her gaze. "What happened?"

"Mrs. Faulkner escaped from the hospital last night. No one knows where she is."

Cassidy's eyes widened. "I knew it. I knew she was going

to get away with it."

"The police will find her."

She shook her head. "Will they? There is no justice, Hunter. I was a fool to think for one second there could be."

"This isn't over yet."

"Isn't it?"

He hated the despair in her voice. "No. Because we have a good lead on someone else who needs justice—Molly. Remember her?"

"We don't know if she's still alive. There's a good chance we'll find out Molly is dead, too."

"Or we'll find out she escaped, just like you did." He put his hands on her shoulders. "Don't give up on me, Cassidy."

"I'm not giving up on you. I just don't know how long I can keep fighting."

"You're not fighting alone. When you get tired, I'll take over."

"But—"

"No, that's how it works," he said firmly. "Whether you want me to stick around or not, I'm going to be there. Now, there is something you can do for me."

"What's that?"

"I could really use some coffee."

She let out a breath. "I can make coffee."

"Let's start there."

Seventeen

—⇒⇒⟪⟪⟪⟪⟪⟪⟪⟪⟪⟪⟪⟪⟪⟪⟪⟪⟪⟪⟪⟪⟪⟪⟪

Cassidy not only made coffee, she scrambled up eggs with fresh vegetables from her garden while Hunter took a shower. Hunter was very good at simplifying things, narrowing the focus of her chaotic brain, which gave her one more reason to like him. He was good for her. She just didn't know how good she was for him. Although, she had made him a lovely breakfast, she thought. That was something.

A familiar knock came at her door, and she hurried across the room to open it, knowing it was George. "Good morning."

"Is it?" he asked with a frown.

"What's wrong?"

"The back bumper on your van is all bent up. Did you get rear-ended?"

"Oh, yes, I did," she said, not wanting to worry George. "It was on my way home last night."

"Did you get their insurance?"

"No. They took off. It was dark. I couldn't see the license plate."

"But you're all right?"

"I'm fine." She cleared her throat as Hunter came into the room, feeling a little like a guilty teenager. She was entitled to have men over; she just never did, and George was going to be curious.

"Hello," Hunter said, his hair damp from a shower. "Am I interrupting?"

"George was just asking me about the car. I told him I got rear-ended." She hoped Hunter could read between the lines.

"We were going to look at the damage in the light," Hunter said.

"It's not good," George put in. "Not that the old van is in tip-top shape; I was more concerned about Cassidy."

"I'm fine. It's all good," she said. "I was just making breakfast. Do you want some?"

"No. I don't want to interrupt. I'll talk to you later." George gave Hunter a speculative look, then glanced back at her. "Let me know if you need anything."

"I will. Thanks for your concern." She shut the door behind George and smiled at Hunter. "I have coffee and breakfast ready."

"It smells delicious." He grabbed her around the waist and kissed her. "But it doesn't smell as good as you."

"That's a nice line," she said with a laugh, unable to stop the happy feeling that ran through her every time Hunter kissed her.

"You look pretty, too."

She'd put on a sleeveless floral dress and wedge sandals since the weather looked nice and they were going to church. Plus, she had wanted Hunter to see her in something other than jeans and a T-shirt, although, he'd seen plenty of her the night before.

He snuck another kiss, and she playfully pushed him away. "No more kissing until we get food."

"As long as there will be more kissing after that," he said, following her over to the kitchen island.

She shot him a smile. "We'll see. In the meantime, you

need to eat your vegetables." She spooned scrambled eggs and veggies onto a plate and pushed it over to him.

"This looks amazing."

"And good for you."

"Aren't you having any?"

"I've been nibbling while I cooked. Bad habit. I'm used to eating alone."

"These might be the best eggs I've ever had."

"You're very complimentary after sex."

He grinned. "If you'd served me this before sex, I would have said the same thing. I guess you learned how to cook in the last decade."

"I actually learned how to cook from my mom, but I didn't have much chance to do it in foster care. When I ended up on my own, I got very creative putting cheap ingredients together. Moving here, with Mary's vegetable garden just outside the door, I had an incredible bounty at my fingertips. I still like a good steak now and then, or a beautiful piece of fish, but vegetables are a mainstay. Do you cook for yourself?"

"Not like this, but I don't starve."

"I remember your mom telling me that she wanted to make sure all her kids, even her boys, could put on a good meal."

"Her boys were kind of hopeless in that department. Dylan and I were too busy to cook, and Ian was more interested in putting chemicals together in science experiments than learning how to make spaghetti. Actually, Kate wasn't very good, either. Or Annie. Come to think of it, Mia is probably the only one who puts on a good meal. We all love to eat, though." He wiped his mouth with a napkin. "I'm hoping Kate will get back to us on Molly, but she's at a bachelorette weekend in Napa with all my female relatives, so that might not happen until she gets back."

"That sounds fun."

"Do you think George is going to give you a hard time for having me over?"

"I'm not sure—maybe. He is protective of me, although he would also like to see me have a life outside of work. I'm not sure he knows what to make of you." She paused. "I didn't even think about there being damage on the van. I should have."

"We'll take a look when we go outside. I think we should take my car to the city. It's a little less obtrusive than your van."

"But then you'll have to drive me all the way back here. Let's take both cars. We can park the van by your place, but that way I can come back on my own."

He frowned. "That didn't work so well last night."

"I can take a different way home, avoid that part of the coastal route."

"Let's see how the day goes. I kind of liked your bed."

"I kind of liked you in my bed," she repeated. "But you do have to go back to work at some point, don't you?"

"Seven o'clock tomorrow morning," he said, not sounding happy about it. "Anyway, are you ready to go to church?"

"I guess. I have to say I haven't been to a church since I was thirteen years old."

"Well, I don't think the Church of the Sky is going to be like any church you've ever been to before."

⇒►◄◄◄⇐

The Church of the Sky was located in an old Victorian house that sat between a large apartment complex and a laundromat. As Cassidy stepped through the front door and into what had once been a living room, she was greeted by an older woman with Native American features, gray hair, and thick black glasses. There were people milling around the room behind her, and she could see a buffet table with coffee and cookies in the next room.

"Welcome," the woman said. "I'm Jolynn. Is this your first time here?"

"Yes. I'm Cassidy, and this is Hunter."

"We're happy to have you here. This morning's service will be in the backyard. It's such a lovely day. We try to be under the sky whenever possible."

"That sounds good. We're actually not just here for the service. We're looking for someone who used to volunteer here quite a few years ago. Her first name was Lily. She had a granddaughter named Molly. I don't suppose you remember them?"

"Oh, my." Jolynn thought for a moment and then shook her head. "I don't recall anyone by those names, but I've only been coming here for about six years. Was it before that?"

"Yes, it was about fourteen years ago."

"Well, there are a few people at the service who have been attending for that long. Perhaps one of them can help you. Can I ask why you're looking for these people?"

"Molly and I were in foster care together. She actually disappeared one day, and I've been worried about her ever since. I recently discovered that her grandmother lived in this neighborhood and came to church here, and while I know Lily passed away some time ago, I thought someone might remember her granddaughter, Molly. I know it's a long shot, but I really cared about Molly."

"Why did you wait so long to look for her?"

"I had to grow up, I guess. And something happened recently to the house where we lived. There was a fire. It brought up the past again, and I haven't been able to stop thinking about Molly since then."

"Fire can be cleansing. It provides the opportunity for rebirth." Jolynn paused. "Your necklace—where did you get it?"

"From a store on Union Street. It's beautiful, isn't it? It reminds me of Molly. She had one just like it."

"It's lovely. Please help yourself to some coffee and food. The service will be starting shortly." Jolynn moved away to greet two other arrivals.

"What do you think?" she asked Hunter. "Did you see the

way she looked at my necklace?"

"I did."

"I know she said she didn't know the names, but I'm starting to get a good feeling about this place."

"Should we check out the backyard?" he asked. "Looks like everyone is heading that way."

She nodded, but before they could move, the front door opened, and a woman came rushing in. She had long, black hair pulled back in a braid, and her dark eyes were a bit harried. But it was the necklace around her neck that made Cassidy gasp.

The woman came to an abrupt stop when she saw them, and as her gaze met Cassidy's, her eyes widened.

"Molly?" Cassidy asked in amazement.

The woman's jaw dropped, but she didn't speak. She abruptly turned and ran out the door.

"That was her," she said to Hunter. "That was Molly."

"We can't let her get away," Hunter said, jogging toward the front door.

It took her a moment to get her body to move. Both Hunter and Molly were halfway down the street when she got out the door. She had to catch up. She had to talk to Molly. This might be her only chance to prove she existed.

The woman was fast, Hunter thought, as he ran down the steep hill in pursuit of the attractive brunette in skinny jeans and a flowy shirt. But he was faster, bridging the gap between them to only a few feet.

Then she darted down an alleyway, and he almost bumped into a kid on a skateboard, as he made the same turn. He thought Cassidy might be behind him, but she'd been paralyzed by surprise when she'd seen the woman she'd called Molly.

He was pretty sure it was Molly, judging by her abrupt exit and her mad dash down the street. He sped up and as the alley narrowed, he saw that the woman he was chasing was about to run out of room as she came face-to-face with a high chain-link fence.

She whirled around, putting up a hand. "Don't come any closer."

He came to a halt about five feet from her. "Molly?"

"Why are you calling me that?"

"Because you're Molly Bennett."

"I'm not. I'm Kenna," she denied.

"Then why did you run when Cassidy called you Molly?" The name Kenna rang a bell in his head. *Wasn't that the name of the jewelry designer, the one who'd designed the necklace that Cassidy was currently wearing?*

She didn't answer his question, but her gaze changed as it moved past him.

He looked over his head and saw Cassidy running down the alleyway. She came to a breathless stop next to him.

"Molly?" she said again, in the same wonder-filled voice she'd used before. "Please tell me it's you. I've been worried about you for fourteen years. It's Cassidy. You have to remember me."

Molly's lips tightened. "I don't remember you."

"You do," Cassidy said, taking another step forward. "I don't know why you're scared of me, but I am not here to cause you any problems. I'm just so thrilled that you're alive. I thought…"

"You thought what?"

"I thought you were dead. I thought the Faulkners might have killed you. I'm so glad they didn't."

Molly licked her lips, dropping her hand to her side. "You really thought they killed me?"

He let out a breath at Molly's words, happy she was dropping the pretense.

"You disappeared in the middle of the night," Cassidy said. "And it wasn't the first time I woke up and you were gone. Something was going on, but I didn't know what. They told me you were transferred to another home, but I thought something bad had happened. I went to my social worker and told her she had to find you. But when she looked into it, she said you didn't exist, that you weren't at the house, and that the Faulkners told her that I'd made you up, that you were my imaginary friend. All the other kids backed up their story. They made me think I was crazy, that we hadn't spent three weeks sharing the same room, talking at night, being each other's friend."

"I always wondered what they'd said." Molly's gaze narrowed. "Where did you get that necklace?"

"In a shop in the Marina. I picked it up yesterday; it reminded me of you, of the one you used to wear—still wear," she added.

Molly's hand went to her necklace. "My grandmother made this one. I made the one you're wearing."

"Oh, my God, you're the designer? The manager told me your name was Kenna."

"It's the name I go by now. I haven't been Molly in a very long time."

"So, what happened? Were you transferred somewhere else?"

"No. I ran away."

"You ran away? How did you survive? You were so young."

Molly hesitated, then said, "I went to the church. My grandmother used to volunteer there, and one of her friends helped me hide. They took care of me until I was eighteen."

"I'm so glad." Cassidy looked at him with a watery smile and said, "She's alive. It's a miracle."

He smiled back. "Sometimes they happen."

"It's a first for me."

"Who's he?" Molly asked, her gaze still wary.

"This is Hunter—Hunter Callaway."

Molly looked surprised once again. "Hunter Callaway? The kid you were so crazy about in high school? You got together? You've been together all this time?"

"No." Cassidy shook her head. "We've been apart almost

as long as you and I have. We reconnected a few days ago when the Faulkners' house burned down."

"What? The house burned down? Are you serious?"

"Yes. It was deliberate. And there's more." Cassidy drew in a deep breath. "After the fire, Tommy's body was found in the walls of the garage. He'd been there fourteen years."

Molly's eyes widened, and she put a hand to her mouth as if she were going to be sick. "What are you saying?"

"I'm saying that Tommy was killed in the house and buried there. You remember Tommy, don't you? He arrived about a week before you ran away."

"Your friend from somewhere else. The skinny kid with the dark-blond hair—I remember. But I don't understand. Who killed him? And you say his body was hidden in the walls? How does that even happen?"

Cassidy gave a helpless shrug. "I don't know, but it did happen. I'm guessing the Faulkners killed Tommy, but the police are investigating. Mr. Faulkner died five months ago and Geralyn had a breakdown when she heard the news. The police were waiting to question her. She was in the hospital, in police custody, but someone helped her escape last night."

"Someone helped her escape?" Molly echoed.

He could see the wheels turning in Molly's eyes as she tried to make sense of what Cassidy was telling her. She was definitely shocked by the news, so stunned that he didn't think she was really taking it all in. He couldn't blame her; it was a lot to process.

"I don't know who helped Geralyn get out, but I think it might have been one of the boys—David or Jeremiah or Quan," Cassidy said. "I saw them last night, and they were worried about Geralyn getting arrested for Tommy's murder."

"You're all still in touch?" Molly asked in bemusement.

"No. We have not been in touch at all. I don't even like them. But David reached out after the police interviewed him yesterday. The police are trying to talk to everyone who lived in the house during that time period."

"Did you tell them about me?"

"I did, but all I knew was your name, and I told them that there was apparently no record of you being at the Faulkners' house."

"Good. I'm glad. I don't want to be involved in any of this. I left that house a long time ago. I'm not that girl anymore."

Watching Molly and Cassidy talk, he couldn't help but think how similar their stories were, how the Faulkners had made them both reinvent themselves. And they were doing well now, because they'd made the choice to run. He wondered if he would have done the same thing. Probably. But he was glad he had never had to face that kind of life-or-death decision.

"What happened to you, Molly?" Cassidy asked. "Why did you have to leave?"

"I just had to get out of there, that's all."

"That wasn't all."

"I don't want to talk about it. I need to go."

"Wait," Cassidy said, moving in front of Molly. "Don't leave. I want to talk to you."

"We don't have anything to say to each other."

"Is that why you ran?" he interjected. "You recognized Cassidy right away, didn't you? So, why take off?"

"Habit," Molly replied. "I've been running away from my past for a long time."

"You don't have to run away from me," Cassidy said. "I left the Faulkners' house two weeks after you did. I hid away, changed my last name, started over. I did exactly what you did."

"I'm glad." Molly let out a breath. "This is stupid, standing here in an alley that smells like garbage."

"We can go back to the church," Cassidy suggested. "Or we could go somewhere else and talk?"

Molly hesitated. "I would like to talk to you, but not at the church, and not here. Why don't you give me your number?" She pulled out her phone. "I'll call you."

"I'd really like to speak to you now."

"I can't. I have to get back to the church. I have a role in the service."

"All right." Cassidy gave her the number, then said, "Why don't you text me now, so I have your number as well?"

"Sure. I should have thought of that." Molly sent a short text. "There you go. We'll talk again."

"I hope it's soon. I'd like you to help me sort out what might have happened to Tommy."

"I can't help with that. Obviously, Tommy was killed after I left. I'm guessing it happened after you left, too. I'm sorry about what happened to him. He didn't deserve that. Anyway, I really do have to go."

He frowned as Molly walked by them. She wasn't running anymore, but she was moving damned fast, and there was something off about the whole encounter.

"That was not the reunion I expected," Cassidy said, giving him a troubled look. "Maybe I was expecting too much. She probably didn't think about me the way I thought about her, because I didn't disappear on her. It wasn't like I thought about the kids I left behind."

"You might have if you'd been better friends with any of them. I know you thought about Tommy."

"I did think about him, yes. We had talked about going to Santa Cruz together, so I kind of expected he'd show up there at some point. Whenever I passed a group of kids on a street corner, saw anyone who looked remotely like him, I'd stop and take another look."

"You never went any further than that?"

"I didn't," she said, guilt in her eyes. "It makes me sound like a terrible person. Here I claim to be best friends with the guy and I never looked for him."

"I'm not judging you. I wasn't in your shoes and obviously the first few years you were just trying to survive and protect yourself."

"I believed Tommy was doing the same, that staying apart kept us both safe. By the time I was old enough to stop worrying about getting dragged back to the Faulkners or some other home, it had been several years."

He put his arm around her. "I get it. And I think that if Tommy hadn't been killed, he would have come looking for you."

She gazed into his eyes. "Thank you for being so understanding, and also for running really fast so Molly couldn't get away. I do not have the right shoes on for a foot race."

"No problem. I was shocked Molly ran the way she did. She was fast, too. Luckily, she ran out of room."

"Street kids run first, ask questions later."

"Let's go back to the car. I don't think there's any point in returning to the church."

"I really wish I didn't have to wait for Molly to get back in touch, especially since I'm not sure she ever will."

"Well, you have her number, too."

"I wouldn't put it past her to toss that phone."

"I hope she doesn't, but it might not matter. The police should be able to track her down now that we know she's the designer named Kenna."

Cassidy gave him a look of alarm. "We can't tell the police about Molly. We can't blow her cover."

"Her cover? What does that mean? She has no more reason than you do to hide anymore. And we need her piece of the puzzle."

"Let's give her a day or two. I don't want to scare her off."

He didn't particularly like her suggestion, but he'd play it her way for the moment. As they walked back to his Jeep, he brought something else up that was bothering him. "Molly said she goes by Kenna now—a name that means fire."

Cassidy frowned. "I know where you're going. I don't like it."

He kept going anyway. "Molly clearly hated the Faulkners, hated that house. She had as good a reason as anyone to burn it down."

"So did I."

"But you didn't do it. We don't know if she did."

"It's more likely that she has never been back to that house. I certainly wouldn't have ever gone there again if it hadn't been for Tommy. She has a good life now. Why would she want to mess that up?"

"Hate can make you crazy. It sounds like she had good reason to hate Donald, and he died under suspicious circumstances."

"Now you're suggesting Molly ran Donald off the road?" She gave him an irritated look as he opened the door of his car for her. "Let's stop pinning every crime on the one person in my past besides you and Tommy who I actually liked. And even if she could have been motivated to start the fire or run Donald off the road, she did not try to do the same thing to me last night."

Risking further annoyance, he said, "How do you know?"

Cassidy frowned, got in the car, and slammed the door, narrowly missing his fingers.

She might be pissed at his suggestion, but he'd given her something to think about—something they both needed to think about.

Eighteen

---⟫⟪⟪⟨---

Hunter's unwelcome suggestions ran around Cassidy's head as they drove back to his apartment. While she couldn't deny that Molly could have hated the Faulkners enough to kill Donald or burn down their house, she couldn't imagine Molly coming after her. And Molly had looked shocked when she saw her in the church. That had felt completely genuine.

Maybe that was because she had tried to kill her the night before.

She frowned at that thought. No. That was crazy. Molly didn't have a motive to hurt her. She'd been the only friend that Molly had had at the Faulkners. If she was on some sort of crusade now to erase her past, she'd go after David or Jeremiah or Quan—maybe Geralyn.

"Let me know which voice in your head wins," Hunter said dryly, as he pulled into his garage.

"It's a tie at the moment. I don't think Molly would have any reason to hurt me or even know where I was yesterday."

"We did stop in at the store where she sells her jewelry. The clerk could have alerted her. She might have even seen us go down the street and into Jack's. If Molly lives anywhere near the store where she sells her jewelry, she could have followed us to the bar, and then here."

"And waited for me to leave? And then stayed on my tail all the way to Half Moon Bay? Why? What reason would she have to try to run me off the road? We didn't say anything to the clerk beyond the fact that we were looking for Molly. You're wrong, Hunter."

"Well, it wouldn't be the first time."

"Sorry, I didn't mean to say that so bluntly. I know you're just trying to help." She got out of the car and they walked out of the garage together. As they reached the sidewalk, she said, "I'm hoping Lindsay doesn't spring out of the bushes again."

"I don't think that's going to happen."

Despite his words, she couldn't help noticing that Hunter took a good look around before opening the door to his building. They made their way up the stairs to his apartment without incident. Once inside, he turned the dead bolt.

She wandered over to the window that faced the street and looked outside. Was someone following her now? They had to have done that last night. How else would they have gotten on her tail? But everything out front looked quiet, normal, a typical Sunday afternoon.

"See anything?" Hunter asked, coming up behind her, sliding his arms around her waist.

"No." She turned in his embrace, so she could look into his eyes. "But I was just going over what you said about someone following me from here to the highway, and it feels like we're leaving out the most obvious person—Lindsay."

Surprise arched his brows. "You think Lindsay tried to run you off the road?"

She shrugged. "She didn't like that we were together."

"Still…"

"You don't think she has it in her?"

"I don't. Trying to run someone off the road is an aggressive, violent, dangerous act. Does that really describe Lindsay?"

"You probably knew her better than I did," she said, hearing the edge in her voice.

"I like it when you're jealous," he said, with a gleam in his eyes. "But I think one of the guys we saw last night is a better suspect for last night's attack."

"Jeremiah always had an ugly temper," she murmured.

"And you made it clear you were against Geralyn, which none of the guys wanted to hear."

"It is easier to believe it was one of them." She put her arms around his waist and rested her head on his shoulder. "I'm tired."

He stroked her hair. "I know. I should have let you get more sleep last night. But you're too damned beautiful."

She lifted her head and smiled. "And you're too damned handsome. I don't have any regrets. Last night and this morning were amazing, but I might need a nap."

"It's a good thing my bed is not very far away."

"I want to sleep, not to…you know."

"I'd let you sleep…for a while." He brushed her cheek with his finger, a warm, gentle, sensuous gesture that pushed the idea of a nap way down on her to-do list.

"Before or after?" she teased.

He lowered his head and gave her a tender kiss. "I could leave that to you."

As she was debating her answer, Hunter's phone began to buzz. "You should get that. It could be Max."

He pulled the phone out of his pocket and frowned. "It's not Max. It's my mother. I'm sure it can wait. It's probably some wedding problem."

"Go ahead and take it. I'm going to lie down for a bit. You can join me when you're done."

"All right."

As she wandered into his bedroom, she heard him say, "Hi, Mom." A pause was followed by some defensive words: "I know you called me last night, but I was a little busy. Yes, it involved Cassidy. And, yes, I know what I'm doing."

She smiled to herself and then shut the door. She not

only wanted to give him privacy, she also didn't want to accidentally hear what his mom thought of her now. She'd had a good relationship with Sharon in high school, but clearly Hunter's mom was now worried about her reappearance in Hunter's life. She couldn't blame Sharon. She was a little worried, too.

Being with Hunter again was a dream come true, and he seemed to feel the same way, but were they both just living a dream? A dream that would eventually end? It seemed likely.

She didn't want to think about that now. Climbing into Hunter's bed, she snuggled under his covers, smelling his scent on the pillow under her cheek. Closing her eyes, she told herself she'd just take a little cat nap. And then they could figure out what to do next.

Hunter had more in mind than a nap when he walked into his bedroom, but Cassidy was fast asleep, and he didn't have the heart to wake her. He gently closed the door and went into the living room.

Taking a seat at his kitchen table, he opened up his computer and checked his email. There was nothing of importance. Tapping his fingers restlessly on the keyboard, he typed in the name Kenna and jewelry designer. A website popped up.

He leaned forward, curious to learn more about Molly, aka Kenna. Her behavior at the church, the mad dash down the street, and her evasive answers in the alley, had left him with a bad feeling in his gut. He didn't know what her truth was, but he didn't think they'd heard it yet.

Whatever had gone wrong in her past, a lot seemed to be going right in her present. She had definitely made a life for herself now, and she was very talented.

He flipped through the jewelry designs, moving to the page that described herself. There wasn't more than a paragraph, but it talked about how Kenna had learned about jewelry making and the legends of silver and turquoise as handed down from her grandmother. She talked about her love of the elements: earth, fire, and water, and how she used them in her jewelry. She spoke about rebirth, cleansing the soul, letting go of the past, opening up to new opportunities. There was no mention of her actual parents or her past.

Clicking out of her website, he tried to find her on social media, but her business page under Kenna Designs only featured her jewelry, with no personal posts. She obviously liked to stay out of the spotlight. He wasn't surprised. People like Molly and Cassidy had learned the hard way that staying in the shadows was the best way to survive.

As he closed his computer, his phone rang. He was not happy when Lindsay's name popped up. He didn't really want to talk to her again, but maybe she had information he needed. "Hello."

"Hi Hunter. Can you talk? Is Cassidy there?"

"I can talk. I'm alone." He didn't mention that Cassidy was sleeping in his bed. He didn't think that would go over well.

"Good. It was a little awkward last night, and I wanted to apologize for showing up at your door like that. Obviously, I put you in an uncomfortable situation."

"It was fine."

"Are you sure? Cassidy didn't seem happy to see me, and yet we were good friends at one time."

"She has a lot on her mind."

"Like Tommy, I know. She really loved him."

He suspected that Lindsay's words were meant to be a reminder to him that Cassidy had chosen Tommy over him. It had been the previous theme of many of their conversations back then. It had taken him a long time to realize that Lindsay had used Cassidy and Tommy to get close to him, to become his confidant.

"Hunter?"

Her voice brought him back to the present. "Did you want something, Lindsay?"

"I'd like to have a conversation with you. I've thought about you over the years. I'd love to catch up."

"This isn't the best time for that."

"Because Cassidy is back?"

"Because I'd like to know what happened to Tommy, and that's all I'm thinking about at the moment."

"Well, I would like to find that out, too. I got to thinking last night that I might know something. I don't want to get into it over the phone. Could we meet somewhere?"

"If we meet, I'll be bringing Cassidy with me. We're working together, Lindsay."

"Working together, or back together?"

"Why don't you just tell me what you have to say?"

"You're not going to like it."

"Just say what you have to say." *Had she always been this cagey and annoying?*

"All right. When we were in high school, Cassidy used my computer one day to research poisonous herbs. I didn't realize what she was doing until after she left, and then I just thought it was for a homework assignment. But now I wonder if she didn't poison Tommy. It could have been accidental. She might have meant it for someone else."

"What the hell are you talking about?" He was incensed by her words. "Are you actually suggesting that Cassidy killed Tommy?"

"I'm just telling you that she was looking that stuff up. You never wanted to believe anything bad about her, but I don't think she's ever been as innocent as you thought she was. Jeremiah told me that the two of them fooled around one night, too."

"You're just making up lies. Why?"

"I'm not making anything up. I'm trying to warn you."

"There is nothing you can say that would make me believe Cassidy is guilty."

"Well, the police might be more interested in hearing what I have to say."

"Is that a threat? What's your endgame, Lindsay? I go out

with you and you stay quiet? Is that the deal?"

"You're making this sound so ugly. I care about you, Hunter."

"And clearly you were never Cassidy's friend."

"I was her friend. She's the one who left without a word. She left you, too. I can't believe you're so eager to trust her. It's like she put a spell on you."

"My relationship with Cassidy is none of your business. We went on a few dates a long time ago. I know you weren't happy when things ended, but why are you getting in the middle of all this? It doesn't make sense to me. You're acting like I broke up with you yesterday." He was beginning to wonder if Lindsay's motives were about getting him back into her life or if she had a completely different agenda that he just hadn't figured out yet. "Do you know who killed Tommy? Do you know what happened in that house? Do you have any real information?"

Silence followed his questions.

After a moment, she said, "I obviously know more than you do. I would have been happy to share, but I'll tell my stories to other people who are interested in hearing them. Good-bye, Hunter."

A dial tone punctuated her final words.

"Who were you talking to?" Cassidy asked, coming over to the table. "I heard you shouting."

"Sorry. That was Lindsay."

"What did she want?"

"She wanted to meet me alone. I said you and I were a package deal, and she got all bent out of shape. She started making up crazy stories."

"Like what?"

He didn't want to tell her, because it felt like Cassidy had been betrayed by so many people, but he could see she wasn't going to let it go. And maybe she had a right to know. "She said you used her computer after school one day to look up poisonous herbs."

Cassidy's brown eyes widened. "What?"

"She thinks you might have accidentally poisoned Tommy instead of your intended victim—like Geralyn or Donald, or one of the boys."

Her face paled. "Lindsay thinks I poisoned Tommy, my really good friend, and stuffed his body in the wall all by myself, in a garage that I couldn't even get into?"

"I told you it was ridiculous. But now I'm concerned as to what she's telling the police."

She sank down in the chair across from him. "Wow. Just wow."

"I'm sorry. I didn't want to tell you. But I don't want you to be blindsided."

She met his gaze. "I thought Geralyn Faulkner was the one I had to worry about, but perhaps it's Lindsay. Maybe it wasn't that farfetched for me to suggest that she's the one who tried to run me off the road."

"Maybe not," he muttered. "She did sound a little crazy today. She also said you and Jeremiah fooled around."

"That's even more ridiculous. I hated Jeremiah. He was always mean and crude in so many ways. I wouldn't have touched him with a ten-foot pole." She paused. "Maybe you should be worried, too, Hunter. Lindsay obviously said those things to change your mind about me."

"I don't get it, though. We really didn't have that intense of a relationship, and it was so long ago. I'm sure she's loved lots of other men since then. Why is she suddenly so worked up about me? Are we missing something?"

"I don't know. Maybe." She gave him a troubled look. "How did you end the conversation with Lindsay?"

"I told her I didn't know what her endgame was but acting like a woman scorned after a few dates in high school is bizarre."

"That should have appeased her," Cassidy said dryly.

He shrugged. "I probably should have played it differently, but she pissed me off. Unfortunately, she said she was going to share her thoughts with the police since I wasn't interested in hearing them."

"That's great. She'll give the police another reason to look at me."

He heard the new worry in her voice. "I can make sure Max knows the whole story about Lindsay."

"It's good we have him on the case."

"It is."

"What else have you been doing?" She tipped her head toward his open computer. "Work stuff or..."

"I did some research on Molly/Kenna. I found her website, but nothing of significance relating to her past, although she does talk about her love of fire and water."

"It's part of her heritage. You're reading too much into it." She got up from the table and moved over to the refrigerator. "Do you have anything to drink?"

"Not sure. Whatever is there, help yourself."

Cassidy grabbed a bottle of lemonade and closed the door, pausing as she read the flyer on his refrigerator. "Hey, Hunter, I think you have something else to do today."

He groaned. "The chili cookoff at Golden Gate Park—I forgot. It's a fundraiser for an injured firefighter."

She came back to the table. "Did you know him or her?"

"I know him, but not well. He works out of another house. He'll be off his feet for a while, and he has three kids."

"Will he be all right?"

"Eventually. Not sure if he'll come back to work, but hopefully."

"I sometimes forget you have a very dangerous job."

"Honestly, most times it's not that dangerous."

"But it can be. Was it difficult for you to go into a fire after you got hurt?"

He thought about her question. "I was a bit tense my first day back, but that was more in anticipation. I'm well aware that a lot of people in my family think I have some kind of PTSD. Burke and Dylan watched me like hawks on my first shift. It probably would have bothered me more if I hadn't been so distracted by finding Tommy's remains."

"So, you don't have PTSD? You're not afraid of getting

caught again in a terrible situation?"

"You know what it really is?"

"No, but I'd like to," she said, meeting his gaze.

"When I fell down that elevator shaft and the fire was all around me, I didn't see my life flash before my eyes, but I did have a shocking moment of wondering if I'd done everything I wanted to do. It was weird, and the thought stayed with me throughout rehab. When I decided to travel, it was because that question was still running around in my head. It was like a constant restless refrain that I couldn't seem to get away from."

"Which is why you've been questioning whether you really want to be a firefighter."

"Yes. But I don't know if it's just the job I'm questioning, or if it's more than that." He ran a hand through his hair. "I'm sure I'll figure it out at some point. Not that I shouldn't have it figured out already. I've been in my career for seven years. It's a little late to just decide to do something else."

"It's not late at all. Being a firefighter isn't who you are; it's what you do."

"I don't know if that's true, Cassidy. When you're a firefighter, especially in my family, it's both who you are and what you do. It defines you."

"So, don't let it."

"It's not that easy."

"I didn't say it was easy. And if you want my opinion, you're looking for one simple answer, and it's more complicated than that. You probably won't be able to figure it out until you stop trying so hard."

She might have a point. "That sounds very Zen."

"I have gotten into yoga the last few years. It helps relieve my tension, stay in the moment, not worry about the past or the future. And I think maybe you need to do that, too, in regard to this big question rolling around your head. You had a near-death experience and it shook you up. It's natural for you to question your choices, the way you're living your life. But whatever you choose should be what you want. No one in your family will think differently about you if you quit."

"I wouldn't be so sure of that."

"Oh, now I get it," she said with a glint in her eyes.

"What do you get?" he asked warily.

"You don't want to look like a coward. You took the temporary job, so people won't think you're afraid to fight fire, even though you might not want to do it for a completely different reason. But first you have to prove your bravery, maybe not just to your family and friends but also to yourself. Then you can walk away."

He frowned as she very concisely articulated some of the thoughts going through his head.

"Well?" she prodded. "Am I close or way off base?"

"You might be close," he conceded.

"You're not a coward, Hunter."

"I would be a quitter. And I never quit."

"Choosing a different path isn't quitting. Has no one in your family ever left the department?"

"Aiden did. He got hurt when he was smokejumping and then he fell in love and decided he didn't want to spend so much time away from Sara."

"Do you judge him for that?"

"No, but—" He wanted to say that was different, but he couldn't. "You're good, Cassidy."

"And you'll figure things out, Hunter."

"I know I will. I've actually been rolling a crazy idea around in my head."

"Really? What is it?"

"You'll think I've lost my mind."

"I seriously doubt that. But let's hear it."

"There's a piece of land in the Santa Cruz mountains that I've had my eye on for a while. There's a big house and a barn, and the property would make a great camp for kids. It's close to the city. The ocean is nearby. There are plenty of trails for hiking, rock climbing."

"It sounds great."

"I'd like to do a couple of free weeks for underprivileged kids and then run regular sessions as well. Maybe include a camp for kids with special needs. My cousin Nicole's son Brandon is autistic, and I know camp is hard for him." He took a breath, thinking about the property. "I could get construction help from my uncle and my dad and my cousins to remodel the house and maybe even add a few other cabins. There's plenty of room." As he spoke, the excitement grew within him.

Cassidy gave him a pleased smile. "I love it. And it's perfect for you. You're great with kids. You've always been like the Pied Piper; people want to follow you. You could make an amazing camp."

He liked her unconditional support.

"But practically speaking, it would cost a lot of money just to get the land and then to remodel. I'd have to find investors, take out a loan, and what do I know about running a camp?"

"You could learn everything you need to know. And maybe you could get investors. You have a lot of connections through your family. If you include at-risk kids, there might be foundations willing to get involved as well."

"Then you don't think it's totally crazy?"

"Not even a little bit. This reminds me of how excited you were when we planned to be camp counselors in Yosemite. You used to tell me how much you loved going to camp when you were a kid."

"I do have great memories of those camps."

"Is the land for sale?"

"It's going to be. The person who owned the property recently passed away, and the family wants to sell."

"How did you find it?"

"I went through Santa Cruz on my way to South America, and on an off-road impulsive adventure, I discovered the place."

"If that's not fate, I don't know what it is," she said. "And, by the way, it's kind of funny to hear you say you went through Santa Cruz on your way to South America, as if they're anywhere close."

He grinned. "You know what I meant."

"You should do it, Hunter."

"I'll keep thinking about it. Thanks for listening."

"Always. It's not like you haven't done more than your fair share of listening to me." She paused. "Changing the subject..."

"Go ahead."

"I'm thinking that I should go home, and you should go to your fundraiser."

Frowning, he didn't like that idea at all. "I have a better idea. Why don't you come with me to the park? You can meet my friends."

"Will your family be there, too?"

"Some of them," he said with a nod, not sure why a shadow suddenly passed through her eyes. "Is that a problem?"

"They probably don't think much of me after the way I bailed on you."

"That was a long time ago, Cassidy."

"And I don't think they've forgotten. I heard you talking to your mom earlier. I could tell she was warning you not to get involved with me again."

"It wasn't exactly like that. And once I have a chance to fill them in on the part of your story they don't know, they'll understand exactly why you had to leave."

"I'll wait until that happens. I know you probably don't think it's a big deal, but I'm not up for facing a bunch of angry Callaways."

"It wouldn't be like that. They might be protective of me," he conceded. "But they would never be cruel to you."

"I'm sure you're right, but I'm feeling very...emotional right now. There's a lot going on. It's a little overwhelming."

"I get that. I'm in this thing, too. In the end, it doesn't matter what my family thinks—only what I think."

She gazed back at him, a question in her eyes. "What do

you think, Hunter? Wait. Never mind. Don't answer that."

"Why don't you want me to answer?" He was surprised by her sudden backtrack.

"Because...I'm not sure what I want you to say."

She didn't know what she wanted him to say? Why the hell not? "You want to explain that?"

"Last night, we were living in the moment, or maybe we were living in the past, I don't know. Our relationship is complicated. You told me not to overthink it, and I think...that we should just let things be and not involve any other people."

He didn't really care for the idea. "That sounds like you have one foot out the door, Cassidy."

"I wouldn't say that, but I don't know where this is going."

"Where do you want it to go?"

She couldn't seem to come up with an answer, and her shrug irritated the hell out of him. But that was Cassidy. She always kept her thoughts a secret. He hadn't realized that when they were teenagers, but he did now. "Why do you have to hide from me?"

"I'm not hiding," she snapped. "Let's not do this now. There's too much else going on. You have your fundraiser to get to, and I have things to do at my house. We can talk tomorrow."

"I start a twenty-four hour shift tomorrow at seven a.m."

"Then we'll talk Tuesday."

"Hang on," he said, getting to his feet. "Is this the way it's always going to be?"

"What do you mean?"

"You get scared. You feel cornered. And then you run. But you don't have to run away from me. You don't have to hide your thoughts." He wasn't just talking about the present; he was also talking about the past.

"You're pushing me, Hunter, and I don't like it. I don't know what this is. I don't know what I want it to be. You like to be in control of everything, but when I left before, I vowed that I would never be under someone's control ever again. I have to be able to leave when I want."

"I'm not trying to control you. I just want you to talk to me, to trust me with your feelings. The way I just trusted you when I shared something very personal. It's a two-way street."

Her gaze was pained. "I know that's the way you see it. But love is control. It's powerful. You can get lost in it. You can make stupid decisions. And it hurts like hell when it ends."

"Not all love ends."

"That hasn't been my experience."

He wanted to say that their experience would be different, but could he really promise that? They couldn't even have a deep conversation. "It hasn't been mine, either," he said. "But I think it's possible. I know it's possible. I've seen it in my own family. You saw it, too—in your parents. You told me they were happy together."

"I thought they were, but I was thirteen when they died. What did I know?"

"Don't do that. Don't rewrite their history. I understand why you're cautious. You've been through hell. And I probably only know a tiny bit of how that felt, because you don't share much."

"I know I have a problem opening up," she admitted. "If I could ever let myself trust someone, it would be you. I just don't know if I can do that, or if I can promise that I'll never get scared and run, because you're right—it is what I do, and you deserve more than that." Her eyes glittered with moisture. "I have to go, Hunter."

His lips tightened. "We're not done, Cassidy. You're still in danger, and we need to find Tommy's killer. I'm sorry I put you on the spot on the personal stuff. But don't make decisions that could put your life on the line."

"You have things to do, and so do I." She grabbed her purse and headed toward the door. "I'll call you when I get home. I'll stay off the coast road."

He followed her down the stairs to her van, regretting

that he'd let their conversation get so off track. "I don't like this, Cassidy. We should stay together."

"It will be fine."

"What about Molly? What about everything else?"

"We'll get back to all that." She drew in a breath and let it out. "I will say this. You're not wrong. I do hide my feelings. It's a habit that came from my need to survive certain situations, and it's difficult for me to change."

"I'm not trying to change you."

She gave him a pointed look.

"Well, maybe a little," he conceded. "But not a lot."

"Let's just take a little time to breathe and regroup, okay?"

He wanted to tell her he didn't need a chance to breathe, he needed her, but she'd gotten in her van, locked the door and started the engine. All he could do was step back and let her go.

He dug his hands into his pockets as he watched her leave. He was about to go into his house when out of the corner of his eye, he saw her van suddenly pull over two blocks away.

Was she crying? Was something wrong? Had she changed her mind about leaving?

After a moment's hesitation, he jogged down the block and saw her on her phone. He tapped the window, and she almost jumped out of her skin. Then she rolled it down.

"You scared me," she said.

"What's going on? Why did you stop?"

"Molly just texted me. She wants to meet."

"Well, that changes everything, doesn't it?"

"Yes, it does."

Nineteen

—➤➤◄◄◄—

Cassidy looked back at her phone, where Molly had sent her a brief but important text: *Meet me at my studio if you want to talk. I'll be there for the next hour.* An address followed.

She was surprised. There was a part of her that hadn't thought she'd ever talk to Molly again.

"Where does she want to meet?" Hunter asked.

"She'll be at her studio for the next hour. That's all she says."

"Let's go. You can drive."

"No," she said abruptly. "I need to talk to Molly on my own."

"Why? We went to the church together."

"I know, but I think she'll be more forthcoming if it's just me."

Her answer did not make him happy. "Look, Cassidy, I know that you're angry with me—"

"I think it's the other way around."

"Fine, but that doesn't matter. We can table the personal stuff and deal with Molly together."

She wasn't really that upset with him. They'd had an

honest and difficult conversation that had needed to be had, and they'd probably have another one at some point, but she didn't think he should be a part of her conversation with Molly. "Try to understand, Hunter. This isn't about us or me trying to keep secrets from you. I just think Molly will tell me more if it's just the two of us. She was skittish earlier today. I need to do this on my own."

"It could be a trap, Cassidy."

"Why would she want to trap me? Or want to hurt me? She and I were friends once. I'm the only one who looked out for her, who tried to find her. She has no motive."

"That you know of. She could be more entangled in this situation than you realize. You don't know that she hasn't spoken to David or one of the other guys. You really don't know anything except what little she told you earlier."

"That's why I need to talk to her now. I want to know exactly why she left the house, what the Faulkners did to her, what she knows about the other kids and the Faulkners' relatives. Maybe she had an interaction with Evan or Colin that would be significant."

"I understand all that, but I can't forget that someone tried to hurt you last night. I know you think I'm being too controlling, but I don't care."

The genuine concern in his eyes made her weaken. "If it will make you feel better, you can follow me to the studio. You can even walk me inside, but then you have to go. You have your fundraiser to get to anyway."

"All right. I'll take the compromise. I'll get my car. You'll wait here?"

"I'll wait."

She rolled up the window as he jogged back to his building to get his car. She texted Molly: *I'll be there in ten minutes.*

There was no answer, but she didn't really expect one. What they needed to talk about was not a conversation that should be had in a text.

She set down her phone, her nerves tingling in

anticipation. She'd spent so many years wondering what had happened to Molly; she was finally going to find out.

Hunter came up behind her in his Jeep. She put Molly's address into her GPS and pulled away from the curb. It took about fifteen minutes to get to the South of Market neighborhood where Molly's studio was located.

Her business was housed in a three-story building that appeared to be a community workspace for various designers. Since it was Sunday afternoon, there was plenty of street parking, and Hunter was able to pull into a spot directly behind her.

As they got out and walked to the front of the building, she noticed Hunter taking a long, sweeping look around the street, but it was very quiet. Most of the buildings appeared to be closed.

She hit the buzzer for Kenna Designs and Molly's voice came over the speaker.

"It's Cassidy. And Hunter. He just wants to say hello and then he's going to leave."

"All right," Molly said.

The buzzer rang, and Cassidy quickly opened the door. The lobby was small and bare, with one elevator, but she opted for the stairs since Molly's studio appeared to be on the second floor.

"Are you feeling better about this?" she asked Hunter, as they moved toward the stairs.

"Not really. I'd like to stay with you."

"I'll be okay. And you should go to your event. It's important."

"It's not as important as this."

She put a hand on his arm as they hit the first landing. "Hunter, wait. I want to get something straight."

"By all means," he said, meeting her gaze.

"I really appreciate your concern. I know you're just looking out for me. And sometimes it's hard for me to accept that someone would want to do that." She paused. "I did have a moment of panic at your house about seeing your family again, and I can't promise that I won't have another one. Hiding my thoughts is part of my armor."

"You don't need armor when you're with me."

"I know, but I'm…a work in progress," she said with a helpless shrug. "One who is really used to not sharing anything with anyone."

"I get that. I'm a work in progress, too, so you're not alone."

The tension between them dissipated as they exchanged a smile. "Let's go see Molly."

When they got to the second floor, Molly was waiting in the doorway to her studio, her long hair pulled out of its braid and now flowing around her shoulders. "I wondered what was taking you so long," she said, a wary gleam in her dark eyes.

"I was just saying good-bye to Hunter, but he wanted to come all the way up."

"You used to take a long time to say good-bye," Molly said. "I sometimes spied on the two of you from the bedroom window. I didn't know how you could kiss for so long without taking a breath. It was fairly amazing."

She flushed a little at Molly's words. "I didn't know anyone was watching."

Molly turned to Hunter. "You're still her protector, aren't you?"

"I haven't been for a long time, but I am now."

"Are you coming in then?"

"Just for a second. I'd like to see your place."

"And then Hunter is going to leave, so we can chat in private," she said, as they followed Molly into her studio.

It was basically one large room with a divider for the bedroom area, a bathroom, and a small kitchenette. Aside from the very small living space, the rest of the room was set up to be a practical workshop. There was a desk by the window with a computer and a stack of files, where she obviously did her business. On the larger tables, there were tools and materials: hammers, pliers, wire, soldering iron, boxes of beads and other miscellaneous items, as well as big lights that could be utilized for detail work. Tall floor-to-ceiling bookshelves along the other wall housed buckets of materials as well as numerous art books.

"This is cool," she said. "It feels very creative."

"It works for me," Molly replied.

"You live here, too?" Hunter asked.

"Yes. I can't afford to rent two places, and I don't need much."

"I'm going to take off," Hunter said, having satisfied himself that she would be safe in the studio. "I'll give you two some privacy."

"You don't have to leave," Molly said.

"I do," he returned. "But I'm glad you two are going to talk. Cassidy, I'll catch up with you later."

She nodded, giving him a grateful smile.

"He still likes you," Molly commented, as Hunter left the studio. "You still like him. So, are you together or not?"

"I told you earlier, we just reunited a few days ago, when Tommy's body was discovered. Hunter actually found the remains. He's a firefighter. He was venting the walls in the garage."

"That's odd and ironic, isn't it?"

"He said it felt a little fateful," she agreed.

"I remember when Tommy first showed up at the house. Hunter didn't like it much. You suddenly didn't have as much time for him."

"He was a little jealous, which was ridiculous, because Tommy and I were only friends, nothing more." She paused. "But I did use Hunter's jealousy to keep him from trying to find me after I ran away. I told him I was with Tommy. It wasn't a lie; I was supposed to be with Tommy, but he changed his mind at the last minute. I guess I could have changed mine, but I didn't. I left Hunter on the day of the prom."

"The prom? That's cold. And you were over the moon to go to the prom with him. Why did you choose that day? Why did you leave then?"

"I couldn't wait. Because I'd raised the red flag about your disappearance with the authorities, everyone in the house was angry with me. They were treating me like a nut case. There was talk of psychiatrists and sedatives. It was very scary, and then Mr. Faulkner pulled me aside and told me that he and I needed to meet privately. He wanted to take me to lunch the day of the prom, and I freaked out. I thought if I left the house with him, I'd never come back. I'd disappear just like you had. I told Tommy, and he said I needed to get out of there. I couldn't wait." She paused. "One thing I don't understand is why the Department of Children and Family Services didn't have any record of you being at the Faulkners."

"That's because I didn't go through them."

"What do you mean?"

"I met David in front of a convenience store. I was begging for money. My grandmother had gone into the hospital several weeks earlier, and the social workers had come sniffing around the apartment. I knew if they found me, they'd put me somewhere else, and I didn't want to leave my grandmother. I thought she would get better, and then I could go home. But it was taking a long time. I was hungry and scared. David told me that his parents took in foster kids. He thought they'd be willing to take me in for a few weeks and not tell anyone. He said they were very kind people. When I met Geralyn and Donald, they seemed nice, and there were other kids there. You were sweet. I thought it was going to be okay. They said they'd let me stay until my grandmother got better, that I'd be safe there." Shadows darkened Molly's eyes. "I need some coffee. Do you want some?"

"No, I'm okay." As Molly walked over to the counter and poured some coffee into a mug, Cassidy said, "I know it's difficult to talk about the past."

"I've never spoken about it with anyone," Molly said, sipping her coffee as she leaned against the counter. "I don't even know why I'm talking about it now."

"Because I'll understand. We're the same, Molly. I ran

away just like you did. I was a little older, but I was just as desperate. After that, I put the past away, and I never wanted to revisit it. But Tommy's body being discovered in that old house changed everything." She moved toward a table for two. "Can we sit?"

"Sure."

She pulled out a chair at the table and sat down, while Molly took the one across from her. "You look good, Molly—happy."

"It has taken me awhile, but I'm in a good place."

She cleared her throat, knowing she was stalling a little. "I don't want to ask, but I have to. Did Mr. Faulkner molest you? I woke up a couple of times at night, and you weren't there, but when I woke up in the morning, you would be back in your bed—except for the last time."

"I was...molested." She stumbled over the word, then squared her shoulders. "That's why I left."

"I'm so sorry."

"I just want to forget about the past. I don't want to be involved in any of this. I called you because I wanted to make sure you didn't tell anyone else you found me. You didn't, did you?"

"I didn't."

"Not even the police?"

"No. But they're going to want to hear from you."

"I have nothing to say. I was out of the house before Tommy died, so I don't know how it happened or who was involved. I'm sad that he lost his life there, but I'm not completely surprised. There was evil in that house. Thank God, both of us escaped."

"We were lucky." She paused. "And I understand your desire to stay out of this, but we might need you to help us figure out the totality of what was going on."

"Does it matter? Tommy is dead."

"I want justice for him."

"You, of all people, should know there is no justice."

"I think there can be."

"Well, I don't. And I have nothing to add."

"David suggested that Donald's brother Evan or Evan's son Colin might have been angry with Tommy over video games. Did you ever witness that?"

"No, but I tried to stay away from both of them. I didn't like them. I didn't like anyone, except for you. The younger girls were all right, but they were tight with each other. The boys were stupid, making dumb jokes, saying mean things." Molly shuddered. "That place was awful. I wish to God I had never met David, that I had never gone with him to that house. And I was so wrong about the Faulkners. They were nothing close to nice." She took another sip of her coffee. "You said you saw all the guys last night?"

"Yes. They wanted me to join with them in trying to protect Mrs. Faulkner from whatever might be coming her way. David used the pretense of wanting to plan a memorial for Tommy to get me there. But as soon as I expressed my conviction that Mrs. Faulkner was guilty of murder, everyone got very hostile, especially Jeremiah. I also couldn't help reminding them that they had lied about your existence."

"Did they own up to the lie?"

"No. They doubled down. Said I'd made you up. I told them I had proof, and I put my hand on this necklace." She mimicked her action from the night before.

Molly's gaze filled with worry. "I wish you hadn't brought me up. Did you tell them about the jewelry store, about my new name?"

"I didn't tell them anything. I just implied I knew more than they did. It was a bad decision. Someone followed me home last night and tried to run me off the road, just the way they probably did to Mr. Faulkner." As she made the statement, she remembered Hunter suggesting that Molly had been the one to ram her car from behind but seeing the shock on Molly's face now put that idea out of her head.

"I can't believe it. Someone tried to kill you?" Molly asked. "This is getting worse and worse. You need to back away, Cassidy. If you want to bury Tommy and mourn him, do that. Don't try to solve his murder. Don't work with those guys. You can't trust them."

"Believe me, I do not trust them. I barely trust anyone."

"Except Hunter."

"Except him," she agreed.

"So, what do you do now?" Molly asked. "If you'll let me change the subject."

"I'm a landscape designer. I work at a nursery."

Molly suddenly smiled, her first real smile since they'd reconnected. "That's perfect. You loved flowers so much."

"It is perfect. An older couple took me in when I was nineteen, taught me the business, and I love it. We both found a way to start over."

"Yes. The church really helped me. One of the older women counseled me on letting go, allowing myself to be reborn, cleansing my soul of all the darkness. It's finally working. I'm starting to feel free. It's amazing how long the ties of hatred lasted for me. So many years of nightmares. But now I'm starting to feel like I can breathe again. I can do what I was born to do."

"Your jewelry is beautiful." She touched her necklace again. "When I saw this, I thought of you. I had to have it."

"Was it just by chance you went to that store?"

"We went to a bunch of stores before that one. All I could remember about you was your silver-turquoise necklace and how you said your grandmother Lily used to work in a shop in San Francisco that sold a lot of Native American-inspired jewelry. So, Hunter and I went looking for such a store on the off chance that we could find it and maybe locate someone who knew your grandmother or knew you. I have to admit I was afraid I was going to find out you were dead."

Molly looked amazed by her words. "I can't believe you went to all that trouble."

"I couldn't do anything to move the police investigation along into Tommy's death, so I went back to you. You were the big question in my head all these years. But even when we found the jewelry store on Union Street, I didn't know you were Kenna. The clerk—Helen—just said her daughter had found you. She didn't seem to know that you were related to Lily or Molly. She told us to go to the church where your grandmother volunteered."

"Helen doesn't know that Kenna is Molly. I wanted to sell my jewelry in that store, but not as Lily's granddaughter."

"I understand. I changed my last name, not my first, although that made me a lot easier to find. Not that I really thought anyone would look for me after I turned eighteen, but keeping secrets was part of my survival plan."

"Mine, too."

"Your grandmother would be proud that you've carried on her traditions."

"I'm just glad she never knew what happened to me. She died while I was at the Faulkners' house. I didn't know it until I left. I missed seeing her by two days. Maybe that was for the best."

"She didn't know you would be left alone when she got sick?"

"She thought she'd get better, but she didn't."

"Why didn't you go to the church in the first place, instead of asking David to take you to the Faulkners?"

"I did go to the church, but the first person I spoke to immediately got on the phone to the police to find out where I should go. So, I ran. For some stupid reason, I thought I would have more control over the situation if I stayed at the Faulkners. That was a mistake. Anyway, when I went back the second time, I managed to get to one of my grandmother's friends, who was willing to take me in, hide me away. I was very grateful to her." She let out a heavy breath. "It's been good seeing you, but I don't think we should talk again, Cassidy."

"Why?" she asked, disappointed by Molly's words.

"Because we'll only remind each other of the pain."

"We could find a way to a new friendship. I'm not interested in rehashing those days. Once is enough. I just needed some answers. We can move on."

"Maybe. Let's see how things go. I definitely don't want to be a part of the investigation into Tommy's death, so when that's over, let me know."

"All right. I can understand that."

"And you won't tell anyone who I am or where I am?"

"I won't," she promised.

"What about Hunter?"

"He'll keep your secret. He'll understand why you want to stay out of it. And like you said, there's nothing you can add that will help since you weren't there when Tommy died."

"Exactly." Molly stood up. "You should go. Hunter is waiting."

"No, he's not. He was going to a fundraiser. He just wanted to make sure that you weren't trying to lure me into some sort of trap, so he wanted to walk me up here."

Molly gave her an odd look. "Why would he think that?"

"Because of what happened last night on the Pacific Coast Highway."

"Right. That makes sense. That makes me even more certain he's waiting downstairs." Molly smiled. "Maybe this is your second chance with him, Cassidy."

"I don't know. We're good together, but I have a lot of baggage."

"Everyone does. It's nice when you can find someone willing to hold the bags."

"I'll have to remember that."

"Good-bye, Cassidy."

"Can we just say see you later?" She didn't like the finality of Molly's words.

"Okay. See you later."

"Definitely." She wanted to hug Molly, but she felt like her friend still had too many walls up to be comfortable with that. So, she just smiled and left.

When she walked out of the building, she found Hunter sitting on the front steps, just as Molly had predicted. He jumped to his feet when he saw her.

"I told you to go to the cook-off," she said.

"This is a deserted area; I wasn't going to do that. How did it go in there?"

"Not bad."

"Not bad doesn't sound great," he murmured, a questioning glint in his eyes.

"It was good. We talked. She told me she was molested; that's why she ran away. She also said David met her when she was homeless, and he asked his parents to take her in until her grandmother got out of the hospital. They agreed, without filing any formal paperwork. I guess that's why David and the Faulkners denied she was ever there. They didn't want to get in trouble and jeopardize the rest of their foster care business. Anyway, Molly doesn't want to be involved in any of this. She made me promise not to tell anyone I'd found her, not even the police, and I agreed."

"Why would you do that?"

"Because Molly was gone before Tommy was killed. She can't help with that case, and she has suffered enough. She has made a new life for herself, and she doesn't need to be dragged back down into the darkness. I understand that. If she could help us find Tommy's killer, I wouldn't keep silent, but she can't."

"I see your point, but she does have knowledge of everyone at the house."

"No more than I do. Can I count on you to back me up on this?"

"I'll agree for now, but I might change my mind. If I do, I will tell you before I tell anyone else."

"All right. I'll take that. You should go to your fundraiser now."

"I really hate to let you make that drive home on your own."

"There's no one here." She waved her hand toward the empty street. "No one is watching us. No one is following me. I'll stay on the busy freeways."

"And you'll text me when you get home?"

"I will. You can't watch over me twenty-four seven, Hunter. You have a job, and so do I. And I'm not going to stop living my life. The Faulkners already took too much from me; I'm not giving them anymore."

"At this point, I don't think it's the Faulkners we need to be worried about."

"Well, if it was one of the guys who took Geralyn who came after me last night, then they don't have anything more to fear from me. I can't speak out about a woman who isn't in custody."

"Sure you can. You can shout your story to the rooftops. You can go to the press. You can cause all kinds of trouble. Don't get complacent, Cassidy. You have good survival instincts. Keep those sharp."

"I will. I won't underestimate anyone."

He walked her to her van. "Do you think you and Molly will see each other again?"

"I'd like to see her. She seemed leery about the idea of us being friends. She thinks we'll just remind each other of the bad stuff, but I believe we could start fresh. Maybe after all of this is over, and Geralyn is in jail, then we'll be free to try again. But even if that doesn't happen, I'm just thrilled that she's alive. That's all that matters. Now, you should go." She started to push him away, but he captured her hand and pressed it against his heart.

Then he lowered his head and kissed her. And despite her earlier intentions to put some space between them, she was immediately lost when his mouth touched hers. She couldn't help but kiss him back. The pull between them was impossible to fight. Her head might be on one page, but her heart and her body were on another.

When they finally let go of each other, she gave him a helpless smile. "I hope Molly didn't see that. She'll think I really didn't change at all. I still can't give you anything but the longest kiss good-bye."

He grinned back at her. "That wasn't one of our longer good-byes, by any means."

"No, but just because we want each other doesn't mean we should have each other."

"It doesn't mean we shouldn't, either. But that's a conversation for another day." He opened her door, so she could get inside. "Lock this and text me when you're safe."

"I will." As she climbed into the van and started the engine, Hunter waited on the sidewalk, and his concern touched her heart. Actually, it wasn't just his concern; it was everything about him: the way he pushed her to be everything she could be, the way he smiled, teased, kissed, loved... *Maybe they could be together.*

It seemed like an impossible dream. *And when had her dreams ever come true?*

Emotional tears blurred her eyes, and she blinked them away. She suspected there might be crying to come later; she wasn't going to start now.

Twenty

———➤➤❮❮❮←———

Monday was filled with fire calls, training drills, and more fire calls. Hunter exchanged several texts with Cassidy, and everything seemed to be fine with her. She'd had no problems getting home the night before, and she was busy working at the estate with two of her coworkers, so he didn't have to worry that she was alone.

But he was still concerned. She might think that Geralyn's escape had taken the interest off her, but he wasn't so sure. And he wasn't going to relax until Geralyn was recaptured and whoever had taken her was arrested. Unfortunately, that didn't seem like it would happen any time soon. He'd already bothered Max several times, and there were no new leads.

As he wandered into the kitchen, looking to grab a late afternoon snack, he was surprised to run into Kate. "Hey, what are you doing here?"

"I wanted to check in before I take off."

"Take off? I thought you were here for the week."

"There's a case I need to consult on down in LA. I'll be back Thursday.

"That's good. How was the weekend?"

"It was great. We had so much fun. Female power."

He smiled. "There's plenty of that in our family."

"Plenty of testosterone, too," she said dryly. "I didn't want you to think I'd forgotten about the favor you asked me. I had a coworker put in the information you gave me, but while she came up with the girl's grandmother, who is now deceased, as you mentioned, we weren't able to find any reference to Molly Bennett after the age of fourteen. No school records, no DMV, no credit cards—nothing. But I will keep looking. I have some other ideas on how we might be able to find her."

He felt guilty that he hadn't thought to update Kate. "We found out yesterday that Molly changed her name. I should have called you last night. I'm sorry. There has been a lot going on."

"Like what?"

"Cassidy and I actually tracked Molly down through her grandmother's jewelry-making business."

"Whoa! You found her?" Kate asked in surprise. "Seriously?"

"You're not the only detective in the family. However, there was some luck involved."

"That's amazing. She's alive and well then."

"Yes."

"Is this woman going to be able to help the current case?"

"No. Molly left the house before Tommy was killed, so she has no idea who was responsible for that, but Cassidy had always wondered what happened to her, and she was thrilled to find out she's alive, especially after what happened to Tommy. I feel badly that I didn't text you to stop working on my favor."

She gave him a careless shrug. "It wasn't that big of a deal, and I meant to call you last night, too, but Mia and Annie and I started talking with Mom when we got back, and things went late into the night."

"I'm sure Mom loved having her girls around."

"She did. The one good thing about a wedding is that it brings the family together."

"This family rarely needs an excuse," he said with a laugh.

"True. I'm going to take off. But before I go, can I just ask—"

"No. You can't ask."

"Come on, Hunter, I'm curious."

"You're always curious. But you can't ask, because I can't answer. I don't know what's going on with Cassidy."

"Except that you still have feelings for her."

"Except that," he admitted. "Everything else is a big question mark."

Kate's mixed feelings showed in her gaze. "I want you to be happy and if that's Cassidy, that's great, but—"

"But you can keep your thoughts to yourself. It's my life, Kate."

"I know, and you're stubborn."

"Like you."

"And the rest of our family," she agreed.

"Speaking of the rest of our family," he said, as Max came down the hall.

"Hunter, Kate," Max said.

"What are you doing here?" he asked. "If you're making a personal call, this can't be good. It's not about Cassidy is it?"

"Not directly."

"Mrs. Faulkner? Have you found her?"

"No, but there has been a development." Max gave him a somber look. "Jeremiah Hunt, one of the individuals we interviewed—"

"I know Jeremiah. Cassidy and I met with him the other night. What happened?"

"I wanted to check back in with him this morning, go over some of the things he'd told us in our previous interview. I also wanted to take a look at his car after the incident on the coast highway the other night. Since Jeremiah owns an auto shop and is very familiar with cars and has in fact done some racing, I thought he might—"

"Be a good candidate for having tried to run Cassidy off the road," he finished. "Great thinking, Max."

"Thank you," Max said dryly. "I do have some skills when it comes to investigation."

"I know. Sorry. What did you find out?"

"There was an SUV in the shop with damage to the front bumper."

His pulse jumped. "Then he did it. Jeremiah tried to kill Cassidy. Did you arrest him?"

"No. Unfortunately, I found him unconscious in his office at the shop. He'd OD'd. He's still alive, but barely. He's in a coma."

"But he's going to survive, right? He's going to go to jail for this?"

"I don't know. Currently, he's in critical condition. And before you ask, we have a guard on his room, who will not be drinking any liquids provided by anyone other than himself, so no chance of a repeat on what happened with Mrs. Faulkner. We're not going to lose Jeremiah. I'll stand by his door myself if I have to."

"I'd sure like to hear what he has to say—if he did it on his own, or if he was put up to it. I have to believe that David and/or Quan have stashed Mrs. Faulkner somewhere."

"David was actually in his office today. I spoke to him before coming here. He has solid alibis for when Mrs. Faulkner left the hospital, and he expressed a great deal of concern as to who might have taken the woman he calls Mom. He suggested again that Mr. Faulkner's brother, Evan, might be involved in this. We have not been able to locate him yet. Quan Tran has also disappeared off the radar, but we're working on finding him as well."

"I keep thinking this is almost over, but the goalposts keep moving."

"They do," Max agreed.

"Thanks for the update."

"No problem. Are you butting in on my case?" Max

asked, turning to Kate.

She made a face at him. "As if I would do that without telling you."

"Are you telling me now?"

"No. But if you need assistance, I'd be happy to give it. I was just helping Hunter look for that missing girl, but I guess that has been resolved."

Max's eyebrow shot up. "Who are you talking about? The girl that Cassidy said went missing from the home, the one that no one else remembered? You found her, Hunter?"

He realized too late he should have told Kate to keep her mouth shut. Cassidy had made him promise not to divulge Molly's whereabouts. He needed to be careful. He couldn't leave Max hanging, but he also couldn't betray Cassidy's trust. It would only push her further away at a time when he was trying to bring her closer.

"Yes. It was a lucky break. We found her through a church that Cassidy remembered the girl's grandmother attending. We went there yesterday. It turns out that Molly ran away from the Faulkners' house. She'd only been staying there temporarily, so that's why there wasn't a record of her being assigned to the house."

"But that doesn't explain why the family claimed she didn't exist." Max's brows pulled together in a frown. "Why didn't you tell me this earlier, Hunter?"

"I should have. It slipped my mind," he hedged.

Max gave him a disbelieving look. "That didn't happen."

He ran a hand through his hair and cleared his throat. "There has been a lot going on. Molly doesn't know anything about Tommy. She left before he was killed. She doesn't have anything to contribute to the case."

"She lived in the house, just like the other kids; I'd like to talk to her. Where can I find her?"

As Max's question hung in the air, the alarm bells went off, and he'd never been so happy to get a call. "We'll have to talk later," he told Max.

"We better," Max said, a warning expression in his eyes.

"You can't hold back on me, Hunter. Let me decide what's important to know."

"Sure," he said. "I will fill you in as soon as I get back. Kate, I'll see you soon."

She nodded, looking a bit perturbed by the conversation she'd just witnessed. She could tell he was being purposefully vague, just as Max could. But he couldn't worry about either of them now.

He put on his gear and jumped on board the truck, as they raced toward a three-alarm fire in a retail building. Smoke was visible almost five blocks away. This was going to be a big one, and he would need to concentrate on the fire and nothing else. It wouldn't be easy to put Cassidy out of his mind, but it was necessary. He just hoped that Max didn't talk to her before he had a chance to explain how he'd let Molly's existence come out after Cassidy had expressly asked him to keep the secret. He wanted her to trust him, and he'd already blown it. Hopefully, he could find a way to make it right.

—➤➤◄◄—

Cassidy didn't hear about the fire that had consumed half of a city block until Tuesday morning when she turned on the news while she was getting dressed for work. She'd gone to bed early the night before after an exhausting day of work and having had too many sleepless nights in a row.

As she watched the video report, she could see several crews were still on the scene, making sure that the fire that had started in a paint store and wiped out three other buildings was finally out. She squinted, wondering if she might see Hunter in the shot, but it was impossible to identify any of the firefighters.

Glancing at her watch, she saw it was almost eight. Hunter had said he'd be off at seven, but maybe the fire had put everyone on overtime.

Now she knew why she hadn't heard from him the night before.

Picking up her phone, she realized she had a missed call, but it wasn't from Hunter; it was from Max. She checked her voicemail and Max's voice come across the line with disturbing news.

"I heard you located your missing friend," he said. "Please call me back; I'd like to talk to you."

She felt a sinking pit in her stomach. *Hunter had told Max after she'd deliberately asked him not to?* A wave of betrayal swept through her. Hunter wanted her to trust him, but he'd just shown her that she couldn't. It was the one thing she'd asked him not to do.

Opening up her messages again, she typed in a text to Hunter: *Why did you tell Max about Molly?* Then she hit Send.

Her phone rang a moment later.

"It's not what you think," Hunter said. "I didn't bring up Molly's name to Max."

"Then who did? He left me a voicemail last night. Luckily, I didn't see it until just now. You could have given me a heads-up. What if I'd answered the phone? I would have been blindsided."

"I know. I saw Max at the station late yesterday afternoon, right before I went out on a call that lasted all night. We just got back ten minutes ago. I didn't have a second to send you a text. I didn't intentionally tell him about Molly."

She heard the weariness in his voice, but she was too angry to care at the moment. "So, what happened?"

"Kate was at the station when Max came by. She wanted to give me an update on her search for Molly. Remember when I asked her to use her FBI resources to help us?"

"Yes. I forgot about that."

"Well, Kate hadn't found anything on Molly and was very curious as to what happened to the girl and was ready to keep looking. I had to stop her. I had to say something. I told her that we'd gotten a lucky break and had tracked Molly down through her grandmother. But I didn't give her Molly's name, phone number, or address, and Kate didn't ask. Unfortunately, Max arrived, and when he jokingly asked Kate if she was going to stick her FBI nose into his case, she said—"

"That she was helping you find Molly," she finished, a bit of her anger receding.

"Exactly. I told Max what you said, that Molly had left the house weeks before Tommy was killed, that she didn't know anything, but he said he still wanted to interview her. Luckily, the fire call came in, and I didn't have to give him any more information. If I'd had time, I would have told you he was probably going to call. I know you want to protect Molly, but I don't know if you'll be able to keep her identity or whereabouts a secret."

"Probably not now. I made her a promise, Hunter."

"I shouldn't have told Kate, but I wasn't thinking that it would matter if she knew."

"I guess I understand."

"What are you going to tell Max when you call him back?"

"I'm not going to call him back yet. I have work to do. Let's see what happens today. Maybe they'll find Mrs. Faulkner, and he won't need to talk to Molly."

"Did he tell you about Jeremiah in his message?"

"Jeremiah?" she echoed. "No. What about him?"

"Max went to talk to him at his auto shop. He wanted to see if his car looked like it might have had some front-end damage, which it did. He's the one who ran you off the road."

Her heart skipped a beat. "It was Jeremiah? Is he in jail, I hope?"

"No, he's in the hospital. He OD'd yesterday morning. Max said he's in critical condition and currently unconscious. At least, that was his status last night."

"Once again, we're waiting for someone to wake up. He'd better not disappear from the hospital, too."

"Max also talked to David yesterday. He said David was very cooperative, but he claimed to know nothing. He also has an alibi for when Mrs. Faulkner disappeared."

"He could have hired someone to get her out of the hospital. Or maybe Jeremiah did it."

"Why don't we meet? We can talk through all this. I just need to go home and shower."

"You probably need to sleep," she said, feeling guilty that she'd forced him to deal with all this when he was obviously exhausted. "You were up all night."

"Sleep can wait. I can meet you in an hour."

"No. I have a lot going on this morning. I have a meeting with a bride and then I need to get out to the Holman's estate. Let's meet later today—tonight."

"You're angry. I let you down."

"I'm not thrilled, but I get it, Hunter. You didn't deliberately betray me."

"I really didn't. I hope you understand that."

"You rest. I'll work, and then we'll get together. Okay? I have to go. I have a meeting. Bye." She ended the call quickly, knowing that any further conversation at this moment would not be productive. While she could see how Hunter had let the information slip out, she still wasn't happy about it. He might have put Molly in danger or back on the run. She wondered if she should contact Molly and warn her that the police might get in touch.

But Hunter had said that Max did not have Molly's real name, and if she didn't call Max back, then Molly would probably stay safely hidden away for a while longer. Maybe once Geralyn was located, Max's need to speak to Molly would go away.

She probably had a little time before she needed to tell Molly she'd broken her promise. Well, Hunter had broken the promise, but that wasn't going to matter to Molly. And she really wanted to keep open the possibility of a future friendship with Molly, so maybe she'd wait.

As she stood up, she thought about the other piece of news that Hunter had delivered. Jeremiah had overdosed. *Had it been deliberate? Had he been suicidal because he'd realized he'd almost killed her? Or because he had guilt over killing Tommy?* Maybe he was afraid he was about to get caught. She couldn't believe the timing of the overdose was a coincidence.

Picking up her phone again, she called David. She didn't trust him at all, and she might be baiting the tiger, but she was curious to hear what he had to say.

"Cassidy? How are you?" David asked, answering her call on the second ring.

"Did you hear about Jeremiah?"

"Hear what? I haven't spoken to him since Saturday night."

"He overdosed yesterday. He's in the hospital."

"What?" Surprise laced his voice. It sounded genuine, but how could she be sure? "Will he be all right?"

"I don't know. It sounded serious. I thought you or Quan might have more information—not just about Jeremiah, but also about Geralyn. I heard she escaped from the hospital with some help."

"And you probably think it was me, but it wasn't. I already spoke to the police about it. I don't know who took Mom, but my gut tells me it was Evan. He's probably afraid she's going to tell the police that he killed Tommy. I'm really worried about her. I've been trying to think of where Evan would take her. Do you have any ideas?"

"No. I don't know anything about him."

"He liked the mountains. I was thinking he might have headed up to the Sierras, maybe some isolated cabin in Tahoe."

"I'm sure the police will look for him."

"I hope they find him before..." His voice trailed away. "I know you don't share my grief, but Geralyn was the only mother I really remember. I was so young when my real mom died."

"Which is why I think you know where she is now."

"I really don't. I wish I did, because I think Evan will kill her in order to shut her up."

His theory made some sense, but she didn't know what to believe. "You're a good talker, David, but you're also a good liar. I saw that when you lied about Molly all those years ago."

"I don't know how many times I have to tell you that that girl didn't exist."

"Really? You didn't meet her by a convenience store and take her to the house?" She realized too late she'd just given a big clue away.

"Who told you that?" he asked sharply.

"Molly did. When we were sharing a room. I didn't remember until recently."

"Are you sure she told you that a long time ago? Did you find Molly?"

"How would I find Molly if she doesn't exist?" she countered.

He cleared his throat. "You're the liar, Cassidy. That was made clear years ago. You have mental issues. It's understandable. A lot of foster kids have problems."

"You might have made me believe that just a little when I was sixteen, but I'm not that girl anymore. And if you had something to do with Geralyn's escape from the hospital, with Tommy's death, with anything that happened to Molly, the truth will come out."

"I'm not worried about the truth, but you should be."

His words sent a chill down her spine. "What does that mean?"

"Maybe the people you think are your friends are not."

"Could you be more vague?"

"We're done talking, Cassidy. Don't call me again."

"Trust me, I won't."

David broke the connection, robbing her of the chance to hang up on him. Fuming, she paced around the room, mad at herself for giving away what Molly had told her about the convenience store. Hopefully, she'd covered it up. David couldn't really be sure when Molly had told her that, but he was definitely suspicious. *Was that because he knew Molly*

*had run away? He knew Donald had molested her? Would
David go after Molly if he thought she was also a threat to
Geralyn, someone else who might have a story to tell that
would hurt the Faulkners?*

Rolling her head around on her shoulders, she let out a
sigh that turned into a groan. Everything was getting too
complicated. Maybe she should get back to work and leave
the investigation to the detectives.

Grabbing her keys, she put her phone in her pocket and
went downstairs to the shop. When Felicia saw her, she gave
her a rather urgent wave.

An older man stood at the counter. He was in his fifties
or sixties. He wore faded jeans and a black T-shirt and had
light-brown, thinning hair. He looked a little familiar, and
when he turned his head, she knew why. It was Donald's
younger brother—Evan.

Her stomach flipped over in shock and dismay.

"Cassidy," he said.

"What are you doing here?" she bit out.

"Looking for you." Anger blazed through his eyes. "We
need to talk about what you've been saying to the police."

"Cassidy, should I call someone?" Felicia asked
nervously.

She actually didn't know how to answer that question.
Evan's face was red, his eyes were jumpy, and his hands were
clenched in fists. He looked like he was about to snap. But he
wasn't going to hurt her in the middle of the store with
witnesses around.

"It's okay," she said, not wanting to involve Felicia in her
personal problems. "Come with me," she told Evan, leading
him into the small room they used for wedding flower
consultations. "Why don't you tell me what you're talking
about?"

"I just spoke to the cops," he said. "They think I killed
some kid fourteen years ago. They think I might have killed
my own brother, too. They said the children who used to live
in the house have all pointed their fingers at me. I need that to

stop."

"Well, I didn't point my finger at you. I don't know who killed Tommy, but my money is on Donald."

"My brother wouldn't have murdered a kid. You're crazy."

"Well, that kid ended up in the walls of your brother's very private garage. How on earth could he have not known about it? Donald was in there all the time." She paused, thinking maybe Evan wasn't such a long shot suspect. He was boiling over with anger, which didn't seem like the reaction of a completely innocent man. "You were in there with him quite a bit. Even Colin got in there, when none of the other kids could."

"You need to shut up." He waved a finger at her, as he moved forward.

Now she was sorry she'd invited him into the very small room. There was nowhere for her to run.

"I do not need this kind of shit," he yelled. "And don't go talking to the police about Colin, either. If you do, you're going to be sorry."

"Is that a threat?" She squared her shoulders and lifted her chin, trying not let him intimidate her, but he was a very scary man at the moment.

"It's a fact." And with those final words, he left the room, slamming the door behind him.

She let out a breath and put a hand on the desk behind her to steady her nerves. She might not have thought Evan was capable of killing someone before, but she did now.

Was David right? Was she wrong about the Faulkners? Was it Donald's brother who was the evil one?

She pulled out her phone and called Hunter. It rang four times, then went to voicemail. He was probably in the shower or asleep. She really wanted to talk to him, but the man was no doubt exhausted, and as soon as she told him what had happened with Evan, he'd jump in his car and drive to Half Moon Bay.

But knowing if she didn't leave a message, he'd only

worry more at the missed call, she said, "Call me later when you wake up. Evan—Donald's brother came by the nursery. We had an interesting conversation. I want to tell you about it." Hopefully, that would bring a call back but wouldn't send Hunter's blood pressure through the roof. She thought about calling Max next and telling him about Evan, but that would bring questions up about Molly.

She was tangled up in too many secrets, which was not where she wanted to be. Instead of calling Max, she tried Molly. Maybe she needed to let her know that everything was starting to unravel, so Molly could be prepared. Again, she ended up with voicemail. Again, she left a short message. "Call me back, Molly. There are some things you need to know. It's important."

The door opened, and she jumped, but thankfully it was just Felicia.

"Are you all right? Who was that man?" Felicia asked.

"Someone I knew a long time ago. And I'm fine. If he comes back, call the police."

"I will. But I'm wondering if I should call the police right now. Are you in some kind of trouble, Cassidy?"

"Nothing I can't handle," she said, wondering if that was even remotely close to being true.

"You're sure?"

"I'm positive."

"Okay, then. Pamela Baker is here for her wedding consult. Are you ready? Or do you need a minute?"

"I'm fine. Send her in." She'd talk about flowers for the next hour, which would calm her nerves, and then she'd drive up to the Holman Estate and work on her garden. Everything else could wait.

Twenty-One

—→⫸⫷←—

Hunter woke up at two o'clock on Tuesday afternoon. He couldn't believe he'd slept for so long. Checking his phone, he realized he had a voicemail from Cassidy. It had come in several hours ago. In fact, she'd called him back shortly after he'd spoken to her. That didn't seem good.

Her voice came over the speaker, and her words made him feel even worse. *Evan Faulkner—Donald's brother—had shown up at the nursery? How had he found her? And what the hell had he wanted?* She'd referred to it as an interesting conversation, but there had been a note of concern in her voice.

He immediately called her back but was frustrated when she didn't answer. They were certainly missing each other today. When he got her voicemail, he said, "Call me as soon as you can. Let's meet up when you're done with work."

Setting down his phone, he wandered around his apartment for a half hour, eating a bowl of cereal, checking his email, changing his clothes, and then decided he was done waiting around. Cassidy had said she'd be working at the estate today. He'd go there first, and if she wasn't there, he'd drive to Half Moon Bay.

It had been too long since he'd seen her. He missed her, and he was worried about her. They had a lot to talk about, but mostly he just wanted to see her. He had never felt so connected to a woman as he did to her. She was constantly in his thoughts. He wanted her to be the first person he spoke to in the morning and the last person he spoke to before he went to sleep.

He just didn't know if she wanted that, too. He thought she did, but she was scared. She was afraid to go for everything she wanted, because she didn't want to fail. She didn't want to get hurt.

The last thing he wanted to do was hurt her, but she was going to have to find a way to trust him, or their relationship would never work.

Grabbing his keys, he headed out the door. When he got to the sidewalk, he saw a familiar figure walking toward him. It wasn't Cassidy; it was Lindsay.

He inwardly groaned. He'd thought he'd made his feelings clear to her.

"Hi, Hunter." She gave him a tentative smile.

"What are you doing here?"

"I have some information that I thought you might want."

He thought her information was just a ploy to see him again, but he couldn't take the chance that it wasn't. "What is it?"

"Can we go inside and talk?"

"I'm on my way out. I only have a minute, but if it's important, I'd like to hear it."

She stared back at him, disappointment in her eyes. "All right. I was at my mom's house earlier today, and we were talking about the fire. It's really strange living next to that burned-down house and knowing someone was killed like ten feet away from my bedroom window."

"I'm sure that is strange and uncomfortable."

"When I was leaving, I went into our side yard. There's a gate between our properties. I figured the police have finished their investigation, so I wasn't disturbing anything."

"And..." he prodded.

"I found something in the dirt. It was actually on our side of the gate. It made me think that the person who set the fire had gone through our backyard. They probably came over the back fence. That's why no one on the street saw them."

"What did you find?" he asked, impatient for her to get to the point.

She pulled something silver out of her pocket. "This."

He looked at the dangly silver earring, and his heart began to pound.

"Do you recognize it? Do you think it means anything?" Lindsay asked.

As he lifted his gaze to hers, he saw something in her eyes that made him wonder if she'd really found the earring in the yard or if it was just one of hers. "I don't know if it means anything. But the police need to see it. Why didn't you call them?"

"Because I know you and Cassidy are working together, and, well, I didn't want to take it to the police on the off chance that it was hers."

"What?" he asked. "What are you trying to say? You think Cassidy set that fire? That she lost her earring in the process?"

"She told me once that Tommy had suggested they just burn the house down, so they could all go somewhere else. I'm not saying she killed Tommy. I know she didn't do that. But maybe she decided to put their old plan into action."

Now he was glad Lindsay hadn't gone to the police with that story. He also wished her words didn't echo what Cassidy had already told him. It gave her idea more weight. He took the earring out of her palm, before she could close her fingers. "I'll ask her if this is hers."

"She'd probably deny it if it is. Unless you don't tell her where it was found. That would make her less suspicious."

"I know what to tell her. And I can read her pretty well."

"Can you?" Lindsay challenged. "You didn't know she

was going to leave you the day of the prom."

"I was younger then."

"I don't understand why you're being so nice to her, Hunter. She hurt you. I was there. I listened to you practically cry about her. How do you just forgive her?"

"I now know more about her circumstances back then."

"And that gives her a pass on the pain?"

"Not a pass, but maybe some forgiveness."

"I don't get it," she said, shaking her head in bewilderment. "She treats you like dirt, and you take her back. And I was nothing but nice to you, and you act like I'm the enemy."

"You were a good friend to me, Lindsay. You were nice." He wanted to find a way to lessen her anger. "And I'm not trying to treat you like the enemy."

"We were more than friends, Hunter," she said, moisture appearing in her eyes. "I loved you. I think now that you're the reason I've never fallen for anyone else. You took my heart, and I never got it back."

"I cared about you, too, Lindsay. You helped me through a tough year." He paused. "But I wasn't in love with you in high school, and I'm not in love with you now. You deserve someone who will put you at the center of their world, and that person isn't me. I'm sorry. I don't want to hurt you, but that's the truth."

"So, it's still Cassidy? She's the one?"

"I think so."

"She's not going to make you happy, Hunter. She can't. She's a broken person, and, ultimately, she'll always choose to protect herself first. Is that really what you want?"

"I don't know. It's not a choice between you and her. Even if she wasn't around, I still wouldn't be the right person for you. And I'm a little surprised you would think differently. What's going on with you, Lindsay? We've been living in the same city for years. Why the sudden rush now to get back into my life? I'm missing something. What is it? Why are you so unhappy and angry?" He paused. "These emotions aren't really about me, are they? What happened to you?"

She shifted her weight and wiped her eyes with her fingers. "I was engaged last year. It ended badly. He cheated on me. Everyone told me I was lucky to find out before the wedding, but it didn't feel like luck; it felt awful. When Mom said she saw you, I remembered what a good person you were, and I thought if you were still single, I should see if there was anything left between us. Maybe we could try again."

For the first time, he felt like he was seeing the real Lindsay again. "I'm sorry that happened to you. I wish it hadn't."

"Me, too."

"But I'm not the one who's going to make it all better."

She drew in a breath and let it out. "I know. I feel like a big idiot for pushing so hard to get you to see me again. You must feel like I'm stalking you. I've been going through a lot of depression the last few months, and I just haven't been handling my life very well."

"We all go through rough times."

"I'm sorry. Anyway, that's it. I won't bother you again."

"Did you really find this earring in the yard?"

"I really did. And I still think it's possible Cassidy burned the house down. I wouldn't actually blame her for that. I know she had a hard time there. But I'll let you two figure it out while I try to get back to my life."

"You're going to be okay, Lindsay."

"I hope so." She gave him a watery smile. "You're a good person, Hunter. But you're a one-woman man, and you found your woman a long time ago. Maybe you will have your happily ever after. Good-bye."

"Bye," he muttered, as she walked down the street to her car.

Closing his fingers around the earring, he headed toward his Jeep, mixed emotions running through him. It felt like he and Lindsay had finally come to an understanding, a place of truth, but he still wasn't sure about the earring, and he didn't think it belonged to Cassidy.

As he got in the car, he set the earring down on the console. The silver caught the light, reminding him of the jewelry he'd seen in Molly's studio.

His pulse leapt. *Had Molly burned down the house? Was that the real reason why she'd begged Cassidy not to tell the police about her?*

He started the engine and pulled into the street. He needed to find Cassidy. They had a lot to talk about.

"That's it," Cassidy said, brushing the dirt off her hands, as she surveyed the plants that her coworker Freddie had just delivered. They now covered almost half of the massive back deck. By the end of the week, she'd have them in the ground, and the garden would really come to life. She could picture the beauty in her mind, and she was impatient to get to the end, but at the same time, she wanted to enjoy the journey.

"You have a lot to do," Freddie commented.

"I'll start on these tomorrow." She'd already finished one area of the garden, and she needed to do some prep work on the next plot of land, but it had been a stressful day, and she wasn't feeling like doing all that now.

"I can help you in the morning. We can't do any more at the Engletons until their water feature is placed," he added, referring to another property that they were landscaping.

"That would be perfect, thanks."

"Great. You need anything else?"

"No, I'm good. I'll be right behind you."

"Then I'll see you back at the nursery."

After Freddie left, she moved some plants into the shade of the deck, then grabbed her purse off the table. Pulling out her phone, she realized she'd missed a call from Hunter while she'd been helping Freddie unload plants.

As his husky voice came over the speaker, her heart twisted with both pleasure and a yearning ache to be with him. It was the way she'd always felt about him, and it didn't look like her feelings would ever change.

So why was she so afraid of something going wrong? Why couldn't she just trust in the relationship they were building? Why did she have to keep pulling back?

Was she testing him in some way? Wanting to see how far back she could pull before he'd give up on her?

Frowning, she thought that definitely sounded like self-sabotage. Maybe she needed to just stop being afraid of feeling happy, being in love. She needed to stop worrying about how things might end and just enjoy them while she had them.

Feeling better about that idea, she put her phone back in her bag and slung it over her shoulder. Then she picked up a box filled with tools that she didn't want to leave in the yard overnight and walked down the driveway to her van. She'd call Hunter from the van, or maybe she'd just drive to his apartment and surprise him.

She opened the back of the van and put the tools inside. As she leaned over, she thought she heard a step behind her.

"Hunter?" she murmured.

Before she could turn around, something hard came down on the back of her head.

She felt a screaming pain that knocked her to her knees and then she fell forward as oblivion claimed her.

—➤➤◆◆◆—

Hunter pulled up in front of the Pacific Heights mansion, happy to see Cassidy's van in the drive. She was here, and he couldn't wait to see her. He jogged down the drive and saw the back of the van was open, and Cassidy's bag and water bottle were on the ground. *That didn't seem right.*

A terrible fear raced through him.

He ran through the open gate and into the backyard. "Cassidy? Cassidy?" he yelled.

He didn't see her anywhere. It was quiet, eerily quiet. He

checked every corner of the yard, wanting to make sure she wasn't in the shed or in the crawlspace by the deck, but she was nowhere to be found.

He pulled out his phone as he headed back toward her van and punched in her number.

A buzzing sound took him to her bag. Her phone was inside. But she was gone.

There was no way she would leave her bag and phone out here. Unless she'd gone in the house? He went up the steps to the front door and rang the bell several times. There was no sign of life. Going around the back again, he tried to find another way in, but all the doors and windows were locked.

He didn't want to jump to the worst possible conclusion, but he couldn't stop himself. *Something had happened to Cassidy.*

But she'd said she wasn't going to be alone today. She was working with a coworker. Where the hell was that person?

He got on his phone and called the nursery. The woman who answered said that Cassidy wasn't there, she was working off site, but she couldn't give him any more information. Since that woman didn't know him, he asked for George. Cassidy would probably kill him for upsetting the older man, but he needed information.

"Hello?" George said a moment later.

"This is Hunter Callaway. I'm at the house where Cassidy is supposed to be working, but while her van is here, she's not. Her bag was on the ground by the back of the van, and her phone was inside."

"What? What are you saying?" George asked with alarm.

"Cassidy might be in trouble. She said she was supposed to be working with someone else here at the house. Who was that?"

"Freddie was with her for most of the day. He just got in. Hold on."

He tapped his foot impatiently, waiting for George to

come back on the line.

"Freddie said she told him she was leaving right after him," George said. "That was about forty-five minutes ago."

"So, she was alone after he left?"

"Yes. What's going on?"

"I don't know yet, but I'm going to call the police."

"The police?" George echoed. "This has something to do with her past?"

"I'm afraid it does. If you hear from Cassidy—"

"I'll call you, and you do the same. I—I love that girl, Hunter. Bring her back to me."

"I will," he promised, feeling more terrified than he'd ever felt in his life.

His next call was to Max, where he repeated the same information.

"I'll be there in ten minutes," Max said. "I'm walking out the door."

"Hurry," he said, barely getting out the word. The idea of standing around and waiting for Max to arrive drove him crazy. Cassidy's life was on the line. Someone could be hurting her right now.

He paced around in a circle, trying to breathe, to calm down, to tell himself that Cassidy could have been killed on the spot, but she hadn't been. That probably meant she was still alive.

But why had they taken her? To shut her up? That didn't ring true. *She didn't know that much, unless there was something they thought she knew?*

He pulled out her phone and tried to open it, but the screen was locked. He stared at the numbers and tried her birthdate, then his birthdate—neither worked.

He'd probably put his fingerprints all over it, too, not that he thought the police would have found any prints since it was in her bag when he'd retrieved it.

Walking down the drive, he waited in front of the house for Max to arrive. Finally, two cars pulled up: one a police car, the other a sedan. Max and his partner Detective Randall got out of the sedan while two uniformed officers stepped out of the police vehicle.

"There's nothing much to see." He led them to her van.

"So, the bag and the water bottle were on the ground, the door was open, and that's it?" Detective Randall asked, as the officers inspected the vehicle and the driveway.

"That's it. I checked in with her business. Her boss and coworker said she had told them she was leaving, but obviously she never did."

Max pulled him aside as the others took a closer look at the vehicle and surrounding area. "Walk with me," he said, leading him back down to the sidewalk.

"They took her, Max."

"Who are you thinking?" Max asked.

"David or Quan or..." His voice drifted away as he remembered her earlier message to him. "Wait a second. She left me a voicemail earlier. She said Evan Faulkner, Donald's brother, had come by the nursery and they'd had an interesting conversation, whatever that means. When I called her back, she didn't answer."

"Okay. Evan must be back in town then. That's good. I'll check in with him and see what that was about."

He wanted to feel reassured, but Cassidy's life was at stake, and Max's calm demeanor was actually making him feel more impatient. "They're going to kill her, Max. They already tried once when they attempted to run her off the road. I never should have let her be alone." Impotent rage welled within him. "I feel so helpless. I need to do something. I'm going to speak to David or I'll find this Evan."

"You're not going anywhere except home. You need to let me handle this. You bungle something with Cassidy's life on the line, and it's over. You understand?" Max said sharply. "I will do everything that needs to be done."

He knew Max would try. "I can't just sit and wait."

"Yes, you can, because that's the best thing for you to do. We will find her."

"How? You have no idea where she is."

"We'll take it one step at a time, follow each clue."

"That could take forever."

"I understand what you're going through, Hunter. A similar thing happened when Emma and I were dating, but the best thing you can do for Cassidy is to let us do our job." Max paused as Detective Randall came down the drive.

"Found this in the shrubs by the van," Randall said, holding a matchbook in his gloved hand. "It's from Harley's Bar in San Jose."

"Harley's Bar?" Max echoed.

"What? What's the significance of that?" he demanded, the name of the bar sounding familiar.

"Evan Faulkner runs Harley's Bar," Max told him.

His heart thudded against his chest. "Then it's him. He's the one who took her."

"Maybe it's him," Max said. "That matchbook could have been planted. Go home, Hunter. Go see your family and let them distract you. I promise to stay in touch with any leads."

He didn't want to leave, but there was no point in hanging around here, and clearly Max would not let him ride along on his investigation. "Can we put out an alert on Cassidy? I know she's not a missing kid, but we need people to be looking for her. We need her photo on the news."

"If we do that, it might put her in more danger," Detective Randall put in.

"How could she be in more danger?" he practically yelled.

"Because it will make the kidnapper nervous," Max said. "Let me have the officers give you a ride home."

"I don't need a ride. I don't need babysitters. Just find Cassidy."

He didn't wait for a response from Max. He strode down the street to his car, got inside and pulled away from the curb with a squeal of his tires. He drove for six blocks before he had any idea where he wanted to go.

As he stopped at a light, his gaze caught on the earring once more. *Molly.* Could she possibly help him find Cassidy?

It was worth a shot.

Unless she was a part of this?

Were they on the wrong track about her? Was it Molly who wanted to shut Cassidy up, so her life would not be put in jeopardy?

He needed to find out.

Twenty-Two

—➤ ➤➤ ◄◄ ◄—

Hunter arrived at Molly's studio at four o'clock. There was more traffic on the street today as the weekday commute was just beginning, but he managed to squeeze the Jeep into a tight parking spot, hoping that the fact that he was a foot into the red wouldn't matter. But he wasn't worried about getting a parking ticket. He'd block the entire street if he had to.

He jogged across the street to Molly's building and pressed the buzzer. When she didn't immediately answer, he hit it again.

"Yes?" she said impatiently, an edge to her voice.

"It's Hunter. Let me in."

"I'm busy. I told Cassidy I don't want to talk about any of this anymore."

"Too bad. You're not out of this. Cassidy is missing. Someone grabbed her."

"What?"

"Let me in," he repeated.

The buzzer rang, and he ran into the building and up the stairs. Molly was once again waiting at the door, a troubled look on her face.

"What do you mean—someone grabbed Cassidy?" she asked.

He pushed past her, just to make sure Cassidy wasn't in the studio, even though he knew Molly wouldn't have let him in if she had been.

Molly shut the door behind him. "You're saying she's been kidnapped?"

"Probably by whoever tried to run her off the road the other night."

"I told her she needed to stay away from the investigation into Tommy's death. I knew no good would come of it. Why are you here?"

"Because I think you know more than you're telling."

"I don't. I don't know anything. I wasn't at the house when Tommy was killed."

"You keep making that point, but there's something in your eyes."

She instinctively shifted her gaze at his words.

"You have to tell me what I'm missing."

"Nothing," she said, forcing herself to look at him again. "You're not missing anything."

"Well, maybe you are—perhaps this earring?" He took it out of his pocket and held it up in the light.

"That's not mine," she said quickly, but he'd already seen the truth in her eyes.

"It looks like something you would make."

"It's just a silver hoop."

"With a tiny line of turquoise, your signature."

"You don't know anything."

He gave her a hard look. "You set the Faulkners' house on fire, didn't you?"

"No. That's crazy."

He didn't believe her for a second. "I don't care about the fire. I'm not interested in getting the person who set it in trouble. I'm happy the house burned down. Tommy's body was found and hopefully someone will pay for killing him. But that fire is what started everything else. It's why Cassidy is in danger. You have to tell me the truth, Molly, because if you don't, Cassidy might die, and I can't let that happen. I don't think you can, either, because she was the best friend you ever had."

He could see the waver in her eyes.

"I don't know where she is," Molly said. "I swear."

"Did you set the fire?" When she didn't reply, he said, "Fine. I'll just show this earring to the police and let them question you."

"Wait! Yes. I set the fire. And that night was the first night I'd slept without a nightmare in fourteen years. But I didn't know about Tommy's body. I didn't know I was setting off a chain of events. I just wanted to destroy the house."

"Did you also want to destroy Donald for what he did to you? Did you run his car off the road?"

"No. I didn't do that. I don't care that he's dead, but I'm not responsible. I almost wish I could take credit for that, but I can't."

He saw the pain in her eyes. "I know Donald abused you. I'm sorry for what you went through."

"Did Cassidy tell you that?"

"I pretty much guessed."

She turned away from him and walked over to the window, her back as stiff as a poker.

"See, now I think I'm missing something again." He walked over to join her. "Molly, what don't I know?"

"I never told Cassidy that it was Donald. She just assumed."

His gut clenched. "It wasn't him?"

"No." She turned to face him. "It was David."

"David?" he breathed.

"Yes."

"That's why he lied about you ever being in the house. Who else knew?"

"His father. I told Donald. I begged him to help me. He slapped me hard across the face and told me to never say those words again or he would turn me over to the police. He would tell them that I had stolen from him. He would make up stories about me. He would make sure that I went to jail. I couldn't stay in the house, so I ran away. That's it. That's the whole truth."

"Why didn't you tell Cassidy that?"

"Because I didn't want to give David a reason to come after me, and I was afraid she'd let something slip if she was talking to him."

"That's why you also didn't want her to tell the police that she found you."

"That…and the other thing."

"The fire." It was all making sense. "What made you do that now?"

"Every time I got even remotely close to that neighborhood, I felt sick to my stomach. I would break out in hives, get horrible migraines. And then I saw David get an award on the news a couple of weeks ago. He's some cyber expert now. All the memories came back. My therapist said I needed to find a way to cleanse my aura, to free myself of the dark shadows that surround me, and find a way to be reborn, to rise from the ashes. Fire is part of our tribal culture. I named myself Kenna because it means fire. And I suddenly knew what I had to do. I made sure that no one was in the house. I watched Geralyn leave. And then I went through Lindsay's backyard, the way we used to do when we were kids. I guess my earring got caught in the shrubs."

She gave him a pained look. "I thought I would feel fantastic when I watched the flames take over the house, but it didn't feel as good as I imagined. I realized too late that I shouldn't have done it, but I can't take it back, and now I'm terrified of the idea that my actions to free myself might put me in jail, and I'll be trapped again."

He didn't know what to say. He hated arson. He was a firefighter. He saw how fire ruined lives, but Molly's story was also compelling, and the Faulkners were evil people. So was David, which brought him back to the present. "Let's put the fire aside and talk about Cassidy."

"I don't know who took her."

"They found a matchbook for Harley's Bar in the bushes by where Cassidy was taken. Apparently, Evan Faulkner runs that bar. And Cassidy left me a message earlier that Evan talked to her. Do you know how he would have found her?"

"No. I haven't seen him since I was fourteen. But it seems kind of convenient for that matchbook to be right next to the van. The most conniving person in that house was David. I think he's behind everything. He hides his sickness very well, but he's a terrible person."

"If it's David, where would he take Cassidy?"

"I don't know."

"It has to be some place secluded, maybe tied to the Faulkners in some way, because I'm guessing Geralyn is there, too. Did they have a place where they went on vacation? A family cabin? Would they have gone to the mountains? To the beach? To the river?"

"The river—the Russian River," she said with a light in her eyes. "David lived there before Donald adopted him, and he used to brag that he was the only one Donald would take there on vacation. Donald and Evan, actually, they always went together. Colin went, too. It was the two dads and the two sons. Maybe they're all in this together."

The Russian River was about an hour north of the city. He'd been there a few times for rafting trips. "Do you know where on the river they would go? Do you know where the cabin was or where David used to live?"

She thought for a moment. "David said his mom was a waitress. She worked at a pie shop. He used to go there after school and do his homework until she got sick. I think it might have been in Healdsburg. I'm not sure."

"That's good," he said with a nod.

"What are you going to do?"

"I'm going to drive up there and find Cassidy."

"She might be somewhere else. My memory is from a long time ago. And the Russian River is huge."

"Yes, but how many pie shops can there be?" He paused

by the door. "Look, I didn't intend to say anything, Molly, but I inadvertently mentioned to my cousin's husband, who is the police detective on the case, that I had found you. I didn't give him your new name or your phone number or address, but he'll probably ask me again at some point."

"Then I'll disappear."

"Don't do that."

"Why not? You're going to tell him I set the fire, too, aren't you? You're a firefighter. How could you not?"

"I'm going to have to wrestle with that one," he admitted. "But I don't have any proof that you did it, and arson is almost impossible to prove. I also need to know that you're not going to do something like this again. You have to go to counseling, someone different, someone who doesn't inspire you to burn down your past."

"I could do that. I'm not going to hurt anyone, Hunter. And I don't have any other houses I want to burn down. If you find Cassidy, it will be because I helped you. That should count for something, shouldn't it?"

"Yes, it counts," he said, knowing that this woman had suffered a lot in her life. "And I want to help you. For now, stay put. You don't have to be afraid. No one is looking for you; they're all looking for Cassidy."

"I hope you find her."

"I will," he vowed. "I'm not going to stop looking until I do."

Cassidy felt sick to her stomach. She'd woken up blindfolded, with her hands tied behind her back, and it was clear she was in a vehicle. *Maybe the trunk*, she thought as she banged around in a small space. She didn't know how much time had passed, but her head was aching, and her stomach was churning, and she really wanted air.

A wave of panic ran through her as she considered what was happening. Obviously, someone had kidnapped her. *But why? And where were they going? Was she just being taken to a more remote location, so someone could kill her?*

It felt like it was taking a long time to get wherever they were going.

She kicked her legs around, trying to find some clue or some sort of weapon, but she came up with nothing. Still, she wasn't going down without a fight. She just didn't know who she was going to fight.

Who had grabbed her? Jeremiah was in the hospital. That left David and Quan. There was also Molly. *Had she misread that entire situation? What about Lindsay?* That girl clearly hated her now and was almost stalking Hunter. *Or was she focusing too much on people her age?* She couldn't forget how Evan had threatened her earlier.

The vehicle suddenly came to a stop and she bumped her already sore head once again. She heard two doors open and close. And then a latch clicked, a rush of air hit her face, and there was light behind the blindfold.

Two hands grabbed her and roughly pulled her out of the trunk. She stumbled as her feet hit the ground. There were clearly men on either side of her, each with a hand on her arm. "Who are you?" she asked. "What do you want?"

There was no answer. She strained her senses for clues. She could feel branches breaking under her feet. The path was dirt with pebbles, and then she was being urged up the steps. It felt like there was wood beneath her feet. Another door opened. She was going into a house. And as one of her captors pushed her forward, she could smell his cologne.

She sucked in a breath as she realized the truth.

And then her blindfold was stripped away from her face. She blinked as David's face came into focus. Behind him was Quan. They were standing in what appeared to be a rustic cabin with wooden walls and a stone fireplace. A couch and an armchair were the only pieces of furniture. The shades were drawn, leaving only one dimly lit lamp to cast light into the room.

"Why am I here? What's going on?"

"You're here because you're a troublemaker," David said. "You always were. So was Tommy. I tried to be nice to both of you, but you weren't grateful."

"Grateful? Why would I be grateful to you?"

"Because I let you run away."

"But that didn't happen with Tommy," she said slowly. "Did it? You killed him." She didn't need him to confess. She now knew that was the truth. "But why? He was your friend."

"He threatened me. I don't like people who do that."

She looked over at Quan. "Did you know he killed Tommy?"

"Not until recently," Quan said, his voice clipped, edgy. "You should have kept your mouth shut, Cassidy. We tried to warn you that there would be trouble."

"You both took Mrs. Faulkner out of the hospital, or you arranged for someone else to do it. Where is she?"

"That's not important." David drew her attention back to him as he pulled a gun from the back waistband of his jeans.

Her heart stopped. "You're going to shoot me? You think you'll get away with that?"

"I might not shoot you, if you help me, if you show me the respect I deserve."

"I don't understand. How could I possibly help you?"

His angry, evil eyes met hers. "You can tell me where Molly is."

"Molly?" She stared back at him in confusion. "Why do you care? She doesn't know you killed Tommy."

"She knows...other stuff."

"Oh, my God," she breathed, the truth hitting her in the face as she saw the fear in his eyes. "It wasn't Donald who abused Molly; it was you."

"What?" A woman's voice came from behind her.

She whirled around to see the woman she had been most afraid to see—Geralyn Faulkner. She'd obviously come out of the bedroom. Her blonde hair had gone completely gray. She was very thin and looked haggard, a little drugged, her brown-eyed gaze cloudy.

"What's going on?" Geralyn asked again. "What is she talking about, David?"

"She's delusional, Mom, you know that."

"She said something about Molly. You didn't hurt Molly, did you?" Geralyn asked.

"Of course not," David said.

"You don't believe him, do you?" she asked Geralyn.

"I always believe my son."

"Go back to your room, Mom. Put on the headphones I gave you."

Geralyn hesitated. "Why do you have a gun?"

"To protect you," David said.

"Oh, you're so sweet."

"Don't leave, Geralyn," she said quickly. "It's clear you don't know that David is going to kill me. You can't let that happen."

Geralyn gave her a bewildered look. "You always make up the most incredible stories, Cassidy. You're such a troublemaker."

"I didn't make up Molly. She was in the house, and David molested her. He also killed Tommy, and Donald helped him cover it up. Don't you see who the real villain is? It's David."

"Mom, go to your room," David ordered. "Quan, help her."

Quan moved over to Geralyn's side and escorted her into the bedroom, leaving her alone with David.

"I'm not going to tell you anything," she said defiantly, facing him once more.

"Then you're going to die, and no one is ever going to find you, not even Hunter."

Her heart broke at the mention of Hunter. She was going to disappear on him again. But this time it wouldn't be her fault. *Would that matter?* It would still hurt him. He'd blame himself for not sticking close enough to her, even though she'd pushed him away.

"Hey, David," Quan said from the doorway. "You need

to calm Geralyn down. She's getting agitated. She wants you."

"Fine. Watch Cassidy," he said, moving into the bedroom. "I'll take care of Mom."

She looked at Quan. "Why are you doing this?"

"Sit down, Cassidy." He pushed her toward a hard chair by the table. "Instead of asking questions, you better focus on telling David what he wants. Or you won't get out of this."

"Even if I tell him, I won't get out of this." She gave him a speculative look. "What's in it for you? You didn't hurt Molly. You didn't kill Tommy. You didn't do anything wrong—until now, did you?"

Twenty-Three

Hunter called Max after he'd crossed over the Golden Gate Bridge, wanting to be far enough away so that he wouldn't be persuaded to turn around and come back.

Without giving away where he'd gotten the information, he told Max that he thought it was possible David had a connection to Healdsburg, and he was going to check it out. Max, of course, did not want him to go on his own, but he promised that he would call in if he found any leads. Max agreed to do the same.

Although there was some traffic heading out of San Francisco, he made it to Healdsburg in under an hour, managing to avoid getting a speeding ticket as he pressed the needle toward ninety for most of the trip. It was past five when he rolled into the small downtown area. He'd checked the internet for a pie shop and since there was only one, aptly named Pie A La Mode, he headed there.

The café was located on the corner of a block filled with small boutique and tourist stores, as well as a bank, a post office, and a fast-food Mexican restaurant.

When he entered the restaurant, the smell of sugar,

cinnamon, and apples almost overwhelmed him. There was a long counter with eight stools and about ten booths in the small diner-like restaurant. A waitress at the cash register was about eighteen. He didn't think she was going to be of any help, but the woman behind the counter appeared to be in her fifties. Maybe she would remember David's mother.

He was a little afraid that he might have used up his luck. Finding Molly had been a remarkable occurrence. And now he was attempting to do the same thing. But it had to work. He had to find a clue to David's whereabouts; Cassidy's life was on the line, and there was no option for failure.

Moving over to the counter, he waited for the waitress to come over. She set down a water glass and gave him a tired smile. "Do you need a menu or are you just here for pie?"

He took a look at the display case of pies in front of him. "I'll take a slice of the apple." He thought she might be more receptive to questions if he was a paying customer.

"You got it. You want that with ice cream?"

"Just the pie is fine."

She sliced him a hefty piece and set it before him. "There you go."

"I was hoping you might also be able to help me."

"With what?" she asked warily.

"I'm looking for someone who used to work here about twenty years ago."

"Well, I've been here since I opened this place thirty years ago. My name is Regina."

"That's great."

"Who are you looking for?"

"A woman who had a little boy named David. He was probably about six at the time."

A spark lit her eyes. "David—with blond hair and blue eyes, a mischievous smile. I remember him."

"You do? And his mother?"

"Yes. Laura was a sweet thing, a single mom. She got sick and died. It was very sad. But David was lucky. His father came back into the picture and took him home with him."

"His father?" he echoed, suddenly wondering if David had been favored by the Faulkners, because there was an actual blood relationship. "Do you remember his name?"

"I don't remember. I'm sorry. Why are you asking?"

"I'm looking for David."

"Is he in trouble?"

He thought about how he wanted to answer that question and decided on a lie. "He's a friend, and I think he's in danger. I was hoping that you might remember where he lived with his mother, or if you know anything else about the mom's family... That might help me find him."

"David and his mother lived in a trailer park about a mile from here, but it was flooded about five years ago and torn down."

Disappointment ran through him. "Oh." He was stymied as to what to ask next. He'd hoped this lead would take him somewhere.

She gave him a thoughtful look. "You seem a little sad."

"Worried is what I am. I know David is somewhere around here; I just don't know where to look. Where do you think David's mom met David's father?"

"Oh, well, I know the answer to that. They met on the Fourth of July at the Riverview Lodge. She said she thought he was handsome and sophisticated. Later, she found out he was married. She didn't tell him she was pregnant, not until she got sick. To his credit, he came and got his boy. And for the first couple of years, he used to bring David back for a summer vacation. They'd stop in for pie and say hello, but then they stopped coming around. Goodness, I haven't thought of them in years."

"Is the lodge still around?" he asked, thinking the place might mean something to David.

"It went out of business two years ago, but it's still there. It's all boarded up."

"Can you tell me how to get there?"

"Sure, but I don't think you'll find David there."

He had no idea if he would, but a boarded-up old lodge seemed like the perfect place to keep Geralyn and Cassidy.

"Are you going to eat your pie?" she asked.

He took two quick bites, then pulled out his wallet and put a twenty on the table. "Thanks."

"I'll get you some change."

"Keep it."

"If you find David, tell him to come by and say hello. I'll make sure he gets a piece of my lemon meringue pie."

"I'll do that," he said, knowing that if he found David, the man was going to end up in no condition to say hello or have pie.

— ·⇒⇐· —

"Quan," Cassidy said, feeling a desperate need to take these moments while David was calming Geralyn to get into Quan's head, to force him to see that he was making a terrible mistake going along with David. "You didn't answer me before. You didn't tell me why you're doing this."

"I owe David."

"Why?"

"He was my protector. He saved my life."

"How? When?"

"When I was fourteen. A group of kids were beating the crap out of me until David stepped in. After that, they left me alone. David told me as long as I was loyal to him, I'd be safe. So, I did what he said."

"That's why you backed up his lie about Molly. Did you know he molested her?"

"I don't think he did that. It had to have been Donald."

"Weren't you listening a minute ago? He admitted it, Quan."

"He didn't say that. He said Molly is going to say he did it. And we have to stop her. And we have to stop you."

"You don't have to do anything. You can let me go and walk away from this. David is the one who killed Tommy.

David is the one who abused Molly. David is the one who wants to kill me."

"Killing Tommy was an accident. David didn't mean to do it. They were fighting. They shoved each other. Tommy hit his head."

She didn't know if that was the truth or just what David had told Quan. "How did you guys get Geralyn out of the hospital?"

"David hacked into the cameras. I put a little something in the guard's coffee, and then I took Geralyn out of there."

"Why? Why do all that for her?"

"Because she was the closest person I had to a mom, and David and I didn't want her to get charged for Tommy's death. She took care of us. We owe her."

She was beginning to see a common thread in Quan's reasoning. "You owe Geralyn. You owe David. What about what you owe Molly? Tommy? Me? None of us hurt you. We were your family, too."

"You hated all of us."

"Only because you all lied about Molly, and because I was scared of Donald. But you and me—we didn't have any problems."

"This is your fault, Cassidy. You didn't want to protect Geralyn. You wanted to talk to the cops. You wanted to find Molly and bring her back to life. All you have to do is tell David where she is. If you prove your loyalty to him, he'll protect you."

"Oh, Quan, that won't happen. As soon as he finds Molly, he'll kill me. And he'll kill her, and he'll probably kill you, because he can't leave anyone alive who knows the truth. But you and I can leave right now. You haven't done anything that you can't come back from. And if you don't want to come, just let me walk through the door."

For a second, she thought she was getting through to Quan, but then he jumped to his feet.

Turning her head, she saw David in the doorway, grinning with confidence. "You really thought that was going to work, Cassidy? Quan would never turn on me. Neither will Jada or Rhea. I have leverage on all of them."

As he spoke of the other kids, she wondered about Jeremiah. "What about Jeremiah? Did he try to run me off the road?"

"Yes, and he was unsuccessful. I made sure he knew of my disappointment."

"Were you responsible for his overdose? You know, he's not dead. He'll recover. He'll tell the truth."

"No, he won't. He tried to die so he wouldn't have to betray me. And if he does recover, he'll keep his mouth shut."

"I don't understand the power you have over everyone."

"I was responsible for how they were treated, Cassidy. I made sure that those who were loyal got special privileges."

"How did you make sure of that? And why didn't Geralyn and Donald see what was going on?"

"My mother sees nothing. She's a sweet, dumb woman, who believed her husband when he told her he'd found a little boy who needed a home. She didn't question how much I looked like Donald. She didn't ask what happened to my parents. She didn't wonder why he found me at the Russian River. She just said they loved me so much, they were going to adopt me. I didn't know the truth until I was fifteen, that my benefactor was not just a kind man who once knew my mother; he was my biological father."

"What?" she asked in amazement. "Is that true?"

"Yes, it's true. Donald and my mother Laura had an affair. And when she got sick and couldn't take care of me anymore, she told him he had to take me, or she would tell his wife everything."

"How do you know that?"

"I found the letter she wrote him, begging him to do the right thing."

"So, your mother died, and he came and got you?"

"And passed me off to Geralyn as just another kid who needed help." Anger burned in his eyes.

She was beginning to realize where some of David's

crazy behavior was coming from. "When you found out, you must have felt betrayed that he hadn't ever acknowledged that you were his real son."

"I was furious. But I quickly realized I had the golden ticket. He would do anything I wanted to keep me quiet. And I used that leverage to protect the other kids—as long as they were loyal to me, too."

"And when you abused Molly and killed Tommy, your father had to protect you. Donald helped you bury Tommy behind that wall, didn't he?"

"There you go. You put it all together. It doesn't matter. You're not going to be able to tell anyone."

"You mean you're not going to let me go if I tell you where Molly is?"

He stared back at her. "I think you know the answer to that."

"I do." She looked at Quan. "Don't you see? You've tied yourself to a murderer. He's not going to stop, and at some point, you're going to be expendable, too."

"You don't need to kill her," Quan said. "And how come you never told me Donald was your biological father?"

She was happy to hear Quan ask a question. It seemed like he might be coming out of his stupor.

A crash made them all turn their heads. Geralyn had come back into the room, and the broken mug at her feet matched the broken look in her eyes. "What did you just say, Quan?"

"Nothing," Quan murmured quickly, looking away from Geralyn.

"He asked David why he never told him that Donald was his biological father," she said to Geralyn.

"Shut up," David said, pointing the gun at her head. "She's lying again, Mom. Don't listen to her."

Geralyn's eyes seemed more alert now. "Donald— you...he laughed when people said you looked like him." She put a shaky hand to her mouth. "Oh, God, it's true. You are his son."

"Welcome to the party, Mom," David said cynically.

"Who—who was your mother?"

"She was a waitress at the Russian River."

"And you knew the whole time?"

"No, I found out when I was fifteen. You know why Dad never wanted you or anyone to go in the garage? It's because he had love letters in there."

Geralyn paled. "Why didn't you tell me?"

"Because then I would have lost my leverage with Dad. But it's going to be fine. I'm going to take care of you. You were good to me, and I'll be good to you. We'll go to another state. No one will ever find us. I have good cyber skills. I can make sure of that. Tommy's case will go unsolved, along with the others. Or maybe, someone else will take the fall."

"You killed Tommy?" Geralyn asked in surprise. "I thought it might have been Donald. He—he spent a lot of time in the garage alone—or maybe not alone, but he never wanted me to go in there. When the police said they found a body…well, what else could I think?"

Cassidy realized that Geralyn hadn't known anything about Tommy until the fire had revealed his body. Or maybe she'd suspected but had just been unwilling to ask any questions. Clearly, she'd been a little afraid of Donald.

"David killed Tommy," she repeated, wanting to make sure that information sunk into Geralyn's head. "He also abused Molly, the girl you said didn't exist."

Geralyn looked at her in confusion. "Not David. David wouldn't do that. He's a good boy."

"He did do it. Look at him; he's not denying it."

"Don't believe her. She's a liar. She always was," David said.

"This needs to stop," Quan said, inching toward the door. "This is messed up. I can't be a part of all this. I won't tell anyone but leave me out of it."

"No way," David said. "No one walks away from me."

As Quan reached for the doorknob, David shot him.

Geralyn screamed. Cassidy didn't know if she screamed,

too, but there was ringing in her ears as shock ran through her.

Quan fell to the floor, blood coming out of his chest. David had shot him in the heart.

"I'll find Molly on my own," David said, turning to her.

She jumped to her feet.

"There's nowhere to run," he said with a laugh. "But give it a shot if you want."

"Stop," Geralyn said, moving in front of Cassidy in a shocking gesture of protection. "Don't kill her, David."

"You hate her. Why do you care?"

"I care about you," Geralyn said. "I don't want you to do this."

"Go to your room, Mom. You don't need to see this."

"This isn't how I raised you," Geralyn pleaded.

As David was distracted by Geralyn, Cassidy saw a movement by the door, the figure of a man, and she knew instantly it was Hunter.

Relief soared through her, followed by fear. Hunter wouldn't have a gun. If he came into the room, he'd get hurt.

She had to disable David before that happened. She moved around Geralyn, hoping to block David's view of the door.

"Stay where you are," David said, waving his gun. "Mom, go to your room."

"I can't let you do this, David. Please."

Geralyn's pleading voice drew David's attention, and Cassidy bolted forward, barreling her head into his chest, knocking him backward.

The gun went off as it flew out of his hands.

Then he turned on her with vicious anger, punching her in the face, throwing her onto her back and socking her in the gut.

As she tried to roll away from him, Hunter rushed into the room, pulling David off her, throwing him against the wall.

She scrambled to her feet, looking wildly around,

wondering if Geralyn would come after her, but then she saw the woman sprawled on the floor, her eyes wide open in shock, blood coming out of her shoulder. When the gun had gone off, the bullet must have hit her.

Geralyn wasn't going to be a problem, but David was. She wanted to help Hunter but with her hands still tied behind her back, she didn't know what she could do.

In the end, she realized that David was no match for Hunter, who was clearly ready to kill David if need be. She'd never seen Hunter so violent, so filled with rage, so determined to protect her. He hit David again and again, fury driving his powerful punches.

When David finally crashed to the floor, blood coming out of his face and mouth, she said, "Stop, Hunter, he's done." While she wouldn't have mourned for one second over David's death, she didn't want Hunter to have to live with having killed a man.

Hunter kicked David one last time in the ribs. David barely flinched as he fell into unconsciousness.

"Now, he's done." Hunter opened his arms, and she ran into them. "Are you okay?" he asked, holding her tight.

His arms, his body, felt amazing and wonderful. She was safe. They were both safe. "Now that you're here, I'm really good." She lifted her head, tears of relief streaming down her face. "You came for me. How did you find me?"

"It's a long story, but, of course, I came for you. Did you think I wouldn't?"

"I knew you would try. I was just afraid David would hurt you."

"I thought you saw me in the doorway. I thought you knew I was coming in."

"I did."

"Then why did you tackle him?"

"So he couldn't shoot you. I thought if I could just get the gun out of his hand, you'd be all right."

He shook his head in amazement. "He almost shot you instead."

"But ironically he shot the one and probably only person he loves." She looked back at Geralyn who was still breathing but also still bleeding. "We should call for help."

Hunter let her go and grabbed the gun that David had dropped on the floor. He called 911. Then, with help on the way, he went over to the kitchen, found a knife and cut through the ties that were binding her hands.

She flexed her fingers in relief, then grabbed towels out of the kitchen and went back to Geralyn, pressing one against her shoulder.

Hunter checked on Quan. As she gave him an inquiring look, he shook his head.

Quan had paid the ultimate price for his loyalty.

"I'll call Max, too," Hunter said.

She looked down at Geralyn, a woman she had hated with every fiber of her being.

"Why are you helping me?" Geralyn asked.

"Because it's the right thing to do," she said. "Why did you try to save me?"

Geralyn sighed. "Because it was long past time for me to do the right thing."

Twenty-Four

$\Longrightarrow \gg\!\!\ll \Longleftarrow$

Within ten minutes, the cabin was swarming with police and paramedics. After briefing the cops on what had taken place and putting them in touch with Max for more details, Hunter took Cassidy's hand as they stepped out onto the back deck overlooking the river. Night had fallen but there was plenty of light coming from the full moon, the bright stars, and the lights inside the cabin.

"How are you holding up?" he asked.

Her brown eyes were still huge when she turned to look at him. "I'm in shock. So, I guess we're at the Russian River."

He nodded, realizing she was still trying to get her bearings. She'd mentioned being blindfolded on the trip from San Francisco. "We are."

"How did you get here? How did you know where I was?"

"I went by the house where you were supposed to be working and I saw your bag on the ground. Your phone was inside. I knew someone had grabbed you. I called Max and the police came. They found a matchbook from Harley's Bar, which apparently Donald's brother owns."

"Evan?" she questioned. "I don't think he's involved in this, although I don't know for sure if he knows what David has done over the years. He came to see me earlier. He thought I was the one sending the cops in his direction, but I'm sure now it was David. He's the one who killed Tommy. Donald helped him cover it up by burying Tommy's body behind the wall."

He nodded. "I suspect David planted that matchbook on purpose to send everyone in Evan's direction."

"He almost thought of everything, but he must have missed something because you're here."

Hunter put his hands on her shoulders. "He missed Molly."

"Molly," she breathed. "He wanted me to tell him where she was. I think that's why he didn't kill me. He wanted to make me talk first. She was the loose end. When Molly said she was abused in that house, I thought it was Donald. I guess she never really said his name, but she didn't correct my assumption."

"She told me that she let you think it was Donald, because she was afraid that somehow David would come after her again."

"That makes sense. Geralyn didn't know, either. She came into the room when David admitted to it. She was stunned. She also didn't know about Tommy. She said she thought it was Donald, but she was never allowed in that garage. I guess I gave her more credit than she deserved. She was blind to David's evil ways, to Donald's devotion and loyalty to his son—his real son," she added. "David was the product of an affair that Donald had with someone in this area. But David didn't find out that he wasn't just another foster kid until he was fifteen. I guess that's when he snapped, when his anger overwhelmed him. He discovered that he could do anything he wanted because his father didn't want him to tell Geralyn about the affair. He had leverage. And the other kids became his pawns. If they were loyal to him, he got them things. That's why Quan was so loyal, even until today.

But I wasn't loyal; I kept talking about Molly. And Tommy hadn't been there long enough to be loyal. He must have found out that David hurt Molly or something... He was going to talk, and David shut him up."

"I know. I'm sorry, Cassidy."

"Me, too. I'm sorry for everyone who was touched by David's darkness. I think the only person he actually cared about was Geralyn, strangely enough."

"I'm not sure he cared, or if he was just afraid she'd eventually figure things out and tell the police."

"That's possible. I'm still trying to make sense of it all." She gazed into his eyes. "But getting back to you—Molly told you about this cabin?"

"No, but she told me that David said his real mother worked at a pie shop in Healdsburg and that he lived at the Russian River until the day Donald came and took him to San Francisco. I drove up here looking for the pie shop. Luckily, there was only one, and the owner remembered David. She said that David's mother met his father at the Riverview Lodge. I took a shot and went to the lodge, which is just down the road, but it was boarded up. I thought I was in the wrong place, but then I saw a path into the woods and realized there were cabins along the river." He took a breath. "When I heard that gun go off, my heart stopped. I knew I was in the right place, but I did not know what I would find. When I got closer, I heard your voice, so I waited, looking for an opportunity." He smiled. "You certainly gave me one, even though it was very risky."

"Things were unraveling fast. David shot Quan, because Quan suddenly spoke up against him. Geralyn had finally caught on to everything. He was going to kill us all, and then he would have probably hunted Molly down, maybe the younger girls, too, Jada and Rhea."

"They'll all be safe now."

"I wonder if David killed Donald—if he ran him off the road. Maybe Donald got a sudden case of conscience, too, and became a threat to David."

"I wouldn't put it past him."

"David said Jeremiah was the one who rammed my car and tried to push me over the side of the road. He suggested that Jeremiah tried to kill himself, so he wouldn't have to turn on David. God knows what other crimes David has committed over the years. I feel like there's more to find out."

"The police can figure all that out. This is over for you, Cassidy." He really wanted her to understand that, to believe it. "You know who killed Tommy. You know where Molly is. Nothing else matters, does it?"

She thought for a moment. "No. Nothing else matters. I'm glad Molly helped you."

"She was reluctant, but I had some leverage over her."

"What?" Cassidy asked in surprise.

"I spoke to Lindsay earlier today. She found a silver earring by the back gate between her parents' property and the Faulkners' house. She suggested it might be yours, that you had set the fire."

"Good old Lindsay. She just keeps coming for me. And she is determined to find a way to get you back in her life."

"I set her straight. We actually finally got to the root of things. She's been going through a lot of depression since her fiancé cheated on her last year. When she saw me, she suddenly got fixated on everything that was wrong in her life, and how it would have been better if she and I had gotten together. But I reminded her that we were never really a couple and that we never would be. She finally seemed to hear me."

"I'm sure that was hard—for both of you."

"I'm sorry I hurt her. I never realized she felt so much more strongly than I did. Although, I have a feeling her recent problems colored the way she was looking at her past. At any rate, getting back to the earring, I knew it wasn't yours, but it sure looked a lot like the jewelry we'd seen at Molly's studio."

Awareness dawned in her eyes. "Oh, no," she murmured. "Not Molly."

"Unfortunately, yes. When I showed her the earring, she

admitted that she burned the house down. She said she saw David getting an award on the news, and she just snapped. She wanted to cleanse her soul, her life, her past, and fire is part of her tribal tradition. She waited to make sure no one was in the house. She didn't want to hurt anyone, at least not physically. She just wanted to destroy the place where the destruction of her soul took place."

"I can't blame her. But now I'm worried that she's going to have to pay for what she did."

"Well, I don't have the earring anymore, so there's no proof she was there."

She gave him a surprised look. "You don't?"

"No, I must have dropped it somewhere," he said vaguely. "No one saw Molly going into the house. I'm not sure there's anything that would tie her to the crime."

"Really, Hunter? You would let a crime of fire go unpunished?"

"She asked me the same thing. It goes against my nature, I'll admit. But what you and Molly and the other kids went through there...I'm glad the house is gone."

"Me, too."

There were so many things he wanted to say to her, but she was still pale, jittery, and there were too many people around. Someone was bound to interrupt them soon.

That thought had barely crossed his mind when Max walked out onto the deck. He'd texted Max the address for the lodge when he'd first arrived and had updated him shortly after they'd called 911.

Max gave them a concerned look. "Are you both all right?"

"We're okay, right, Cassidy?"

She nodded, still looking strained, but very, very brave. "I'm sure you want to know everything that happened, Max."

"Definitely. Geralyn Faulkner and David Bellerman are on their way to the hospital, in separate ambulances. The coroner will be picking up Mr. Tran's body. Want to tell me who shot who?"

"David did all the shooting. He shot Quan when it looked like Quan was going to bail. And when I rushed him, the gun went off, and the bullet hit Geralyn. Then Hunter came in and took care of David."

"I figured that was your work, Hunter," Max said dryly. "I'm sorry I tried to stop you from getting involved earlier. Your gut instinct probably saved Cassidy's life. But you never told me how you got the clue to come up here."

He didn't want to lie to Max, but he also didn't want to give Molly up. "I remembered hearing about David's adoption story, how he lived here in the Russian River with his single mom, who worked in a pie shop. When she died, Donald Faulkner adopted David. I thought if the pie shop was still in existence, someone might remember where David lived or where Donald had spent his time when he was up here. It was a long shot. And it was also possible that David was nowhere near this area, but somehow it all worked out."

"Interesting," Max said. "I don't believe you, though. Yesterday, at the firehouse, Kate said you'd found the missing girl, and we haven't had a chance to talk about that. Was she your fountain of information?"

He felt torn. He'd promised Molly. He'd promised Cassidy. But Max was not just a friend; he was family.

"It's all right," Cassidy cut in. "We did find Molly. She ran away from the Faulkners when she was fourteen because she was abused by David, and his father refused to do anything about it. I asked Hunter not to tell you because Molly has changed her life around, and she didn't want to take the chance that David would find her again."

Max slowly nodded. "I understand. I still need to talk to her. She may want to press charges against David for what he did to her."

"I think she just wants to forget," Cassidy said. "But will you let me give her your name and number? Maybe we could meet away from the police station. Perhaps her name could be kept out of this story."

"We can do all that. I don't really need her story right

now. David is going to go down for murdering Mr. Tran, for his kidnapping of you, and attempted murder of Mrs. Faulkner."

"She'll never testify against him," Cassidy said.

"I don't think we need her."

"What about Tommy? David admitted that he killed him," Cassidy added. "And it didn't look like Mrs. Faulkner knew that. Perhaps Geralyn will be willing to go against David now."

"I think we can make her see the advantages of that," Max said. "Do you know who kidnapped you, Cassidy?"

"David and Quan. I was leaning into the back of the van and one of them hit me on the head with something hard." She put her fingertips to the back of her head and winced. "I've got a pretty good bump. I was knocked out. They put me in the trunk of a car, blindfolded me, and tied my hands."

She was speaking pragmatically, but Hunter was sure the experience had been terrifying.

"I woke up a few minutes before we arrived at the cabin," she continued. "I didn't know where we were. The shades were drawn. I'd never been there before. I didn't realize Geralyn was there for a few minutes. She was in the bedroom. She was still a little out of it. She came out once and David took her back into her room. I tried to reason with Quan, but it was clear he'd been David's loyal soldier for so long, he didn't know how to be anything else. David manipulated everyone in that house, Max. He's a sociopath —charming on the outside, evil on the inside."

Cassidy shivered, and he quickly put his arm around her. "Are you okay?"

"I'm suddenly cold."

"That's probably the shock." He looked back at Max. "We already spoke to the local police. Can we go now? Can we follow up with you tomorrow, in San Francisco?"

"I think I've got what I need for now. I spoke to the local detectives and filled them in on what's been going on. You can take Cassidy home. I'll be in touch tomorrow."

"Thanks."

As they walked back through the house, Cassidy stopped by Quan's body, which had been covered with a sheet by the paramedics. For a moment, he thought she was considering pulling that sheet back, but she just gave his form a long look and then walked past him.

He led her through the dark woods to his Jeep, keeping a tight grip on her hand. As soon as they got into the vehicle, he turned on the heat. "It should be warm soon."

"I know it's not that cold; it's just me. It's all sinking in—everything that happened. I feel relieved but exhausted."

"You can sleep on the way back."

"I don't know if my mind will slow down long enough for that to happen."

"Are you hungry? Do you want me to stop for food?"

"No. I don't think I could eat anything right now. Maybe when we get back to the city. But if you're hungry—"

"I'm good. I had a few bites of pie earlier."

She gave him a shaky smile. "I was fighting for my life and you were eating pie?"

"I was getting information, and I didn't finish it. As soon as I got what I wanted, I came looking for you."

"You saved my life."

"You were halfway to saving your own."

"I don't think I could have beaten back David if you hadn't shown up."

"I'm just glad I got there before he could hurt you."

"You're a pretty good detective, Hunter. If you're still thinking about changing careers…"

"No way. I do not want to do this for a living. I kept thinking on my way up here that maybe we had used up our luck. We found Molly by trying to locate her family, and I was doing the same thing with David."

"It worked." She paused. "We all thought we were separated from our pasts, from our real families, when we were at the Faulkners, but the ties were still there. We just didn't know it. Maybe the only way we were going to find

Molly was by finding who she was before she went to the Faulkners. And the same was true for David. It's weird how a series of unrelated events put us all in that house at the same time."

"I think you're right. Sometimes you have to look to the past for answers."

"Even if you don't want to." She sighed. "Molly isn't going to want to talk to Max, but I'll have to persuade her."

"He may not care that much about following up with her if she doesn't want to press charges. She's really not a witness to anything but what happened to her."

"That's true. I hope that's the way it works out. She has suffered enough. And we don't have to talk about that earring Lindsay found, unless, of course, Lindsay decides to bring it up."

"I think we've seen the last of her, and I never told her it belonged to Molly, or even suggested that. She'll probably continue to think that you burned the house down."

"I'm okay with that."

As he got onto the highway, Cassidy settled into her seat. The shivers seemed to have stopped. And as the minutes passed, he noticed her struggling to stay awake.

"You can sleep, Cassidy."

"Maybe just a minute," she said.

Within seconds, she was asleep. He smiled to himself, happy that she'd given up the fight to stay alert, in control. He'd like to see her do that more often. Maybe she would now that they'd exorcised the ghosts of her past.

She'd told him that he'd saved her life, and maybe he had. But he also had a feeling she'd saved his, too, in ways she couldn't even imagine.

Cassidy barely remembered getting out of Hunter's car and walking up the stairs to his apartment. She'd been too sleepy to complain about not going all the way home. She'd tumbled into his bed and fallen back asleep before her head hit the pillow.

Now, the sun was streaming through his bedroom windows, on Wednesday morning, and she smelled bacon.

Glancing at the other side of the bed, she saw the tangled covers, and as happy as she was that there was breakfast coming, she kind of wished she'd woken up in his arms.

Climbing out of bed in the clothes she'd worn the night before, she used the bathroom, taking a minute to wash her face and brush her hair, before going out to the kitchen.

Hunter was standing by the stove in jeans and a T-shirt, his hair damp, his face shaven, his clothes clinging to his masculine body in a way that immediately made her want to strip them off of him. She gulped at that wicked thought.

Hunter raised his gaze to hers and gave her a slow, intimate smile that only made her desire for him deepen. It wasn't just desire, though; there were a lot of feelings running through her, emotions she wasn't entirely comfortable with.

"Good morning," he said.

"Morning. It smells good in here."

"There's coffee if you want it. I've got eggs and bacon coming up."

"It looks good," she said, moving into the kitchen. She took a mug out of his cabinet and filled it with coffee.

"I didn't have many vegetables to throw in. Hopefully a few mushrooms and onions will spice up the scramble."

"It will be perfect. I'm starving."

"I figured." He put several strips of bacon onto a paper towel and put them in the microwave. While the bacon was cooking, he grabbed the bread out of the toaster and buttered it. He was moving fast and efficiently, and she liked watching him work.

"Can I help?" she offered somewhat halfheartedly.

"No. I've got it covered. Take a seat."

She sat down at the adjacent kitchen table and glanced out the window. The sun was shining. It was a new day. She had work to get to, a garden to plant, and probably a police interview to get through, but she wasn't in a hurry to get to any of it. She was happy being exactly where she was. In fact, she could imagine more mornings like this. But imagining that was also scary. Opening herself up to the possibilities meant exposing herself to potential pain.

Hunter set down her plate along with a glass of orange juice, then returned with his own breakfast plate. "Dig in."

She smiled and put a napkin on her lap. The first forkful of eggs was delicious and flavorful. "Excellent. You've been busy this morning. You already took a shower, too. I feel like a mess."

"Eat. Don't worry about how you look, because you look great. You always look great."

"I don't think so. You're laying it on a little thick."

He grinned. "I'm just happy."

"I feel pretty good, too. I'm a little afraid of the feeling."

"There's no reason to be afraid anymore." He got up as his phone began to buzz and retrieved it from the counter.

"Is that Max?" she asked.

"No. It's my mother."

"You should take it."

He returned to the table. "I'll talk to her later. I have a feeling that will be a long conversation. Max will have told Emma everything that happened, and she will have set off the family tree of phone calling."

"There's a tree?" she asked, thinking how amazing it would be to have a family so big it warranted a tree.

"Not an official one. But news seems to spread quickly."

She wiped her mouth as she finished her eggs and took a long drink of her orange juice. "That hit the spot."

"Good. Do you want more?"

"No. That was the perfect amount."

He pushed their empty plates aside and reached across the table to cover her hand with his.

Her heart sped up at the look in his eyes. *Was she ready for whatever was coming next?*

"I want to talk to you, Cassidy. About us."

She drew in a quick breath. "I want to talk about us, too, but I'm a little scared."

"Me, too."

"You? My fearless hero? I don't believe that."

"I can run into a burning building. I can take down a psychopath like David. But that's all physical stuff. Putting my heart on the line, that's something else."

"Especially when the girl you're talking to already broke your heart once."

He met her gaze. "Especially then," he agreed, his fingers tightening around hers. "Today is a new beginning for you, Cassidy. You don't ever have to worry about your past again. You can be yourself. You can be free. You can live your life without any clouds hanging over it. You don't have to look over your shoulder. You don't have to wonder what happened to Molly. All of your questions have been answered."

"It's going to be strange to let go of it all. I thought I had before, but when all this started up again, I realized that I wasn't really over my past; I had just locked it away."

"That's understandable. I locked you away, too. After that first year of anger and unhappiness, I tried not to think about you. I didn't believe I would ever see you again. I certainly had no idea you were as close to me as you were."

"I sometimes wondered if I'd accidentally run into you in the city—what I would say, what you would say. I never imagined it would happen the way it did." She swallowed hard, wanting to get out the words she needed to say. "When you just talked about my past, you left out the most important part—you. You're part of my past, part of my present."

"I'd like to be part of your future."

"I'd like to be part of yours, but everything is moving fast."

"We don't have to rush, Cassidy. We can go as slow as you want."

"Do you think you can trust me, Hunter? And don't answer too quickly. When we first reconnected, you made me promise to tell you if I was going to leave. I know that deep down you're not very sure of me."

"I wasn't when I asked you to make that promise. But a lot has changed since then." He tilted his head, giving her a thoughtful look. "It's not just about me trusting you. It goes both ways. Can you trust me? And don't answer too quickly."

She met his teasing smile. "Can I trust you? The man who just saved my life?"

"I'd like to be your hero, but I'd also like to be more. I want to be the person you can talk to, really talk to. The one with whom you can truly be yourself."

"I've kept my secrets for so long, it might take me awhile to really be free of them, but I want to be free. And I know I can trust you, Hunter. You are an amazing man. I knew that when I was sixteen, but I know it even more now. You care so much about people. You have the biggest heart. You're adventurous and funny and kind. I feel incredibly lucky to have you in my life."

"I feel the same way about you."

"Me? With all my baggage?"

"Yes. You impress the hell out of me. You've survived terrible things, more tragedy and heartache than most people see in a lifetime. You might have run away, but you didn't quit. You built a life for yourself. You found a way to make your dreams come true on your own."

Her eye blurred with tears at his words. "You're being too nice."

"I'm not being nice. I'm telling the truth. You were a scared girl when I knew you. I saw glimpses of the woman you would become, but you were still hiding in the shadows. You're not doing that anymore. You're strong, independent, creative. I don't want to control your life; I just want to share it. I think we make a good team."

She smiled with joy. "I think we do, too. I love you, Hunter." She was happy to say the words first, because it needed to be that way. She was the one who had run out on him. "I never told you that when we were together. It was too difficult for me to say. I was afraid of love, but now I feel like it's the best thing I could have, so I'm not going to push it away anymore. I'm going to open up my heart—to you—my first love, my only love. No one has ever come close."

"You're my first love, too." His blue eyes darkened with emotion. "I've loved you since the first minute we met—when I knocked you over."

She laughed. "I've been trying to get up ever since."

"I'll always help you up. I might have saved your life yesterday, but you've also saved mine."

"How have I done that?"

"I told you I've been lost in a feeling of restlessness, a gnawing need that I have not been able to get rid of. But I haven't felt that since you came back into my life. I know what I was missing all these years—you." He paused. "You always encouraged my dreams. I could always talk to you, tell you anything. I could be my real self with you. And while I know I have the support of my family, you were an inspiring person in my life, and I missed you when you were gone. I missed the person I was with you."

"I'm not that same person," she reminded him.

"Neither am I. And that's good. I like the people we are now. I think we're ready for the rest of our lives."

"So do I." She drew in a shaky, emotional breath. "What now?"

"I'm thinking we start with a kiss, and then we go into the bedroom."

"I did miss waking up with you this morning."

"And then we do what we do—together. I'm not going to rush you, Cassidy. You don't have to commit to anything beyond loving me."

"I can definitely do that. I want the rest, too. I want the happily ever after. I never thought I could have it, but you always made me believe I could."

"You can—*we* can." He leaned forward and kissed her with so much love and tenderness, she almost wanted to cry. The happiness she'd been chasing for years was finally going to be hers.

Epilogue

⟶⟫⟪⟵

Three days later, Cassidy and Hunter drove to the church in
the Presidio where Griffin and Annie would say their vows on
Saturday afternoon. It was four o'clock and the ceremony
would take place at five, with a dinner reception to follow at
the yacht club.

She was looking forward to the happy event, a nice
change after many police interviews as well as an emotionally
charged conversation with Molly. Neither she nor Hunter had
told the police that Molly had set the fire, but Cassidy had a
feeling that Molly might eventually do that herself. The guilt
at what she had done was eating away at her, and she was
beginning to realize she would never be free if she didn't let
go of all her secrets. But Cassidy was going to leave that up
to Molly.

"You okay?" Hunter asked, breaking into her reverie, as
he pulled into the parking lot by the church. "You've been
tapping your fingers for the last five minutes."

She suddenly became aware of the beat of her fingers
against the clutch purse resting in her lap. "Oops. Sorry. Just
thinking."

"About everything that has happened?"

"That and the fact that I'm a little nervous to see your whole family." While Hunter had done the rehearsal dinner the night before, she had decided to only go to the wedding, not wanting to draw attention away from Annie with her sudden reappearance. She would have skipped the whole weekend, but Hunter had insisted.

He put a reassuring hand on her leg. "They already know we're together. They're happy about it."

"You're probably glossing over the part where they asked you if you're out of your freaking mind getting back with the woman who broke your teenage heart."

He grinned. "There might have been a little of that, but it's my heart, and they could see I'm crazy about you."

"Or just crazy."

He shook his head. "No way. You never really did anything wrong, Cassidy. You just protected yourself. Everyone understands that, and they are ready to embrace you, so be prepared for a lot of hugging. The Callaways are an affectionate group. I, frankly, can't wait for everyone to see us together. They're going to love you, just the way I do."

The happiness in his blue eyes, the confidence in his tone, made her realize she was looking for problems where they didn't exist. "Okay. I'm ready."

"You look beautiful."

She flushed as desire crept into his gaze. "Thanks. You look very handsome in your suit."

"I'm just glad Griffin didn't put us all in tuxes. Are you ready to go? I may get swept up in some pre-wedding and post-wedding photos, but I'll try to be as quick as I can, so you're not on your own."

"Hunter, you do not have to worry about me. I might be a little nervous about your family, but I can talk to people, even people I don't know. I can take care of myself. I want you to be a part of this celebration in all the ways that you need to be. Please, don't worry about me, not even for a second."

He smiled and gave her a kiss. "I'm not worried about

you; I'm just going to miss you."

"I think you'll survive."

As they got out of the car, another handsome man with dark hair and blue eyes approached, and while there were a few Callaways fitting that description, this one was Dylan.

"There you are," Dylan said. "Long time no see, Cassidy. I'm glad you came."

"Thanks. It's good to see you."

"The photographer wants to take a few photos of the wedding party before the ceremony," Dylan said. "I need to steal you away, Hunter. Sorry, Cassidy."

"Not a problem. You two go and do what you need to do. I'll see you in the church."

As Hunter and Dylan walked away, she felt a little awkward standing by herself, especially since it was still a little early, but she'd just told Hunter she could take care of herself, and she needed to prove that was true.

"Cassidy?"

She was both relieved and unnerved to hear her name called.

Turning around, she saw a petite blonde approaching, as well as a familiar man with brown hair and green eyes— Emma and Max. She hadn't seen Emma since high school. Max, on the other hand, had been a familiar companion the past few days.

"Don't worry, I have no more questions," he said with a smile.

"Good, because I have no more answers."

"I don't know if you remember me," Emma said.

"I do, and I've seen your photo on Max's desk, too, as well as pictures of your beautiful kids."

Emma gave her a beaming maternal smile. "Aren't they adorable? Shannon is eight. We adopted her from Ireland about sixteen months ago—long story. She's actually one of the flower girls, so she's doing the pictures right now. Our baby, Nora, is thirteen months. She's with two of my sisters-in-law, Jessica and Maddie, who both volunteered to watch the babies during the ceremony. They'll be coming to the reception later. My family has been very busy having kids the last few years. Anyway, I'm rambling on. I'm so glad you're all right. Max told me what happened to you, and it must have been terrifying."

"Fortunately, Hunter came to the rescue."

"Hunter said you were halfway to saving yourself."

"I did what I could do, but he was the real hero."

"It sounds like you two make a good pair," Emma said with a sparkle in her eyes.

"We are good together," she admitted.

"I'm so glad you found each other again."

"Me, too. The circumstances could have been better, but it has all worked out. I'm glad that Tommy's body can now rest in peace. David will pay for his crimes, and hopefully Geralyn will pay for hers."

"We're going to make sure of that," Max put in.

"Unfortunately, we may not be able to close the arson case," Emma said. "But since it's clear that it was probably a one-time personal act of revenge, I'm not too concerned that we have an arsonist on the loose."

She was very pleased to hear that. She didn't know if ultimately Molly would confess, but she was not going to worry about it. "I'm happy that house is gone. Too many bad things happened there. Did you ever find out if someone killed Donald?" she asked Max.

"No one has confessed. It's possible that it was an accident."

"My money is on David. Donald probably got tired of being used by David to cover up his crimes."

"Well, David is going to go away for the rest of his life, so he will be punished." Max paused as two women joined them, one blonde and sharing Emma's features, the other a pretty brunette.

"This is my sister Shayla," Emma introduced, nodding to the blonde. "And this is my sister-in-law Sara. She's married to Aiden."

"Nice to meet you both. I'm Cassidy."

"Hunter's date," Emma added.

"We heard a lot about you last night," Sara said with a warm smile. "Welcome to the family."

"I'm not officially family."

"I have a feeling you will be soon," Emma put in, a sparkle in her eyes. "When Hunter wants something, he doesn't stop until he gets it."

"That's true of every last one of you Callaways," Max said with a laugh.

"He's right," Shayla put in. "We're a stubborn, determined bunch. Anyway, we should go inside and nab some good seats."

Cassidy got swept up in the group as they headed into the church and were eventually joined by more Callaways. She was introduced to so many people her head spun. But it was the genuine friendliness, easy acceptance, that really got to her. By the time she was sitting in a pew next to Emma, she was starting to feel tears welling up in her eyes, and the ceremony hadn't even started yet.

She'd loved not only Hunter but also his family since the first minute she'd met them. She'd always wanted to be part of their circle, but she'd never ever thought she could be, not even before she ran away. She had always felt like an imposter, someone who would probably be gone before they even realized she was there. But now she was starting to feel like she really belonged.

As Hunter's mother, Sharon, was escorted down the aisle by his brother Dylan, the crowd began to hush. Dylan took his place at the altar with the groom, Hunter, Hunter's brother Ian, and another man she didn't know. Then the music began, followed by the arrival of two adorable flower girls.

"The redhead is mine," Emma whispered.

"She's adorable."

The bridesmaids were next. She recognized Kate and Mia, Hunter's twin sisters, who hadn't changed all that much since she'd hung out with Hunter and his family in high school. Two other women followed, who were probably Annie's friends or related to some other branch of the family.

The music changed to the wedding processional, and the crowd rose to their feet. She turned her head to see Annie and her father, Tim, come down the aisle.

Annie looked beautiful in her lacy bridal gown. As she took her place at the altar and stared into the eyes of her soon-to-be husband, her face was an expression of pure joy. She was truly marrying the man of her dreams.

Cassidy felt the tears coming back into her eyes, especially when Hunter's gaze sought hers. Everyone else was watching the bride and the groom, but he was looking at her. He was sending her a promise, and she was sending him one back. There were no more secrets between them.

When the ceremony ended, the bride and groom greeted their friends and family on the church steps.

Cassidy moved off to the side, watching from under the shadows of a tree as the Callaways greeted their newest member.

Hunter wanted to get to Cassidy, but he kept getting caught up in hugs and conversations and more photos. As he paused on the steps to the church, his gaze swept the crowd, and he didn't immediately see her. But he wasn't worried. A feeling of joy followed that thought. He knew she was somewhere nearby. He trusted her, and she trusted him. And the hole in his gut that had been bothering him for years was no longer there. He didn't know why it had taken him so long to understand that the only one who could fill that need for him was her, the only woman he'd ever really loved.

"Relax," Dylan said, joining him with a knowing smile. "She's under the tree over there."

He looked over to the patch of trees where Dylan was pointing and saw not only Cassidy but his sisters Mia and Kate.

"She might be getting a grilling," Dylan said. "But she's definitely not gone."

"I wasn't worried."

"Sure you weren't."

"I wasn't. Cassidy and I are together."

"You have no doubts?"

"Not one. You might think that's crazy—"

"No, I think that's love. Before you join her, I heard you talking to Dad about building a summer camp. What's up with that?"

"It's an idea I've been pondering for a while."

"Can I be a part of it?"

He was surprised at his brother's request. "If you want to."

"Why wouldn't I?"

"I didn't think you'd be thrilled about me changing careers. I know you and Burke got me the temporary assignment, so I could get my foot back in the door. It's not that I don't like being a firefighter—"

"You don't have to explain," Dylan said, cutting him off. "I want you to be happy, Hunter. If doing something else is the answer, then do it. You only get one life. We know how fast things can turn. I'm confident you're going to do great things whatever you do."

"I hope so. And I appreciate your words. I've been conflicted."

"Clearly. You can walk away from firefighting without walking away from the family. I hope you know that."

"I do know that. It wasn't really the family that was holding me back—it was myself. I didn't see a clear path until now. Anyway, the new idea is still in the idea stages. There are a lot of hoops to jump through."

"Nobody better for jumping through hoops than Callaways. Cassidy is on board, too?"

"My biggest cheerleader."

"I always knew you were going to end up with a cheerleader."

He grinned. "Not that kind of cheerleader. At any rate, I want you to know that nothing is happening soon. I'll work the job until MacKinney is ready to come back."

"I wasn't worried. So, when are you going to marry Cassidy?"

"One wedding at a time," he said with a laugh.

"You'll be the last one in our family. What will Mom do?"

"Probably start hounding everyone for grandchildren."

"She has already started—as if we need more Callaways." Dylan waved his hand at the crowd. "Look at all these people. We have an amazing family."

As he perused the group in front of them, he felt a swell of love in his chest. "We really do. I never really knew how lucky I was until I saw our family through Cassidy's eyes."

"She's going to make a nice addition." Dylan paused, as one of their cousins on their mom's side came over to join them.

"Lizzie Cole," Hunter drawled, giving the attractive brunette with the beautiful green eyes a hug. "When did you grow up?"

"Same time you did," she returned. "I'm only three years younger than you, Hunter."

"How is everyone in your family?"

"They're good. I wish more of them could have made it today, but we're all spread out."

"Where are you living now?" Lizzie's parents had taken Lizzie and her four siblings to Colorado ten years earlier. "Still in Denver?"

"I'm actually making a move. I got a new job. I'm going to manage an inn at Whisper Lake. It's in the mountains of Colorado, and it is the most inspiring place. I can't wait. You should come visit sometime. We're only two hours out of Denver. There's everything you could want there—boating, paddle-boarding, fishing, hiking, climbing, biking. You name it, we've got it."

"That does sound like everything I could want," he said.

"Good luck with the job."

"Thanks. I've been wanting to manage an inn since I got my degree in hotels and hospitality, and this is a dream come true. Plus, there's something about the town that's kind of magical, mystical."

He exchanged a grin with Dylan, then said, "You never change, do you, Lizzie? You might have been the last one of us to stop believing in Santa Claus."

She made a face at him. "Not everything always has to make sense. Sometimes things happen you just can't explain. By the way, I heard from Kate that you just got reunited with your high school sweetheart. That's cool."

"It's very cool." He was about to excuse himself to join Cassidy when his mom clapped her hands and hushed the milling crowd.

"We're going to take one big family photo," Sharon said. "Anyone who is related, come to the steps."

A crush of Callaways gathered around him: Jack and Lynda, Burke and Maddie, Aiden and Sara and their two kids, Nicole and Ryan and their two kids, Drew and Ria and her niece and daughter, Sean, Jessica and Kyle, Shayla and Reid, and Colton and Olivia. And then his family gathered around: Dylan and Tori, Ian and Grace, Mia and Jeremy and their daughter Ashlyn, Kate and Devin and, of course, Annie and Griffin.

Lizzie stood next to his mom and dad while a few other Callaway cousins joined the photo on the other side of Jack and Lynda. And finally, the two most important people came to the bottom of the steps—his grandparents, who had left quite a legacy behind them.

But the picture wasn't complete—not to him.

To his mom's dismay, he broke away from the crowd.

"One second," he yelled, jogging down the steps to grab Cassidy's hand.

"No, I'm not family," she protested.

"Yes, you are." He gave her a pointed look. "I want you there, Cassidy. You're with me."

"Come join us, Cassidy," Annie echoed, followed by a chorus of others, who started chanting her name.

At one time in her life, Cassidy probably would have run away from all that attention, but now she took his hand and smiled. "Okay. I'm with you."

He led her into the middle of the group and held her hand as the photographer ran them through a series of photos. And then it was time to go to the reception.

As he and Cassidy walked down the steps, his mom stopped them.

"After this, we can start talking about the two of you tying the knot," his mother said.

"Mom, I haven't even proposed."

"Haven't you?" she said with a sweet, loving smile. "I'll see you both at the reception."

"You don't have to propose," Cassidy said quickly, as they walked toward the Jeep.

"Don't worry. When I do it, I'm going to do it right."

"What does that mean?"

He paused by the car. "It means it's going to be our day, our moment, and it won't involve the family. I'll let them come to the wedding."

"I'm sure they would insist on that."

"I don't know. Kate ran off and got married."

"We could do that. It's not like I have family to fill a church."

"I've got enough family for both of us, and I don't really care where we do it, but I don't want to skimp on it. I want you to have your dream wedding, whatever that is."

"As long as you're the one I'm marrying, it will be my dream."

He cupped her face. "I love it when you say things like that."

"And I love you, Hunter. Sometimes, I'm sad about all the time we missed together, but then I think maybe this was always meant to be our time."

"It was. No more looking back. We've done enough of

that. It's all about now and forever more. I'm going to make you happy, Cassidy."

"I'm already happy. I want you to know that I'll never leave you. You're stuck with me for the rest of your life. I hope you can trust that. I probably still have something to prove, but—"

He put his fingers against her mouth. "You have nothing to prove. I know you won't leave. And I won't leave, either. No more secrets between us."

"No more secrets," she promised. "Just love."

"Just love," he echoed.

THE END

———→→≫≪←←———

If you love romantic suspense, don't miss out on Barbara's new *Lightning Strikes Trilogy*:

Beautiful Storm (#1)
Lightning Lingers (#2)
Summer Rain (#3)

———→→≫≪←←———

About The Author

Barbara Freethy is a #1 New York Times Bestselling Author of 66 novels ranging from contemporary romance to romantic suspense and women's fiction. Traditionally published for many years, Barbara opened her own publishing company in 2011 and has since sold over 7 million books! Twenty of her titles have appeared on the New York Times and USA Today Bestseller Lists.

Known for her emotional and compelling stories of love, family, mystery and romance, Barbara enjoys writing about ordinary people caught up in extraordinary adventures. Barbara's books have won numerous awards. She is a six-time finalist for the RITA for best contemporary romance from Romance Writers of America and a two-time winner for DANIEL'S GIFT and THE WAY BACK HOME.

Barbara has lived all over the state of California and currently resides in Northern California where she draws much of her inspiration from the beautiful bay area.

For a complete listing of books, as well as excerpts and contests, and to connect with Barbara:

Visit Barbara's Website:
www.barbarafreethy.com

Join Barbara on Facebook:
www.facebook.com/barbarafreethybooks

Follow Barbara on Twitter:
www.twitter.com/barbarafreethy

Made in the USA
Lexington, KY
14 September 2018